CANADA
GHOST
TO
GHOST

SHEILA HERVEY

Stoddart

Published in 1996 by
Stoddart Publishing Co. Limited
34 Lesmill Road
Toronto, Canada
M3B 2T6
Tel. (416) 445-3333
Fax (416) 445-5967

Stoddart Books are available for bulk purchase for sales
promotions, premiums, fundraising, and seminars. For details,
contact the Special Sales Department at the above address.

Canadian Cataloguing in Publication Data

Hervey, Sheila
Canada ghost to ghost

ISBN 0-7737-5830-5

1. Ghosts – Canada. I. Title

BF1472.C3H47 1996   133.1'0971   C96-931246-6

Cover Design: Bill Douglas @ the Bang
Text Design: Tannice Goddard
Computer Graphics: Mary Bowness

Printed and bound in Canada

*Stoddart Publishing gratefully acknowledges the support of the
Canada Council and the Ontario Arts Council in the development
of writing and publishing in Canada.*

Creating a book is a time-consuming and demanding task that involves both desire and sacrifice on the part of the writer. Simultaneously, one's family is called upon for understanding and a degree of devotion to an often irrational urge.
So this book is for the ladies in my life, daughters Karen and Stacey, who have been through this process more than once. And for Sarah, the newest arrival.

CONTENTS

INTRODUCTION

During the 1970s, I embarked on a voyage of discovery about Canada's ghost population. The result was *Some Canadian Ghosts*, a collection of true stories of the supernatural from across the country. The book sold extremely well and created an ongoing stream of correspondence between its readers and me. Letters came from small towns and large cities, from grade-school students and senior citizens. They arrived in the form of typed narratives and hasty, semiliterate scrawls, some with painstakingly created maps and diagrams.

Over the years, my files of ghost stories continued to grow. I felt it was time to update the original material and add some that was new — hence this book.

In recent years, ghost-hunting has been complicated by the fact that the average family can simply move away when it encounters a supernatural phenomenon. Many fascinating ghost stories of the 1970s, 1980s, and early 1990s end abruptly when the central family leaves the scene of a physical disturbance in order to find a bit of peace and quiet. Fear is stronger than curiosity in this sort of situation. People pack up and run, sometimes with very little justification, rather than stay and face something they can't understand.

In earlier times, there was no such opportunity for escape. People derived their livelihood directly or indirectly from the land or the sea. Their neighbours were not mere strangers; they were relatives and friends in time of trouble. For such firmly rooted families, moving would have meant serious economic, physical, and emotional upheaval. It was something to be avoided at all costs.

Entire communities, then, became involved in local hauntings. More knowledgeable and experienced individuals tried various tactics, from gentle persuasion to orders backed up by the Bible or holy water to, in extreme cases, exorcisms, against an unknown entity that appeared, often without warning, in their midst. It is to their courage that we owe much of our knowledge today about psychic phenomena.

Those of our ancestors who were afflicted with ghostly difficulties were not dismissed as crackpots as easily as they often are today. Communities often worked together to rid a family of an unwanted spirit; ghosts were accepted as very real, possibly dangerous, and a direct challenge to all concerned.

I have re-created some of these historical accounts, and added reports of some more modern ghostly visitations and supernatural events that have occurred in Canada. Some of the incidents in this book I researched in library and newspaper files in those areas where the actual experiences took place. Others are totally new and come directly from people who were personally involved in unusual events not covered by the various news media.

Dates and locations are as accurate as possible. The names of those involved are, for the most part, genuine, although in a few cases, I have changed the names of individuals who felt, perhaps correctly, that they had experienced enough difficulty already without adding more notoriety to their troubles. When small towns are involved, some names and sites have been deliberately omitted to avoid arousing too much neighbourly curiosity. The stories are as they happened. For the most part, the identities of the people involved are of secondary importance.

In any collection of ghost stories, a number of remarkably similar points link the separate experiences. Some of the tales are almost identical in detail, although they may be poles apart in time and distance. This collection is no exception. For example, the fact that an animal can sense the arrival of a ghost is illustrated in several of the stories selected to show entirely different characteristics of the supernatural.

A note about the term "supernatural," while we are on the subject. I have used it throughout this book, but the correct word should really be "supernormal." Most of what we consider unnatural is merely something we can't fully comprehend. Yet if I am knowingly perpetuating the use of a misnomer, it is because the popular term "supernatural" is easier for most readers to understand.

The incidents in *Canada Ghost to Ghost* represent almost all sections of the country, from coast to coast. The final judgement as to their veracity is left up to the reader, whom I ask to bring an open mind, and his or her experience to the reading of this book.

As we move along, I think you will come to agree with me on a number of basic points. Ghosts do exist and are very real to those who encounter them. We have with us representatives of the immediate past, as well as some from the earliest days of Canada's history. Human experiences with supernatural phenomena are as common today as they were one hundred years ago.

Personally, I find the subject of ghosts and the supernatural an enchanting, though disturbing, mystery, something that must give us pause to think and reflect on what we really *know*, as opposed to what we sense or feel. The appearance of a spirit being in the life of someone you know well can be like the discovery of ancient Troy in the exact spot where Homer said it had once existed. What was thought to be a fable or a blank has been discovered, or has made itself aware to one or more of us human beings.

There are times when fiction does indeed reveal itself as fact, when some of life's puzzles suddenly and unexpectedly are solved, and we have to reassess our conventional world and its constant challenges. Quite possibly, there are more than the three dimensions that we are comfortable with, and sometimes a select few of us step across the invisible boundary.

I

WEST COAST VISITATIONS

VEIL OF FEAR

In September of 1989, Blair and Nadine "Deanna" Farling moved with their three children into a one-and-a-half-story residence located in a small town on the coast of British Columbia. At the time, Mandy, the elder daughter, was eighteen, Debbie was sixteen, and Dean, the only boy, was ten.

The Farlings loved the area, and had no reason to believe that their new house was anything other than perfectly normal. Built in 1915, it could have stood a coat of fresh paint, and the semi-finished basement left something to be desired, but there was nothing intimidating about the place. However, their purchase had a feature that was not included in the real estate listing: it was haunted.

There were three bedrooms in the house. Blair and Deanna had the master, the two girls shared the next largest, and Dean had a room all to himself. This was considered an excellent arrangement by the entire family, since Dean's legendary untidiness meant that no one would have wanted to share any space with him.

The basement area was a constant and general aggravation to Deanna. It was necessary to hang clothes down there to dry during inclement weather, which was frequent, and she stored fresh produce in a cold-storage room off to one end. The concrete floor was both hazardous and unsightly, being not only severely cracked but covered with numerous large splotches of paint seemingly thrown about at random. The air in the basement was stale, musty, and rather suffocating.

One section of the cold-storage room was used by Blair for keeping various possessions that had once been his father's. Preston Farling lived in the same district, but he lacked adequate space for his collection of old tools, ladders, and other "stuff" that a family man acquires over a lifetime. Preston was very ill with cancer and wasn't likely to require the implements again, but the younger Farling couple kept everything, just in case.

It was an uneasy time for the family. Blair's mother, Ardelle Farling, who had borne and raised eleven children, had died in July of 1988 after a long fight with Alzheimer's disease. For several years she had not recognized members of her own family, and Preston, unaware that he was also ill, had found himself a lady companion. As is often the case in such an emotionally charged situation, none of the children took to the new addition to their father's life. They claimed that Lottie Demetrov interfered in affairs that were none of her concern, that she kept them and the grandchildren from visiting Preston, and that she was horribly spiteful. The hope that Preston might come by and see Blair, his third child and eldest son, was thus yet another reason for keeping all of Preston's paraphernalia.

While Deanna did not object to providing the storage space, she hated that particular small room. It was dark, cold — of course — and somehow eerie. Every time that she went in it to get potatoes or other vegetables, she felt a presence, as if she were being watched.

A few small but disconcerting incidents soon made the family feel that perhaps their new residence was something out of the ordinary. Mandy was the first to experience anything really odd. About six months after the move, on April 29, 1990, she awoke one night to discover a woman, all dressed in black, standing beside her, holding her hand. Mandy snatched her hand away and shrunk back to the far side of her bed. The woman vanished, leaving the girl to wonder if the incident had been part of a realistic but bad dream. Debbie, undisturbed and asleep in the next bed, slept on unawares, so Mandy said nothing about the incident.

Mandy was never to see the strange apparition again: instead, the woman in black fixated upon Deanna. The ghost ensured that her presence was felt, and let Deanna know that neither she nor her family was welcome in their new home. At no time was the face of the visitor visible. She always wore a small black hat with an attached black veil that hung dramatically over her hidden features, like some spinsterish maiden aunt in the deepest of mourning. Deanna felt certain the creature was evil.

Matters changed abruptly for the worse in early January of 1991. It was about two in the afternoon and Deanna's sister,

Rosemary Cleef, was over for a visit. Usually she brought along her tiny daughter, Marta, but for some reason she had not done so that day. Deanna, Rosemary, and Mandy were sitting quietly at the kitchen table planning the guest list and menu for an upcoming anniversary party.

Suddenly the three women just looked at each other in horror. They all felt a fourth presence in the kitchen with them, so strongly that it took their breath away. Rosemary said later that she had never encountered such a terrible and paralyzing sensation of cold in her life. She was unable to move; they were all in fact frozen in place, each trying desperately to rise up out of her chair but finding it impossible.

Mandy gazed over at her mother and saw the colour slowly drain from Deanna's face. Standing between their two chairs was Ardelle Preston. But Ardelle had been dead for more than two years. She had never even visited the house in which they now resided.

Mandy was the first to regain her feet, and she began to cry — low, deep, coughing sobs. She swayed loosely, seeming about to faint. The sight of her niece helped to get Rosemary up from her chair, and she hurried over to support Mandy beside the kitchen counter.

Deanna lurched roughly to her feet, with such force that her wooden chair tumbled backwards to the floor. She seemed possessed. In a deep voice, strange and terrifying, she told Mandy that her grandmother was standing at the bottom of the basement steps, waiting to see her.

Mandy, clinging tightly to Rosemary, refused to go. "No! I don't want to see her!"

Deanna, who remembers nothing about this early dialogue, stared straight ahead, almost as though listening for someone to tell her what to say next. Then, her voice continuing in strange deep tones, she announced that Ardelle was coming up the stairs.

Mandy, by now nearly hysterical, kept yelling, "No! No! I won't see her!"

There was a brief pause. Perhaps Mandy's refusal had made an impact? Deanna then uttered words to the effect that Ardelle had returned to the basement and was awaiting Mandy down there. Suddenly, and this part Deanna remembers, she yelled out loudly, "Get out! Get out now!"

Mandy and Rosemary did not wait to be commanded a second time; they fled from the kitchen out onto the front porch, gasping with exhaustion and relief.

Deanna then recalls being summoned to the basement in terms she was unable to refuse. It was as if someone else was activating her body. When she reached the bottom of the stairway she found that an ordinary old wooden chair had been placed on the floor in front of her, about a metre from the last step. From behind her, she felt hands, at least three of them, pressing down on her shoulders, forcing her to sit in the old chair.

A clothesline hung in the basement; Deanna had hung some dishtowels and clothes on it to dry earlier that day. Suddenly she heard a great howling sound and a fiercely gusting wind began to churn through the area. The clothesline quivered as the washing flapped about, and flailed against the ceiling.

As Deanna struggled to get up from the chair, she saw Ardelle Farling, a frightened gaze frozen onto her face, struggling against the wind, her hands raised protectively across her body. Ardelle backed away slowly until she was crouched immediately opposite the door to the dreaded cold-storage room. At that moment a brilliant ray of red light streamed straight through the closed door. The noise reached a crescendo as the light seemed to pierce Ardelle's body, which slowly backed away from the door. In that instant, both wind and noise ceased. Everything was deathly still, and Ardelle gradually faded from sight.

Deanna just sat and stared, riveted in the chair and dumbfounded by what had taken place. Ardelle had seemed so solid and real, and yet she was dead. How could she have appeared, seeming quite alive, then just evaporated?

Several minutes passed and Deanna slowly realized that she could move again. Her entire body felt frigid from the cold of a few short moments ago and all her joints felt cramped and stiff. As fast as her trembling legs would carry her, she limped up the stairway and scurried through the kitchen to find her daughter and sister waiting anxiously on the front porch. As Deanna described the incident, she received another shock. To her, that fearful interlude in the basement had seemed an eternity, but both Mandy and Rosemary told her it had only been a matter of a couple of minutes at most. From the outside of the house they had heard no noise, and felt no wind.

Ardelle's ghost seemed to have joined up with that of the strange lady dressed in black.

Deanna Farling chaired a meeting that evening with her husband and daughter to review and discuss the bizarre and frightening occurrences. They were gathered at the kitchen table, having made sure that Dean was occupied with his computer games and that Debbie was spending the evening at a friend's house studying for a test. There seemed to be no point in upsetting and frightening the two younger children with tales of ghosts and penetrating beams of red light. After that afternoon's incident, Mandy could scarcely be excluded.

The little group spent a long time discussing what had happened, then turned to the question of why Ardelle's spirit was there in the house with them. Although she had died prior to their move, it seemed possible that she had somehow managed to locate Blair, with whom she had always been extremely close. Deanna and Blair felt that the years of confusion caused by Alzheimer's, and the pain of her actual death from pneumonia, might have carried over for Ardelle into a form of afterlife. Since she had depended largely upon the guidance of her husband, she might be waiting for him to join her. Preston's illness made it likely that their reunion was imminent. Deanna had felt no threat from Ardelle's ghost, just a sense of distress.

The darkly clad, veiled apparition, on the other hand, concerned the family much more. Should they stay and fight something they did not understand, should they flee? Blair, who had not personally experienced any of the supernatural apparitions or howling winds and penetrating light beams, was nonetheless the most inclined to place the house on the market immediately. But Deanna reluctantly suggested a wait-and-see approach for a limited period, and Mandy agreed to try to live with the situation on two rock-hard conditions: that she would not have to venture down into the basement for any reason whatsoever, and that the family would move if the intruder in black reappeared in the bedroom that she shared with Debbie.

For the next several weeks there existed an uneasy peace between the family and the apparitions. Ardelle's ghost was seen on numerous occasions by both Mandy and Deanna, but she seemed to be merely studying them as they went about their daily chores, and showed no inclination to interfere. They could have done without her presence, but she was after all a member of the family, or had been. Deanna wondered whether Ardelle had tried to move in with her husband, only to discover that she had been replaced by Lottie Demetrov. Such a discovery might have been the final shock that had driven her to the new home of her eldest son. Deanna came to feel sorry for the sad little shadow that flitted about the house.

Then, suddenly, the strange and frightening spirit in black began to torment Deanna once again, popping up in front of her unexpectedly or hovering over her shoulder. Whenever this ghost was nearby, the air would turn frigid — something that did not occur when Ardelle came near. Soon a pattern began to emerge. Deanna noticed that her late mother-in-law was usually seen shortly after something uncomfortable had occurred. She appeared to be trying to offer support and reassurance after the extreme antics of her fellow spirit. Deanna believed that Ardelle would not allow any harm to befall her or any of the other family members. It was strange to feel safer from one ghost because of the presence of a second!

In early 1992, a third apparition moved in with the besieged Farlings. This one was male, tall and slender. Deanna felt that this third spirit might have been the husband of the woman in constant mourning, while Mandy assigned him the role of the black-garbed woman's brother. Unlike the veiled woman, he always appeared friendly. And rather than move freely about the house, he seemed content to make himself at home in Dean's messy room, where he would stand silently for long periods of time, gazing quietly out of the upstairs window at the sea. Thus Dean was drawn into the secret of the house. He did not show any fear of the newcomer at first, but one night, Dean was awakened from his sleep by something grabbing at his right arm. He saw no one in the darkened room, nor was anything visible when he arose and turned on his desk lamp.

Throughout this uncomfortable period, Deanna felt that the family was coping extremely well, although she was beginning to get very tired and worn down. On one occasion, while preparing salads in the kitchen with Rosemary for a church event, she suddenly burst into tears. Ardelle Farling's ghost stood over by the kitchen sink, gazing at them, while the mourning lady stood guard in front of the door that led to the basement.

Deanna could tolerate the presence of Ardelle most of the time, but the extra woman and the quiet man upstairs in Dean's room tried her patience. It was as if the house no longer belonged to the Farlings, who had no control over the comings and goings of the unwanted guests. Deanna felt like a stranger in the home. She was in that sort of mood late one February afternoon when she had to venture down to the basement to collect some potatoes and a large onion for the evening meal. When she went to open the door to the cold-storage room, a big, swirling ball of reddish-black fire and flame seemed to hurl itself at her from the top left corner of the ceiling, barely missing her head.

That was the final straw! The house was placed on the market and sold within a two-week period. The Farlings had listed the property at as low a figure as they could afford in order to conclude a sale as quickly as possible.

Their new house is also haunted, but only by Ardelle, and so they are a family once again. The other visitors were left behind, and Deanna is fairly certain that the ghost of Ardelle will leave of its own volition upon the death of Preston

Farling. In the meantime, she feels, living with the ghost of one's mother-in-law is not so bad, compared to what they had endured before.

Young Dean has been very relaxed about what happened in their house by the sea; he has no problems with ghosts, as long as they keep their hands to themselves. Two or three times when Dean has been alone in his room, he has heard his grandmother's voice calling his name. This is generally when he is playing with his computer games instead of doing his homework; Grandma is an invisible spy!

Debbie, who insists that she never saw anything unusual during their stay in the last house, still has occasional nightmares about the place. A strange lady clad in black features strongly in many of the dream sequences. She will admit that she always felt herself to be under observation by some invisible presence during that unsettling period, and has finally accepted the fact that there were ghosts about the house. No one has told her, however, that one of the apparitions was the spirit of her late grandmother, and that it still shares a roof with her and the rest of her family.

WALD⊕

Living with a ghost in the crenellated shambles of an ancient castle or in a rambling, ivy-encrusted mansion is one thing. But sharing accommodations with one in a tiny residence can become unbearably crowded.

That's what painter Eric Henderson and his wife, Caitlin, discovered one memorable summer. The couple thought they'd struck a fine bargain indeed when they were able to rent a small house in the village of Waldo, in northwestern

British Columbia, for under a hundred dollars a month. Because it was right next to the local public school, the house was often rented out to teachers during the school year, but it was vacant now for the summer vacation period. The small house was well-kept and came fully furnished. There were gaily coloured curtains on the windows, a wide selection of hardcover and paperback books on the shelves, and even an upright piano in the living room. A disembowelled but finely polished cherry-wood grandfather clock stood guard near the front door.

When Eric Henderson came down from Fort St. John, where he had been painting, to see the quaint little house, he was so pleased that he rented it for the full two-month summer period. He and Caitlin had heard vague rumours around the village that the house was haunted, but they dismissed these as mere idle gossip. Anyway, at the asking price, the house was worth taking some degree of risk. As far as Eric was concerned, the excellent fishing in the area was just too good to forfeit over a possible ghost.

From the moment that the Hendersons moved in, however, until the day they departed to return to Fort St. John, the house was the site of a series of strange happenings for the temporary tenants. For one thing, there was the bedroom. "The house had two bedrooms," Eric recounts, "but both my wife and I had an uncomfortable feeling whenever we entered one of them. I can't explain it even today, but we decided not to use that particular room." Then there was the clock. Every evening, usually around ten-thirty, the ornate grandfather clock, in clear defiance of common sense and the principles of mechanical theory, would strike, despite the fact that it lacked the internal machinery to do so.

The chiming clock was often followed by the determined

closing of a couple of doors within the house. Eric and Caitlin could observe them shutting slowly, moving silently across their respective patches of floor, to click shut. There was no breeze or other visible cause for this; the Hendersons were all alone in the house.

This was all the more curious because only the door to the bathroom and that to the unused bedroom moved. These doors were slabs of solid pine, far too heavy to have been moved by an errant draft, even had there been one. As an added accompaniment, windows would be raised within their frames, then drop back into their closed positions with loud crashing sounds. An unseen force would flip through the pages of books lying about the room. And for a most unusual finale, the reels on Eric's fishing rods would spin of their own accord until the lines were hopelessly snagged and tangled.

Although there was nothing particularly evil or dangerous about these various manifestations, they did make life more than a little upsetting. How could one invite guests over for dinner? Would it not seem rather odd if the Hendersons insisted that the visitors leave before ten-thirty? So Eric decided to do a bit of careful investigating. Perhaps, he thought, someone was playing an elaborate practical joke on him. Or there might be some natural explanation for the unusual events.

"Both Caitlin and I checked the house thoroughly. It seemed to be structurally sound," Eric recalls. "But sometimes earth tremors are blamed for door-closing and window-rattling. We wanted to make sure that wasn't the problem. But nobody in the neighbourhood was using explosives and there were no reports of earthquakes or land shifts. We agreed not to touch the objects being moved about, but still they shifted position. Books, papers, and fishing gear were never the way we left them."

Caitlin Henderson believed that the ghost was searching for something in the books, since it was most persistent in its attention to them. Was it seeking a particular passage in a specific book?

The local postmistress told the intrigued couple that their nocturnal visitor was reputed to be the spirit of an older man who had died alone and destitute in the house many years ago — in the bedroom they didn't use.

The Hendersons remained in the house until summer's end. Eric's painting went well and the fishing was every bit as good as he had hoped. But he was annoyed at himself for his failure to solve the mystery of their invisible guest. He and Caitlin moved out reluctantly to make room for two young, recently married schoolteachers. Eric asked a couple of his friends to keep an eye on the little house when he and Caitlin moved back to Fort St. John.

The newcomers didn't know anything about the reputation of their residence and, being occupied at school most of the time, they had little opportunity to mingle with their neighbours. Since they were planning to remain for at least the entire school year, they rearranged the furniture in the living room, including the bookcases, and in the bedroom that had been unused by the Hendersons, to suit themselves.

The townspeople watched and waited, wondering what would happen and when. From the sidewalk, passersby could see that one of the bedrooms had been turned into some sort of study.

Not long after the couple had moved in, at three o'clock one quiet September morning, the piano began to play of its own volition. The young wife, awakened by the discordant thumping sounds coming from the living room, ran screaming out into the street, her long hair tumbling out of its curlers, crying that the house was haunted. She was quite appalled when the immediate neighbours, disturbed by her shrieks, appeared and calmly assured her that she was quite correct. The house was indeed haunted, and they all knew it.

The couple refused to return to the house. They stayed with another teacher for the remainder of the night, and then found other, more orthodox, accommodation considerably farther from the school. Unlike the Hendersons, the schoolteachers were not prepared to cope with a resident ghost in return for a convenient, low-cost place to live.

Although no one ever saw the ghost in Waldo, there was no doubt in the minds of the tenants of that cozy little house, nor in the minds of many townspeople, that some sort of spirit occupied the place. This belief was evidently shared by the owner of the house, who continued to ask for an extremely low rental fee.

THE ROSEWOOD BED

It is not often that a single, powerful, inexplicable manifestation takes place, then suddenly disappears entirely. One night in Vancouver, however, a dozen people witnessed a bizarre occurrence that brought an abrupt end to a happy party and caused a young couple to sell their house immediately.

Although fear and shock kept the people who saw the vision silent for many years, they have recently felt free to discuss the incident, now that the house that serves as the focus for this story has been levelled. The land on which the place once sat, combined with several adjoining properties, has become a condominium site. Their tale can now be added to the ghostly folklore of Canada.

A middle-aged man and his slightly older wife moved to the Vancouver area from their former home in Edmonton, Alberta. They built a large house in the west end of the city. The woman was friendly and outgoing, but her husband was not interested in cultivating a relationship with the neighbours and forming social ties. He made it quite clear that he wished to be left alone. He refused all invitations without explanation and never issued any of his own. If he found his wife chatting near the front door, he would brusquely order her back into the house. While there was no sign that he physically abused her, she was always quick to obey him, scuttling back meekly and shutting the door softly behind her.

The couple had only been living in their new home for about seven months when the woman suddenly became very ill; shortly thereafter, she died. The husband advised the local doctor who had attended the scene that his wife had suffered from a heart condition. The death certificate listed coronary attack as the cause of death.

The husband lost no time in selling the large house and moving away from the district. If they had bothered to give the matter any thought at all, the neighbours would have said that the man was grieving for his late wife and simply wanted to leave the scene of her untimely death. They did find it odd, however, when the postman said that he refused to leave a forwarding address.

A young married couple, Adrian and Shawna Paradine, purchased the home and moved in. For the first few weeks they liked it immensely. However, they began to sense something unusual about the house, an atmosphere that made them ill at ease.

Since the Paradines were complete strangers to the psychic and supernatural worlds, they were unable to explain their increasingly strong feeling that something was wrong in their lovely new home. They found themselves especially uncomfortable in the large room on the main floor that had been used as the master bedroom by the first occupants of the place.

Shawna and Adrian decided to remodel the entire house from top to bottom, linking their uneasiness to the decor, which was not at all to their taste. It was a massive and very costly undertaking for such a young couple, but with the physical assistance of a few close friends and financial help from both of their families, they set to work. They undertook to knock out two walls in order to enlarge the drawing-room area. The new, more spacious room would include the former main-floor master bedroom. They hoped this major structural change would alleviate the discomfort they had felt about this room almost from the very beginning. The furniture, carpeting, paint, and wallpaper were all completely done over; only the exterior of this part of the house remained the same.

When the renovations were finally complete, the Paradines decided to hold a house-warming party. They wanted to celebrate their apparent success in removing all visible signs of the former owners. Six couples, all close friends who had been instrumental in the work, were invited, and until the midnight hour the occasion was a most festive one. Good food and wine, and lots of laughter and goodwill among friends were the order of the day. There was no premonition of trouble.

In the midst of this relaxed gaiety, an icy and ominous chill suddenly descended upon the occupants of the room.

No one spoke or moved. The attention of all was riveted on the far end of the dining room.

Suddenly, the vision of a massive rosewood four-poster bed appeared. Lying in the bed, and dwarfed by it, was a small, pale woman, with gaunt cheeks and feverish, sunken eyes, who was obviously near death. She stared in silent terror at a man who sat in an old rocking chair alongside the bed. The man's face revealed a tight, self-satisfied smile.

"That's the man who built the house!" exclaimed one of the guests. "And that's his wife. She died right here in the house. But why is she looking at him like that?"

"That's where the master bedroom used to be," whispered Shawna in reply.

The horrifying vision faded as silently as it had appeared. Afraid of being accused of excessive drinking, everyone present pledged to keep the bizarre and frightening apparitions strictly secret.

Oddly enough, no one seems to have thought of informing the local police authorities so that the woman's death could be properly investigated. But then, who would have believed the "evidence"? Perhaps the decision to remain silent was a prudent one.

The house was sold within a few weeks of that fateful party. The buyers were not told about any of the strange happenings. The Paradines' lawyers handled the transaction. Apparently the new owners experienced no difficulty. All of the Paradines' lovely new furnishings were given over to an auction house for prompt disposal.

Today only two of the guests that evening remain alive, but both confirm that the story happened exactly as related here. One of them, a woman who was perhaps a little braver, or simply more curious, than the others, attended the auction sale. She saw the new carpet that had been laid down in the drawing room just prior to the party. There were four deep, clear indentations visible in the carpet, as if a heavy object had once sat upon it. The woman took the trouble to examine these depressions with some care. She could scarcely believe her eyes. They formed a large, perfect rectangle, the size of a great four-poster bed.

NANNY GHOST

Freddy Dressler was engaged to marry Frances Crisp. While Frances had met most of Freddy's relatives early on in the relationship, he was only just now getting to know the members of the Crisp family.

One clear early winter's evening the young couple drove the several miles to visit with Audrey, Frances's oldest sister. Audrey and her husband, Greg Stivers, were living with sixteen-month-old Natalia in a renovated farmhouse several miles northeast of Kelowna, British Columbia, the remains of an old dairy farm that had been forced to close when its owner retired.

Frances and Freddy arrived just as Audrey was tucking the baby into her cot. After making sure that the little one was secure, the four adults went into the living room, which was on the same floor as the nursery, but towards the other end of the old house. Audrey would easily hear Natalia if she required attention.

After only a few minutes of conversation, Freddy heard Natalia begin to fuss and fret off in the distance. Neither Audrey nor Greg paid any attention to the baby's complaints, however. Freddy wondered how the child's parents could ignore the rising signs of unhappiness coming from the rear of the house. Finally, Freddy felt that he had waited quite long enough. "Look," he said, "don't you think it might be a good idea if one of us went and checked on Natalia? Maybe just read her a story or something?"

Greg and Audrey just laughed. Frances grinned at Freddy. But when the three of them realized Freddy was truly concerned and angry, they tried to reassure him. Audrey gestured towards the baby's room. "Not to worry. Someone will be with her soon."

Freddy was now very confused. The farmhouse was not very large, and he hadn't been aware of anyone else staying with the Stivers or visiting them. Perhaps a grandparent had been resting quietly in an upstairs room and was going to tend to little Natalia?

After a few more minutes went by, the crying tapered off, then finally stopped altogether. Sensing Freddy's bewilderment, Audrey suggested, "Why don't we go and listen."

Leaving Greg and Frances to sort through some compact discs in the living room, Freddy followed Audrey down the darkened hallway. The two of them came to a stop just outside the partially closed nursery door. From within the room came the soothing voice of an older woman. The child burbled happily in response several times, and then was silent. The woman's voice also ceased.

"Go ahead," said Audrey. "Have a look."

Freddy cautiously poked his head in through the doorway. Except for the now silently sleeping child, the room was empty.

That was Freddy's introduction to the family secret. He learned that the ghost had never been seen, at least by any adults; perhaps Natalia could see her. She had first visited the baby shortly after Audrey had returned from the hospital after giving birth. Originally the parents had been alarmed, but there seemed to be nothing threatening about these soothing visits. Each night, shortly after the baby was put to bed, the spirit would stop by and spend a few minutes in the room, calming the restless Natalia, talking her to sleep.

Freddy was sworn to secrecy. The family believed that this unusual circumstance must be kept from the ears of strangers. It was a happy situation for all concerned, and they did not wish to risk spoiling it.

The gentle ghost continued to visit Natalia until the child was almost two years old. At that time, the little girl went to stay for two weeks with her maternal grandmother while Audrey accompanied Greg on a combined business trip and holiday to California. When they returned and reunited with Natalia at home, the nighttime visitor was gone.

The Stivers accepted the loss of their ghostly visitor philosophically. The old woman had been extremely helpful to them, and perhaps she had moved on to a family that required her more than they did.

Freddy was the person most upset by this turn of events. He had hoped that the nanny ghost would stay to help Frances and himself with any children that they might have!

THE PAINTING THAT CHANGED

Well-meaning and genuinely interested people sometimes throw total confusion into the detailed investigation of a supernatural manifestation. Upon learning about a reported haunting in their area, incredible numbers of people immediately gather at the scene. While they mean no harm, wanting only to satisfy their curiosity, their mere presence can hinder or prevent the necessary and impartial examination of the property involved, and can destroy attempts to obtain calm and full reports from the people who have experienced the occurrence. The following case is an example.

Chilliwack, British Columbia, is a relatively small town situated about one hundred miles from Vancouver in the lower Fraser Valley. The area is noted for its high level of agricultural development and diversification, including beef cattle, raspberries, peas, beans, corn, and an impressive hops crop for the brewing industry. It is generally not known, however, for the production of psychic phenomena.

But in December of 1965, when Douglas and Hetty Frederickson purchased a twelve-room house on William Street North in Chilliwack, the town and the Fredericksons were soon catapulted into an unnerving experience that finally forced Douglas and Hetty to move away to Sayward on Vancouver Island.

Hetty Frederickson was at the centre of the turmoil. She had a series of vivid and recurring nightmares about the body of a woman lying on the floor in a hallway, although it was not a hallway she could recognize from her house. Describing the woman in her visions, Hetty reported, "She always wears a red dress covered with yellow flowers, and her face reveals that she is terrified."

The nightmares were often followed by odd daytime occurrences. In one of the upstairs bedrooms, which was furnished but not used, the bureau drawers kept opening and shutting. An old bedstead in the room mysteriously moved from one spot to another, as though an interior decorator were trying to find the most aesthetically pleasing location for it.

Not one to be easily frightened, Hetty was determined to discover what was going on in her home. She kept vigil in the empty bedroom for three nights in a row, hoping to catch a glimpse of the intruder, her only light coming from a single white candle. On the third night she spied what appeared to be a misty figure standing beside the window. The shape was too ill-defined, however, to allow her to compare it with that of the woman in her nightmarish dreams.

Hetty Frederickson was an artist. Born in Indonesia, she had spent three years at the Academy of Creative Arts in The Hague. She decided to put her talents to work in solving the mystery that existed in her house: she would paint the woman she saw in her nightmares. Perhaps someone would recognize the person. In May of 1966, Hetty began to sketch an impression of her nocturnal visitor. But she was in for yet another shock.

"The woman's face kept changing into that of a man," she explained. "I didn't touch the painting; it changed all by itself. It's all very disturbing!"

If Hetty had ever read Dickens's *The Secret of Dorian Grey*, or seen the classic movie based upon the novel, she would have known that there already existed a fictional precedent for a portrait that alters itself over time. But the apparent change of sex on the part of the subject was a most unusual and bewildering development. The Fredericksons began to speculate as to whether their ghost might not be a male trying to communicate with them. Or perhaps there were two spirits fighting for domination. In either case they were left with the puzzle of the woman lying in a strange hallway.

Finally, Hetty pronounced her portrait complete, but she was not at all satisfied with the result: "Sketching the woman was not easy. Every time I tried to paint, the face would start out as that of a man even though I was attempting to paint a woman. But I really fought it and concentrated with all my power, until at last I was able to paint the likeness of a woman. However, now that it is finished, the painting is altering itself back to resemble a man."

Then the excitement began in earnest. News of the strange painting had leaked out through the neighbours to the press, and a major hunt began for the most recent occupants of the big house. It turned out that the place had previously been used as a boarding house, with such a high turnover of occupants that there was no serious hope of reconstructing its history. A few former residents did telephone Hetty and her husband with one piece of interesting information: that a series of secret chutes ran from the top of the house to the bottom. All attempts at locating these were foiled, however.

Meanwhile, the haunting continued. Whenever Hetty tried to catch up on sleep that she had missed, she would be disturbed by the same nightmare. And the furniture in the same upstairs bedroom continued to move about.

It was discovered that a man had committed suicide in the house ten years earlier. And then there was a story involving a woman who was allegedly murdered in the house and whose body was said to have been cemented into a chimney, but the bewildered Fredericksons felt that an overly fertile imagination was probably the author of this latter tale. The press had by this time reported fully on Hetty's visions of a woman in trouble, and it seemed logical that someone might have been trying to provide a colourful explanation.

Meanwhile, it was readily apparent that Hetty's painting of the woman's portrait would be useless for identification purposes, since the face was changing all the time. Hetty was so distraught that she threatened to remove the painting from the house.

At this point, there were some questions being asked about Hetty herself. Some wondered if she was trying to somehow increase the value of her art; others indicated that perhaps her mental elevator didn't go all the way to the attic. But all attempts to blame the artist for the problems were soon forgotten once a serious examination of the house was undertaken.

A door was discovered, concealed behind some old oak panelling, that led directly into the bedroom where all the strange noises had been heard, the same room where the bedstead and bureau drawers moved without human intervention. The actual opening of the doorway was right beside the old bedstead (when it wasn't moving about).

A cramped passageway was also found, leading to a turret at the top of the house. But it contained only the usual insulating material that one would expect; no raccoons or rats' nests or bat droppings, only a few spiderwebs that lay in haphazard abandon. The dust under the turret had not been disturbed for years.

The patient searchers moved through the house, tapping at walls and panels, anticipating hollow hidden recesses but finding none. They pulled furniture out into the centre of rooms, removed musty books from shelves, checked underneath carpets for telltale signs of hidden stairs, but nothing else unusual was found. Hetty followed silently, moving forward to join the searchers as they approached the attic. Suddenly she stopped abruptly, feeling at once faint and yet exhilarated. "This is the place, this is where I see that woman in my dreams!" Hetty exclaimed.

This entrance to the attic, a sort of hallway, dimly lit, had been the backdrop for the recurring dream.

Since the press had begun to file daily reports on the hauntings, people had begun to treat the Frederickson house as something of a tourist site. They turned out in droves, completely uninhibited and very persistent, impatient, and demanding. One Sunday over seven hundred visitors showed up, eager to view the secret passages, study the portrait that changed, and catch a glimpse of the ghost. Hetty even applied for a commercial licence that would have allowed her to charge admission to the house to capitalize on the crowds, but the town council turned her down. Her immediate neighbours were by this time getting quite fed up with the clamour.

In desperation, the Fredericksons simply decided to move. They were making no progress in solving the mystery, and could no longer endure the steady stream of traffic and the deluge of telephone calls demanding the latest news. The couple relocated to Sayward, a small logging community some two hundred and fifty miles north of Victoria. Fortunately they each possessed skills that allowed them to find employment immediately; Douglas was a logger and Hetty could teach art anywhere.

The house in Chilliwack stood empty for some time, the target of vandals and determined ghost-hunters. Then in 1968 a group of musicians moved into the derelict building, cleaned up the property, mended the broken fences, and fixed up the trampled flower beds. There were no further reports of ghosts and the furniture in that one bedroom no longer moved about. Things were back to normal!

And what of the painting? Hetty donated it to the Haunted House exhibit of radio station CKNW in Vancouver, a fund-raising endeavour for their Orphans' Fund. After that, it was loaned to a Japanese exhibition.

Opinions differ as to the credibility of the Frederickson haunting. Many contended at the time that there was nothing amiss with the large Chilliwack house. Doubters point out some aspects about Hetty's story that seem a bit odd, such as the fact that she had not considered the attic as a possible setting for her dreams until led there by the searchers. And John Plul, who was the promotion manager of CKNW, says that despite Hetty Frederickson's claims, her painting clearly depicts a woman.

"The painting is about eight feet high by five feet in width," he recounts. Done mainly in a multitude of shades of orange and in black, it reveals a woman gazing out of a bedroom window. She has her arms tightly folded before her. The left side of her face and a piercing left eye are painted in, but there is nothing showing on the right side."

The right-hand side was supposed to have mysteriously filled in by itself at the height of the haunting. Some tests on that portion of the portrait have indicated a complete absence of paint pigment. The canvas has been "worn down" by the friction of the fingers of curious gawkers.

Yet John Plul firmly believes that Hetty Frederickson was sincere about her dreams and that there was no attempt on her part to mislead the public. And skeptics might have reconsidered upon learning, a few years later, that a new group began to experience difficulties in the house. Nightmares feature prominently in both cases, and other details of the two hauntings are comparable.

In the spring of 1972, five years after the Fredericksons' departure, a family new to the area purchased the controversial Chilliwack residence. The family, which included eight children and several four-legged members, was too active to take serious note of anything strange at first. The large house seemed a perfect place for the sprawling brood, whose parents professed not to believe in ghosts. But soon they were forced to admit that something about it was most peculiar indeed.

Several of the younger children began to have nightmares, much like those that had frightened Hetty Frederickson so badly. Doors banged throughout the house for no apparent reason. And the family dogs, normally quite fearless, were discovered hiding under beds, cowering and whimpering.

For reasons they couldn't explain, the new owners were reluctant to go down into the basement at night. This fear was quite pronounced when they first moved in during the springtime, though it lessened when the strange phenomena decreased during the summer months. But with the approach of winter the doors began to bang anew and the basement once again acquired a frightening atmosphere.

The adult members of the family came to believe that three separate ghosts shared the rambling house with them. One was a female spirit, whom they blamed for setting the thermostat up to thirty degrees Celsius on several occasions. Her presence was also sensed by the family when they were watching television late at night. The second ghost, a male who seemed to have a childlike mentality, was held responsible for the early morning door-banging sessions.

The last of the phantom trio was more disturbing than either the door-banger or the television freak. This ghost had badly frightened several members of the family who had encountered it in dimly lit corridors and stairways. It greeted humans with a singularly icy chill that settled upon their backs and literally held them frozen in position for several long and agonizing minutes, until they were suddenly released, shivering and feverish, from its grasp.

Men often tend to be skeptical of hauntings, and the man who headed up the large family in the Chilliwack house was no exception; he did not believe in ghosts. It is even more impressive, therefore, that he took to sleeping with a fully loaded .38-calibre revolver tucked beneath his pillow — although it is hard to say what he expected the firearm to do against the supernatural.

The hauntings in Chilliwack have never been satisfactorily explained, and now it is likely they never will be. Recently the Chilliwack haunted house, complete with its secret passageway leading to the dusty turret, has succumbed to the wrecker's hammer. Its unsolved mysteries are now safe from prying eyes, and its ghosts can sleep undisturbed.

BY LOVE POSSESSED

Joseph and Barbara Grissum dwelt in a small community just outside of Victoria, British Columbia, with their children, Emma, aged nine, and Sandy, who was seven. To all outward appearances they were an ideal couple. Joseph was a successful real estate salesman who somehow managed to bring home a very handsome paycheque despite a volatile housing market. Barbara remained home to care for her family, which she loved dearly and of which she was very proud. To keep herself busy and to supplement the family's income, she operated a small day-care centre from the house during school hours.

In 1992 a sudden illness struck Barbara and she was forced to give up her day-care centre. It now required all of her waning energy just to deal with her own children. She went to a doctor, who prescribed tonic, vitamins, and more rest. But after battling the illness for several months, she was too weak even to go out grocery shopping. One of her neighbours, a close friend, stopped by twice a week to pick up a grocery list, and purchased whatever items Barbara needed. During these get-togethers the two women would stop to catch up on neighbourhood gossip. One day Barbara's friend let slip that she had seen Joseph having lunch with a lovely young blonde woman on several recent occasions. Who was she — a client searching for a new house?

Barbara realized that her friend probably meant no harm. Nevertheless she felt a little alarm bell at the back of her head. Joseph had always been a gregarious sort, more so than herself, but he had never shown any signs of straying from his marriage vows. That evening, after the children were tucked into bed, Barbara reluctantly asked Joseph in a tentative voice who this young blonde woman might be.

Her husband responded with an explosive outburst of embarrassment and anger. Phoebe Berrington worked in the office with him. She was originally from eastern Canada, Ontario he believed, and was just a business colleague. They often went to lunch together and it was nobody else's affair. Phoebe was new to the real estate firm and to the area, and he was simply helping her to learn the ropes.

Barbara accepted Joseph's explanation, although his attitude and manner struck her as being overly defensive. After all, she truly did want to believe him. However, it wasn't too long before she began to notice a marked increase in the number of evenings he worked late, and trips to visit clients out of town. Occasionally Joseph was away from home for two or three days at a time, something that had never happened before the appearance of Phoebe. When he was at home, the telephone rang with unusual frequency; if

Barbara managed to answer, the caller would hang up immediately. The atmosphere in the Grissum household was getting decidedly chilly: conversation was stilted, and young Emma and Sandy had noticed the change that had come over their parents.

Barbara finally confided her increasing worries about both her health and Joseph's unusual and furtive behaviour to Winnie Raphaels, her friend and next-door neighbour. Barbara trusted Winnie, a tiny, elderly widow, not to gossip about her difficult domestic situation. Winnie often took care of Emma and Sandy for a couple of hours after school so that Barbara could rest from her illness, which was getting progressively worse. The older woman also arranged for Barbara to see another physician for a second opinion on her condition.

In early 1993, following an extensive battery of blood tests ordered by her new doctor, Barbara was diagnosed as having a rare and untreatable serological infection. Devastated and depressed, she prepared to break the news to Joseph. She listened for his car in the driveway and went to greet him at the front door when she heard it arrive. But before she could make her announcement, he made one of his own: he was moving out, taking an apartment downtown; he and Phoebe were in love and she would be moving in with him.

This news shattered Barbara, who was already in a fragile state. Barbara collapsed on the hallway floor. Joseph called for an ambulance, and after seeing his wife safely out of the house, asked Winnie to baby-sit the children. He left that same evening, calling Winnie later to offer a stilted explanation of what he was doing and saying he would be in touch the following day.

To Barbara, Joseph's actions were monstrous. While she recovered somewhat during a ten-day stay in the hospital, both her physical and mental health had suffered to a point where it was now only a matter of waiting until the end. From the moment that Barbara regained consciousness in that sterile hospital room until the very last instant of her life three months later, she was determined to repay her husband, vowing that he would curse the day that he had deserted her and the children.

Upon Barbara's death, Joseph moved back into the family home, bringing with him the fair-haired Phoebe. She began working only part-time at the real estate firm in order to tend the children.

Emma and Sandy were still in a state of grief over their mother's death and shock over the new domestic arrangements. They had mixed feelings about Phoebe; she was very pretty and could be a lot of fun when she really tried. But other times she acted as though she didn't like them very much. She would sit silently at the kitchen table, smoking cigarette after cigarette and gazing out the window, ignoring them completely. Phoebe was almost useless when it came to helping with their homework assignments, and her cooking was an affront to the ingredients.

Joseph was certain that Phoebe would be fine with the children once she got to know them better. Plenty of other people went from one relationship to another and their children usually adjusted. But instead of getting used to things, Phoebe began to change for the worse. She became increasingly short-tempered and nervous, frequently accusing Sandy or Emma of taking her personal possessions and hiding them about the house. She said that they played tricks on her, like turning off the bathroom light when she was in the shower, or scrambling the cosmetics she liked to display on her dresser, or rearranging the clothing in her bureau drawers.

The children denied doing any of these things. They felt that the accusations were foolish and mean. How could they have turned off the bathroom light when Phoebe always barricaded herself behind the security of a locked door when she showered? And what would they want with any of her things?

Phoebe was seldom home after school any more and the children spent all of their free time over at Winnie's house. She would take them over to the small local park where she could keep an eye on them from a wooden bench in the shade of a huge oak tree.

The situation at the Grissum house deteriorated further. Every meal that Phoebe served tasted heavily of salt. The children half-heartedly pushed their food about on their plates, while Joseph ceased coming home for his lunches altogether. He suggested that Phoebe take a cooking course or watch specialty programs on television. He removed the salt shaker from the kitchen table and hid the large package of salt from the spice cupboard. Yet the food prepared by Phoebe continued to arrive at the table heavily dosed with the mineral.

The dial on the home's thermostat began shifting between extreme settings, so that it was always either unbearably hot or terribly cold. Joseph discovered a dusting of talcum powder between the layers of socks in his dresser drawer one day as he was getting ready for work. Bottles of cologne seemed to spill of their own accord, and the master bedroom now had the sickish-sweet stench of a department-store perfume department. Phoebe placed the blame for all of these unexplained incidents on the two children, whom she felt must be acting out of spite. Joseph scoffed at her. Emma and Sandy had been visiting their maternal grandmother when many of the incidents took place, and the children continued to deny any involvement in the mischief.

By the fall of 1994, Joseph and Phoebe were quarrelling constantly. He accused her of making no effort to improve her atrocious cooking, and ranted at her for being a messy housekeeper and incompetent at dealing with Emma and Sandy. She replied with brittle anger, eyes aglow, that he was insensitive, had spoiled monsters for children, and was never at home anyway. During these increasingly frequent verbal mudslinging matches, the two children would head dejectedly over to the quiet sanctuary offered by Winnie Raphaels.

Phoebe Berrington was no longer living in the Grissum house when Christmas arrived that year. It was a subdued and deeply troubled Joseph who greeted the festive season, attempting to explain to his two confused and unhappy children just what had happened and why.

A full-time housekeeper has now moved in to care for the children, cook, and manage the Grissum household. There is never too much salt in the food anymore, although the shaker is back on the kitchen table. Winnie Raphaels still sees the children regularly and will be watching with great interest to see if Joseph ever again attempts to bring home a replacement for his dead wife.

It is, of course, quite impossible to know if Barbara Grissum had anything to do with the dramatic ousting of Phoebe Berrington from what had once been her house. Yet she had vowed that she would repay her husband; if it was her actions from beyond the grave that brought about the destruction of the relationship between Phoebe and Joseph, her dying promise was fulfilled.

2

IS IT A GHOST?

A GHOSTLY CHECKLIST

Do you think that you or someone in your family or circle of friends has a problem with ghosts? It may very well be so. But before jumping to conclusions, take a little bit of time to eliminate the more common misconceptions. It helps to know a few characteristic signs of the occult, to avoid being deceived or honestly mistaken.

The following is a brief, simplified checklist that could be applied to an "average" haunting to reduce the chance of error.

1. Who says you have a ghost in your home? One person, two, or many? Do these people know each

other? Have you brought in individuals who are unaware of the problem and watched their reactions?

2. Does the difficulty date back through several ownerships of the premises? Is there a history of the property changing hands frequently over the years? If so, speaking to some of the previous owners about their own experiences may be helpful.

3. Have all the natural possibilities been eliminated? Could structural peculiarities such as the settling of the house or land shifts account for the phenomena?

4. Have you considered simple fraud? Does anyone want your house or land sufficiently to try to bring about a forced sale?

5. Is the chill you experience genuinely unearthly, or is your present heating system inadequate?

6. Could there be a practical joker taking advantage of the situation, or perhaps contributing to it?

7. How do animals react when the phenomena occur? Are there specific areas in which their behaviour varies widely?

8. Are there children between the ages of five and fifteen living in the house? (Children can activate hauntings or create their own.) Do the incidents occur in their absence?

9. Is there any reason for an individual in the house to feel a need for more attention?

10. Is there anyone within the affected area who has become overly absorbed in the supernatural to the exclusion of all other subjects and interests?

THE SNAKE CURSE

Sometimes, in the course of checking out various stories about the occult, one hears of individuals who determinedly make mountains out of molehills, creating problems where there are none. Such was the case of "snake curse," which involved a young couple living outside of Kleinburg, just north of Toronto.

Connie and Mike McTague had inherited their small home from Mike's elderly aunt, Marcia Kaufman. She had left it to them in return for their many acts of kindness during her last years. But there was a catch, at least in the eyes of Connie and Mike. The old lady had said, perhaps in jest, that should the couple ever decide to sell the house, she would return in the form of a snake to haunt them.

Not long after they moved in, they began complaining of a supposed infestation of supernatural snakes. Mike discovered one at the foot of the cellar stairs, another in the stonework of the living-room fireplace, and a third which lay lurking in wait just outside the kitchen door. Connie hated snakes with a passion.

Perhaps you are having second thoughts already? One little old lady and three separate snakes? The elderly aunt had said nothing of a plague of the scaly creatures. Yet the McTagues claimed they were being haunted by Marcia Kaufman, and they desperately wanted to rid themselves of the snakes.

The house was old, with a stone foundation. A brief check with other residents living in similar houses revealed that snakes nest in these old foundations as a matter of course. A single pairing of these reptiles, which are quite harmless, can produce an awesome number of offspring.

The curse laid down by Marcia, if indeed there was one, specified a haunting if the house was offered for sale. This had not been the case, indeed the McTagues had not even considered it. There was every reason to believe that the snakes seen by the McTagues were perfectly ordinary local creatures. Yet their appearance sent the McTagues into a state of unreasoning terror. Had the couple taken the time to research the situation with their neighbours, the entire matter could have been resolved in a few minutes. Connie may never like snakes very much, but she doesn't have to concern herself with stepping on the spirit of Mike's aunt.

Some occurrences are truly beyond the usual. But one has to be careful to eliminate natural and human factors before shouting "GHOST!"

RUMOURS

How easy is it to start a false ghost story? Quite easy, apparently. At a discussion group in Kettleby, Ontario, a quiet and gentle lady arose suddenly before some twenty-five fascinated people to admit that she had done just that. Her tale illustrates the perhaps too-willing acceptance of ghost stories lacking any solid basis and unobserved by reliable witnesses.

The woman involved purchased, along with her husband, a house formerly owned by two elderly ladies of the highly reclusive type one periodically reads about in the human interest section of the newspaper. As the years passed them by, they went out less and less, and became mindless of sanitation. They allowed their garbage and the other debris of life to accumulate both inside the house and around the property. Eventually, the two old women died.

During the course of settling the estate, it was necessary to clean out the house and the adjacent front and rear yard areas. The neighbours were shocked to discover the conditions under which the two elderly women had been dwelling. They felt guilty for not having realized the situation earlier and offered assistance.

The house was resold, and new owners refurbished it and moved in. A couple of local children dropped in, as they will, to check out the place and its new residents. One of the children, a girl of about nine, asked where the two old ladies had gone. Busy in the kitchen and not wanting to get into a discussion about death with strange children, the new owner said lightly that she thought they were upstairs in the garret room playing cribbage. And that was her mistake.

There was absolutely no reason to suspect a haunting. No one had ever reported seeing either of the two ladies after their deaths. It was not known if they had ever played cribbage or any other card game, and as for being in the garret, their last few years had been spent entirely on the main floor as the stairs had become too difficult for them to ascend.

Still, years later, if you ask anyone in that neighbourhood if there are any haunted houses nearby, chances are that you will be directed to the house once owned and inhabited by the two quiet old women. Marvellous detail has been added bit by bit over the years, until today a great "mystery" exists. The present owner of the house now regrets her flippant remark. It is hard to believe that the tale gained credence based on one remark made so lightly to a small child.

N⊕ISES

The presence of inexplicable noises has led many people to believe that they were under attack by the supernormal. From our youth, we have learned to isolate each new sound we hear and mentally identify its source. When this totally automatic reaction becomes impossible for some reason, we have a tendency to blame our inability to place the noise upon occult interference.

Sometimes this is just plain silly. People who have spent all their lives in a large city may find the tapping of a wood-pecker or the singing of pond frogs frightening. A country person may panic at the rumblings of the subway or the early morning whir of a machine cleaning the streets. When one changes surroundings, it is best to be careful about jumping to the wrong conclusion about a noise in the night — as the following story shows.

For years, there was one sixty-hectare parcel of land in Peel County, northwest of Toronto, that everyone in the neighbourhood believed to be haunted. Children hurried past it after school, and even adults could be observed stepping smartly along when they reached that area.

It was rumoured that a man, an early settler, had been slain on the property. The sound of a rattling chain served to re-enforce this belief again and again. News of this "haunting" persisted for many years, passing from genera-tion to generation.

One crisp, bright, autumn afternoon during the deer sea-son, a local hunter armed with a bow and arrow wandered into the underbrush toward the centre of the "haunted" property. He stumbled over an ancient piece of farm machinery, overgrown with weeds and thistles. It turned out to be an old combine, rusted and forgotten, its rear hauling-chain banging forlornly against the main body of the wreckage.

The hunter realized that he had discovered the source of the odd clanking noises that often reached the side-road on windy nights. Delighted, he related the story of his find to any number of his neighbours. Yet people are funny about such things. The old haunting story was too good to be allowed to die. To this day, children are still cautioned to hurry home past this property, with the threat that the ghost will get anyone who is tardy. And the rusty old chain still bangs forlornly whenever the wind is right.

ANY TIME, ANY PLACE

What is a ghost? The meaning of the word depends largely upon the area in which the sighting or occurrence takes place. It can also be influenced by the background, religious upbringing, or national origin of the persons directly involved in the actual manifestation. But generally the term refers either to the ethereal presentation, whether seen or merely sensed, of a dead person to the living, or to what we might call an apparition.

A broader interpretation of the term "ghost" includes all psychic manifestations and their related phenomena. In this latter category, one finds incidents of telepathy, clairvoyance, hindsight, astral wanderings, and all the different versions of the unpopular poltergeist.

The primary characteristics accorded to ghosts are internationally consistent to a very great degree. The Chinese, for example, firmly believe that all creatures have spirits, so it is not surprising that their ghosts often appear in animal form or shape. While, for the most part, Canadian ghosts tend to assume human form, our folklore also supports the theory that all creatures have spirits. We have laid claim to a demon dog, ghostly horses, cats, and dogs of every description, and even the occasional spirit-bird. Stories about a mighty spirit-wolf are related by many French Canadians.

The ghosts of the Chinese are often indistinguishable from living persons. Once again, the Canadian experience is similar. People have been known to walk right past apparitions without being aware of the startling significance of their experience until a later time.

Contrary to popular belief, ghostly appearances are not restricted to the hours of darkness. They can and do occur anywhere, at any time, day or night, and with great unpredictability. Supernatural experiences may occur singly, in a series, or widely separated in time, and they are frequently accompanied by other disturbing and unusual sensations.

No haunting is ever totally like any other. Since ghosts differ from each other as much as living persons do, the characteristics of individual manifestations vary markedly. A ghost can become known by the secondary traits that accompany its appearance. For example, observers have reported odd smells, ranging from sickly sweet to subtly floral. Some spirits even smell of wood-smoke or burning leaves. Frequently, visual, audible, and tactile experiences are all involved in a single sighting. A ghost is like a very talented musician — it can play with striking effect upon many human senses simultaneously.

A ghostly assault upon the ears can be most impressive. All manner of sounds echo up from the past into the present. The sounds of digging, fighting, screaming, banging, and invisible musical renditions are among the most commonly

experienced. Not too many ghosts drag chains like Dickens's
Joseph Marley.

F☉☉TST℮PS

The sound of footsteps is another spectral favourite. Trying
to follow ghostly footsteps can be an unnerving experience.
This is especially true when they seem to move from one
part of a house to another as soon as the first has been thoroughly checked out; the investigator knows that, somehow,
the invisible noisemaker has passed right by, or even
through, him or her in the connecting corridor. A relatively
common occurrence in hauntings, this is the sort of incident
that can utterly devastate people who are used to believing
only in things they can actually see or touch.

Toronto's Old City Hall, a Victorian structure located in the
downtown core, has caused many arguments in its time. Is it
a beautiful example of Victorian architecture or an aesthetic
horror? It is certainly old enough and sufficiently intricate in
design to make ghosts feel at home. So it isn't altogether surprising that Old City Hall started yet another controversy
when a ghost began lingering on one of its back staircases.
A ghost with those maddening footsteps! Two judges who
conducted court in the building witnessed the haunting —
you can't ask for more objective observers than that.

Provincial Court Justice S. Tupper Bigelow was the first
to notice something peculiar: "My office was located on the
second floor. I began using the staircase, which is a convenient way to go downstairs to our common room. On more
than one occasion I heard those footsteps. I couldn't see
anything, but I could feel my robes being plucked. There

was no chance that the robes could have caught on anything as I walked downstairs."

Judge Peter Wilch used the same staircase. He too heard the mysterious footsteps. On one occasion he heard them walking up just ahead of him. It is difficult to imagine a dignified judge chasing up a flight of stairs, courtly robes billowing, in hot pursuit of an unseen intruder; but that is exactly what Judge Wilch did. He swiftly followed the sounds right up to the top floor, where he began a careful search of the entire area. There was no one there.

Had the invisible being turned around and passed Judge Wilch silently on the staircase? Or was it standing there quietly, enjoying watching the bewildered judge's search?

The footsteps, which are still heard sometimes at Old City Hall, are light, suggesting those of a child or a woman. They appear to be confined to the one staircase, and there seems to be no harm intended by the haunting. The activities of this spirit have been restricted to stair-climbing and the plucking of passing judicial robes.

No one knows where this ghost, if indeed it be one, originates. There is no record of a murder or even an accidental death taking place on this staircase of Old City Hall. Could it be that some long-ago civil servant actually enjoyed her job in life so much that she is returning to it after death? And, if this be true, is she also fulfilling a frustrated lifelong urge to tug at a judge's stately robes of office?

CHILDREN FROM BEYOND

Apparitions involving children are frequently preceded by the sounds of light running footsteps and childish laughter or giggling. This is particularly true if the house has been a happy place in the past.

Buildings assume an atmosphere consistent with their history. Hence, some dwellings seem welcoming and comfortable as you enter them. Others are downright frightening, with a dark and foreboding air that makes you regret passing through the front door. For not all small figures from the spirit world bring joy and merriment with them. The sound of crying can be heard late at night, and concerned listeners may experience a strange feeling of deep sadness, even depression, if their house is occupied by an unhappy young spirit.

The number of sightings of ghost children has greatly decreased over the years. This is only natural, since child mortality rates are lower. Still, we continue to receive reports of children appearing from the past, including many who died long ago. Clothing and hairstyle help us date the apparitions in certain cases, but often there is no accurate way of determining a spirit's origin.

Some child ghosts are accompanied by the spirits of older persons who may have died at the same time. It is possible, but as yet unproven, that some of these mature apparitions are relatives from even further back in history.

Occasionally people have trouble with an empty cradle. It will suddenly begin to rock as if it were occupied by a baby; attempts to stop the rocking motion are met with a definite resistance, and the cradle's action continues unabated.

WOMEN ON THE MOVE

There are many women wandering about on the astral plane. In fact, it sometimes seems that there are many more female ghosts than male. Any number of reasons can be offered for this apparent anomaly, but no one theory satisfies it completely. Perhaps female ghosts are simply more active and sociable than their male counterparts?

Some spirit women merely appear along the side of a quiet road, usually at dusk. Others, bolder, have been known to hitchhike to the place where they once lived. They then vanish between the source of their ride and the front door of the building to which they were travelling. Unless the driver has a specific sensation that leads him to make inquiries of the present occupants of the house, he may never know or even suspect that he has driven a ghost home that evening. In a classic story found in numerous cultures, a female spirit leaves a glove or a scarf behind in the vehicle. This necessitates a check at the residence and leads to the discovery of the nature of the passenger transported earlier that evening.

A sense of duty seems to motivate many female ghosts. Some women come back to care for small children that death has forced them to leave behind. This phenomenon is most common when the child is being raised poorly or is mistreated by a stranger.

Women who were inclined to meddle during life sometimes just don't cease with death. In a few reported cases, men have remarried only to be caused great embarrassment and personal distress by the hauntings of their first wives. Writers of fiction have created some marvellous material by working with this idea. The possible storylines are numerous; imagine a woman living with her present husband and his first wife, now deceased!

GH☉STLY LIGHT

A persistent belief in Canadian folklore is that a patch of strange, glowing light may be a prelude to the visual manifestation of a spirit. These illuminated sightings have been attributed to the presence of marsh gases in the area, a theory that does have some basis in scientific fact. Sudden flickers of light can be generated by methane, which is the main component of marsh gases.

In other instances, unnatural light supposedly created by the forces of the supernatural may have been caused by luminous phosphorous issuing from rotting tree stumps.

An example of the kinds of debates that unusual lighting effects can provoke can be found at Candle Lake, Saskatchewan. This is a beautiful body of water, surrounded by evergreens, located just to the east of Prince Albert National Park. The lake drains into the Torch River, which in turn flows into the mighty Saskatchewan. On the east side of Candle Lake are two islands, named the "Curly Islands" after the wife of an early settler.

The name Candle Lake is derived from an old Cree legend that a strange light can be seen on the lake's surface in the evening. It appears between the two islands, casting a great shadow on the water in the shape of a flickering candle.

Although there is no Indian settlement in the area now, there was once an Indian campground where Fisher Creek is now located, and some graves dating back to the original Indian settlers can be found today along the north shore of Candle Lake. Some claim that the Indians refused to remain in this haunted spot. They continued to hunt within the district, but rejected the idea of keeping a settlement there.

The land around Candle Lake is totally unsuited for agriculture, so most of the white settlers who followed the Indians made their livelihood through trapping, fishing, or logging. They, too, believed that spirits abounded when the water shone eerily at night, assuming that the Indian gravesite was the source of the strange glow.

There will likely never be total agreement on the fascinating light shows at Candle Lake. Recent investigators have tried to account for the unnatural light by attributing it to phosphorescence from decaying logs floating in the water, or the spontaneous combustion of swamp gases. Swamp gases can resemble lighted candles, or balls of fire flitting over the water. Candle Lake is surrounded by swamp and bog.

Yet while marsh gases and phosphorescent rotting wood are both perfectly logical explanations that could well account for a certain percentage of the strange stories that are told of supernatural illuminations, some sightings have been recorded and investigated in areas where no such stumps or gases exist. In these cases, it is harder to dismiss the possibility of a spirit connection . . .

A CHILL IN THE AIR

Ghosts are cold. Those encountering psychic phenomena often notice sudden, inexplicable chills or pervading drafts during the course of a manifestation. Cold is one of the most common characteristics of apparitions — a frigid cold that feels unnatural, uncomfortable, even unhealthy.

It may be that spirits gain energy by draining warmth from their surroundings. Since sudden temperature changes can be fatal to fish, it is not too surprising that goldfish and their ilk are often found dead after the appearance of a spectre in their immediate vicinity.

This unnatural chill is often described as producing "goose bumps," or making "the hair stand up on the back of my neck." The individual is simply reacting physically to the abnormal temperature in the environment.

WHAT TO DO?

Attempts to shoot, injure, or otherwise deter a ghost can prove both frustrating and ineffective. How can you possibly impede something that is already dead and has no physical being? To shoot at a spectre is not only useless, it can be dangerous. The discharged bullet could ricochet off a wall and hit an innocent bystander or even the person who fired the gun.

Some people believe it is helpful to ask a wandering spirit to reveal its purpose "in the name of God." Others think that you should simply ignore the apparition and hope that it will go its own way.

On occasion, psychics and mediums use a series of word pictures that seem to release earthbound spirits. They emphasize the soothing ideas associated with the colour green, gently suggesting that the troubled spirit imagine green leaves, green grass, and green trees. They then direct the ghost to follow the soft light above the trees to freedom and "home."

There are no hard and fast rules for ridding oneself and one's home of an unwanted spirit. Exorcism appears to be effective only if a ghost has completed its task and was a religious person in life; even then, there is no guarantee of success. If you are rude to a guest in the hope that he will realize he is no longer wanted and should leave, the guest might take offence at your bad manners and decide to stay out of sheer spite. Similarly the exorcism rite, which attempts to expel a spirit by means of invocation, may only anger the ghost and increase its level of abnormal activity. Its effects cannot be predicted with any degree of accuracy; they can often be quite devastating.

WHO WILL COME BACK?

There does not seem to be any reliable formula for determining who can or will return from the dead. For all we know, these apparitions may be merely in a state of transition prior to their reincarnation. If this is the case, the length of this period of transition or ghosthood can vary markedly, from a single short appearance to a great many years and numerous sightings.

Certainly we would be in an impossible situation if all those who died tragically, or in great physical or mental agony, were to suddenly reappear in our midst. Some areas would be totally overrun by ghosts, a veritable infestation of lost spirits, because of a single large and violent historical event. The vicinity of all former battlefields would be unfit for human habitation. And almost every house would have at least one spectre left over from somewhere in the past.

Fortunately, however, this does not seem to be what actually happens. Many individuals have died unpleasantly, in both peace and wartime, and the vast majority of them have never been reported as ghosts. Nor are all the wrongdoers haunted and persecuted while they remain near the scenes of their prior criminal activities. It would be quietly satisfying to imagine that the inhabitants of the spirit world pursue and heckle all evil people, but this simply doesn't occur.

If it did, a man like Henry the Eighth, who executed two of his wives, would have had a frightful time pursued by their ghosts. Yet as far as we can determine, neither returned to demand retribution from him. One of them, Anne Boleyn, is reported to pace the ramparts of the Bloody Tower even today, startling the guards, but she apparently did not trouble Henry during his remaining years and marriages.

FOURTEEN WHITE HUSKIES

Sometimes, however, wicked lives end not in the supposed tranquility of the grave but in the vicious circle of perpetual penance exacted for past sins. Labrador has such a spirit. The ghost known as the Trapper was the cause of much heartbreak, great physical suffering, and the deaths of many people. He supplied bad, often fatal, wood-grain alcohol throughout the northern territories. He attacked local women when their men were away tending to traplines in the bush. He evaded and outsmarted the police officers sent to try to capture him, leading them on merry chases before losing them altogether. The Trapper was a storybook villain with no redeeming qualities. People who knew him could only revile him.

The Trapper died a natural death, far away from any outposts of civilization, including the police, but he has since been seen by many people. Every story about the Trapper contains similar information. He is observed driving a sled pulled by a matched team of fourteen pure white huskies, rushing furiously through the snow. This detail is consistent with reports that, while alive, he took great pride in his sled dogs, a collection of rare white huskies.

All those who come across the mysterious Trapper are aided by him. His apparent task is to guide travellers and trappers to safety through the mighty blizzards that roar in the north country. This feat accomplished, the Trapper then disappears back into the raging storm. Credited with saving many lives, the phantom Trapper was last reported making his ghostly rounds in the early 1970s. On that occasion he helped a young American reach the shelter of an unoccupied hunting lodge. When the man turned at the door to thank his benefactor, the Trapper had vanished into the swirling snow.

Ghosts have been known to make requests for special, sometimes unorthodox, burial arrangements. A group of five people living in a small northern Manitoba community claimed that they were being haunted by the ghost of a dead relative. The woman, they reported, appeared nightly, claiming she was unable to rest in peace because her family had buried her in the same grave as her estranged husband, who had predeceased her by six years. She hadn't liked him when they were both alive, and nothing had happened to make her change her mind in death.

Local civil and clerical authorities were consulted, and much discussion and heated argument ensued over whether living humans should be controlled by the dead. Eventually, permission was granted to the dead woman's relatives to meet the unhappy spirit's demands. Her remains were exhumed and placed a few feet away in an adjacent grave owned by the same family group. Since that time, her relatives claim that they are able to sleep through the night unmolested.

It is not usually that simple to translate the wishes of a spirit into deeds. Some apparitions cannot be placated, having returned just to create a bit of confusion, such as casually occupying a favourite rocking chair or fireside corner. These visitors seem to relish listening to their surviving relatives discuss stories of their past. However, if they hear themselves mentioned in disparaging terms, they can react violently, often throwing objects about the room. Other spirits, of a kinder, gentler disposition, desire only to be allowed to remain quietly for a period of time until their spectral needs have been fulfilled.

WICKEDNESS REVEALED

Many reported cases of ghostly vengeance have been attributed to the guilty consciences and vivid imaginations of those involved in the original offence. It is almost certain that those who believe in curses, hexes, and angry ghosts are more likely to be struck down by them. The mind that believes itself deserving of punishment can exact a fearful price from its possessor. Occasionally a profound sense of shame or guilt has resulted in a total loss of sanity.

But there are also numerous sightings in which quite innocent persons have been led by spectral figures to the hitherto undiscovered scene of some ghostly crime.

Apparitions generally appear in places where their living predecessors were happiest, or most miserable, or were directly and seriously involved in some major occurrence. They have revealed accurate information too many times in numerous places to be dismissed as mere hallucination or imagination. In many cases their actions seem calculated and deliberate.

Anyone considering committing an offensive or wicked act might be wise to pause and consider this particular aspect of the supernatural. There is no guarantee that killing an individual will stop him or her from all future activity. Many wrongdoers have experienced horrifying ordeals, showing that the dead can, and sometimes do, return to provide unorthodox but convincing testimony against those who persecuted them in life.

PACTS

The general format of a death pact is quite regular. The first person to die agrees to attempt to communicate by any means available with those who have been left behind. Those who remain are to be available, alert, and receptive to the message. The contents of the communication may have been agreed upon beforehand.

Perhaps we ought to pay more attention to people who vow to return from the grave, for it would appear that this sort of prearranged communication can actually be effected. The appearances of such death-pact spirits are usually of brief duration, seldom developing into a full-scale haunting. Once the required message is communicated, acknowledged, and understood, the faithful spirit seems content to leave of its own volition.

A classic example of pact fulfillment occurred in Halifax, Nova Scotia. It involved two women, Rita and Agnes. They had gone through public school together, remained together through high school, and then worked together in the same large office in that city.

Both being of a somewhat imaginative and romantic

nature, they vowed that if one should die first, she would return and make herself known to her surviving friend. This, they agreed, would prove conclusively that ghosts did exist.

Both girls married. Rita remained in Halifax while Agnes moved to Sydney with her new husband. When she was only thirty-two, Agnes died from a sudden illness.

One particularly warm June evening, Rita found herself alone in her two-story house in suburban Halifax. It was a charming, clapboard house with an especially attractive feature, a pleasant little alcove situated beside the oak stairway. The alcove was in deep shadow, yet a faint wash of fading daylight reached out toward the stairway. Rita was about to climb the stairs when she saw a shape in the alcove.

Her immediate reaction was fear: a prowler, perhaps, had broken into the house. But as the blurred shape took on a clearer form she saw her childhood friend, Agnes, looking young and serene. Agnes smiled. Rita tried to speak to her friend, but before she could utter a word, Agnes vanished. Still, it was enough to convince Rita that her friend in life had returned from the grave to keep the childhood pact that they had made so many years before.

While the casual pact between the two Nova Scotians worked, others of a more serious nature have failed miserably.

Because of the dangerous aspects of his work, master magician and escape artist Harry Houdini took a deep interest in the possibility of there being life after physical death. He deplored the fact that no one had returned to inform him as to what was waiting if he made an error in one of his routines. He set out specific and very complicated instructions as to what he wanted done when he passed away, for he firmly believed that he would be capable of returning. Times and locations for séances were established and lists were made of those who were to attend the gatherings.

In due course, Houdini met his death, although not, as it turned out, during a staged performance. His edicts were followed to the letter, under the leadership of his widow. Everything was done exactly as he had demanded, but Houdini never attended any of the many séances conducted over the years. The secret words that he was to have uttered to identify himself conclusively to those in attendance have remained unspoken to this day.

3

SPIRITS OF THE
NORTH

THE HAUNTED WAITING ROOM

Frank Scott was born in England about six miles west
of Newcastle-upon-Tyne, and attended medical school in
Newcastle from 1951 to 1956. After the required year of
internship, he did his stint of army service, spending three
years as Regimental Medical Officer of the Depot, the
Brigade of Gurkhas, at Sungie Patani on the mainland near
Penang, Malaysia. He then spent two years as an assistant in
a general medical practice in Lagos, Nigeria.

This brief biography is presented to establish that Dr.
Scott is not some impressionable character apt to be upset
by unusual events. He had seen plenty of them in his life,
such as the following tale brought to him by one of the

junior officers of the brigade in Sungie Patani.

The young man was driving back to camp late at night from Penang, and when he reached the Merdeka Bridge, a concrete suspension bridge, a Malay girl flagged him down and requested a lift. The young officer agreed, and she climbed into his car, a sporty MG. When he arrived at Sungie Patani, she was no longer in the vehicle. She had vanished during the drive without any physical trace — but leaving behind a strange, cloying smell.

Some of the older officers in the regiment dismissed the story as a far-fetched tale cooked up by a young subaltern to explain a sexually transmitted disease he might have acquired. Dr. Scott felt that the tale had been truthful, and he was bemused by the reaction of the other men. After all, there had been nothing in the story suggesting sexual activity; the subaltern had simply claimed to have given a young woman a lift. Two doctors questioned the man thoroughly and conducted an extensive physical examination. The story did not change, and the subaltern proved not to have a "social disease."

After his experience overseas, Dr. Scott had no intention of settling down behind a desk in England, so he cast about for an alternative and interesting position. At that time, Graham Spry was Saskatchewan's Agent General in London. The two men ended up getting together, and Mr. Spry showed the intrepid young doctor a map of his home province. There were sixteen towns in Saskatchewan that had a hospital but no doctor, and a new hospital was to be constructed the following spring at a place called Loon Lake. After analyzing the map and questioning Mr. Spry extensively, Dr. Scott concluded that if he couldn't find good hunting and fishing in the Loon Lake area, he was unlikely to discover them anywhere. The two men made a deal. For Scott, it was next stop, Saskatchewan!

Frank Scott arrived at Loon Lake at the end of September 1962. The town was located some five hundred kilometres northwest of Regina — the end of the world for most Canadians. It had no conveniences and was about a hundred and fifty kilometres from the nearest paved road. Scott's initial impression was that he might be able to survive for about a year there. But he grew quite fond of the place over time, and to this day maintains a summer home in the area.

The town of Loon Lake owes its existence to the "mythical railway" of the Depression era. The Canadian National Railway line from North Battleford reaches through the province as far as St. Walburg. During the 1930s, a make-work project was planned to extend that line north through Loon Lake, and then west through Pierceland to Cold Lake, Alberta, where it was to link up with the line running from there to Edmonton. It was an enormously ambitious under-taking, calling for an immense amount of manual labour to prepare the roadbed grade and to cut the ties. Loon Lake was to have been a major watering and shunting terminus between the town and the nearby lake. But no steel was ever shipped in, and no track ever laid. When the deal failed to materialize, a local Indian band reclaimed that land surround-ing the town. The town of Loon Lake became an island within the body of the reserve.

When Dr. Scott moved to Loon Lake, the population was about four hundred for the town proper, with a similar num-ber of inhabitants on the reserve. The town provided a house cum office unit for rent where Dr. Scott was expected to live. The accommodation had been used as a granary in the 1930s, when Loon Lake was first settled. The old building had been added onto on all four sides, adding little to its appearance or functionality. There was a small office with an examining table, and a tiny waiting room that could accommodate six people in a pinch and a squeeze. There was no room for a nurse or secretary. Nor was there any provision for heat or lighting in the narrow waiting room, so until Dr. Scott managed to remedy the situation the place was always gloomy and there seemed to be ice covering the floor all the time.

The building had no proper basement, just a roughed-in hole in the ground housing what had once been a coal furnace, since converted to burn oil, and a concrete cistern that served as a source of water. The town had neither paved streets nor a sewage and water distribution system.

Shortly after his arrival, Dr. Scott started hearing voices in the waiting room in the evenings when he was off duty and relaxing in his sitting room.

"I could never make out any conversation," he explained, "just the sound of voices. Every time, I *knew* that I had locked the door onto the street when I finished up in the office, but I would still get up and go to investigate. There was no one there. The office and waiting room were both empty, the outside door was securely locked, and the street outside was deserted."

Soon after he settled in, Dr. Scott acquired a roommate. Sandy was a yellow Labrador retriever, an excellent gun dog who was so even-tempered that he travelled constantly with his owner, and had come to consider the luggage door of a Cessna 172 to be a dog door. Sandy had never shown any signs of fear. But when the disembodied voices were heard, he would stand in the sitting room with his hackles up, growling deep down in his throat, as he gazed towards the waiting room.

The noises persisted, night after night. They made Dr.

Scott extremely uneasy, especially since Sandy appeared to be so unsettled by them. But Scott did not feel physically afraid of whatever was apparently sharing the house with himself and Sandy: "There was never any feeling of threat, just the unintelligible conversation. No screaming or banging, nothing dramatic. And this phenomenon continued for the entire two-year period that I lived in the place."

When Dr. Scott moved to another, more spacious and comfortable, residence, he kept an interested eye on the people who took over the old granary. They were the parents of the local Baptist minister. When Dr. Scott asked them if they had noticed anything out of the ordinary about the house, the couple replied that they were protected from "things like that" by their religion. This cryptic reply left him wondering why they felt they needed protection. Did they fear the source of the strange voices?

Some time later, the house was purchased from the town and the new owners embarked on an extensive renovation program, including combining the former waiting room and office into a single bedroom. They reported no problems and no voices.

Frank Scott went into semiretirement in 1990, but he still visits his summer home on the lake to the north of the town of Loon Lake. And, no, he still hasn't been able to figure out why he was the recipient of invisible patients or callers long after he had closed his office for the night.

THE STRANGE GUIDE

Near Whitehorse, in the Yukon, a man was saved from possible injury and serious difficulty through the intervention of a ghost from nineteenth-century Canadian history. The man was in his mid-thirties, a war veteran, and neither highly imaginative nor nervous. At his request, I shall refer to him simply as "Jerry" throughout this story.

Early in the fall, Jerry set out with his dog, Max, on one of his frequent prospecting trips. He entered the desolate country near a place called Pelly Crossing, which is located north of Whitehorse, inland along the Mayo Dawson Road. It is an extremely isolated area where only someone with a good deal of outdoors knowledge and skill would go alone.

As Jerry wandered through the scrub brush, he became engulfed in muskeg. Muskeg is a complex phenomenon caused by permafrost. In the north country, below a certain depth, the ground never thaws. The water from annual thaws on the surface cannot drain and becomes trapped. Vegetation often grows over this water, and when it dies, settles, forming bogs. In appearance, muskeg usually resembles flat, open land, with a few scraggly trees scattered here and there. Often it is firm enough to walk on until you hit a thin spot — but dig down a foot or so and you will find water. Seismic crews working in muskeg areas frequently have large machines, such as Foremosts or Caterpillars, which break through the surface and disappear entirely, never to be recovered.

With every step that Jerry took, he ventured farther into this seemingly endless muck. He was determined to go on, but could find no way to proceed without becoming even further ensnared. Even retracing his steps seemed impossible. Being unfamiliar with the area, he had no alternative but to continue plowing on stubbornly through the muskeg. He was in a great deal of trouble!

Eventually, Jerry came to a small elevated area where

there was just enough wood to allow him to build a small fire. By this time it was growing dark, and he decided to make his camp here on the hillock, in relative comfort and security. The problem of trying to find his way out would have to wait until morning.

Jerry managed to collect enough wood to keep his little fire going for some hours. After preparing and eating a small meal, he fed Max and then wandered over to sit beneath the only tree that was situated on his "island." Tired and discouraged after the adventures of the day, Jerry sat there quietly with his head drooping onto his knees.

Suddenly, Jerry's dog became very agitated. It snuggled in as close to its master's legs as it could get, making soft whimpering sounds. Jerry lifted his head from his knees to see what was upsetting this usually calm animal. He could not believe his eyes. In front of him stood four men and a girl of about seventeen years of age. All of them were ghosts.

"I can't explain how I knew they were ghosts," said Jerry. "I just knew they were, and so did Max."

One of the four men began to speak to Jerry in a tongue utterly unknown to him. But to Jerry's utter amazement, he found that he could understand exactly what was being said.

"There they were, all five of them, right in the middle of nowhere," he recounted. "And they weren't Indians. Their skins were white, three of them had blue eyes, and they appeared to me to be Anglo-Saxon. But the language that they were speaking certainly wasn't English, or even French. I'd have recognized either one of those two languages."

One of the ghosts appeared to be the leader of the quintet. He began to shout at Jerry, apparently furious at what he believed to be a deliberate intrusion and some sort of challenge. Jerry, with the benefit of his wartime experience and training, was quick to respond. He jumped to his feet without really contemplating his next move, and started after the offensive spirit. The five ghosts then disappeared as suddenly as they had revealed themselves.

Jerry and Max settled down again, thoroughly confused, but convinced that the strange incident was over. Yet a short time later, the dog started to act upset and worried again. Reluctantly, Jerry raised his head, and there they were anew: the same group of five spirits, standing quietly on the hillock, staring expectantly at him.

The spokesman, the same one as previously, once again began to shout. But this time, as his tone became increasingly violent, the female ghost tried to intervene on Jerry's behalf.

Jerry rose slowly and deliberately to his feet and resorted to some rather abusive language of his own as he demanded that these strange beings go away and leave him alone. Instantly, they vanished into the night.

For the third time, the tired prospector settled down with his head on his knees. Once again, Max began to shiver and whimper softly with fear. When Jerry looked up this time, however, he saw only the girl standing there in the dark. He spoke to her in English, and she responded to him in the strange language that he could understand but not identify.

She said that she realized Jerry was lost, and proceeded to give him explicit instructions on how to make his way out of the muskeg in the morning. She then quietly disappeared.

Jerry and his dog did not see the ghosts again, although the balance of their night in the wilderness was far from restful.

Shortly after dawn, Jerry packed up his few belongings and prepared to leave the hillock. He decided to gamble that the entire incident hadn't been just a figment of his weary imagination, and took the route that the girl had described.

Soon he came upon landmarks that she had told him to watch for: small stones, occasional tiny stunted trees, etc. Finally he was free from the mire.

The first time I heard this story, I figured that it was going to bother me for a long time. Encountering ghosts at any time is most unusual; to deal directly with white-skinned spirits speaking in a foreign tongue in that isolated part of Canada's Northland is unique. But the story has the ring of truth to it. No one would likely come up with a piece of fiction that strange. But from where did this quintet of ghosts come?

The closest I came to identifying those spirits was to place them among the scattering of Europeans who filtered through the North in the 1880s. Since then, a number of people have stepped forward to help with the puzzle.

A Serbian family, including a daughter in her early teens, is said to have passed through Fort Edmonton, now Edmonton, Alberta, around 1874 or 1875, heading for the country of the Yukon River. They were seen over the next two to three years by Indians and a few hardy prospectors in that general area, but then all reports of this family ceased. The last sighting of them occurred in the Fortymile area, not very far from where Jerry had his eerie encounter. There were only about six or seven surviving members of the family when they were last seen alive.

KEELY'S STORY

Keely Osland moved with her parents and older brother, Nolan, from Churchill, Manitoba, to Whitehorse in the Yukon Territory in 1990, when she was eight years old. For their first year in the new area, the family lived in a trailer home. After that, they moved into a house located in the Riverdale district.

The split-level home was quite spacious, and seemed even more so after the time they had spent in the trailer. On the main floor, upstairs, were a dining room, a living room, kitchen, and a bathroom. Keely's parents had their bedroom on this level, and Keely's bedroom was just across the hallway from them. Downstairs, on the lower level, was Nolan's bedroom. There was also a spare bedroom, a second bathroom, and the family room with wet bar, and a laundry room.

The first objection to the move was registered by the family's two cats. It was clear that the pair of them were very upset by something. As Keely described it: "They started to act really strange. Puss, the older, had always been a lazy character, who did nothing all day but lie around. Now he began to dart up and down the stairs. And our other cat, Chucky, he was usually too fat to even get up when it was time for him to eat. But, nevertheless, he started to try and do the same thing as Puss — up and down the stairs."

The two cats continued to behave oddly for some time, burning off energy that neither of them had ever possessed before. Chucky even lost a bit of weight. This strange activity could have been due to the novelty of their new spacious surroundings, but Keely didn't think so.

She herself felt uncomfortable in her new home from the very beginning, although there was nothing she could put her finger on until 1992. By then, she was ten years old, and Nolan, her elder by nine years, had moved out.

On December 13, 1992, the house occupied by Keely's aunt and uncle and their two children burned down. Temporarily homeless, that branch of the family moved in with the Oslands while their residence was being rebuilt. There was plenty of room for everyone, since Nolan's departure had brought the number of empty bedrooms up to two.

Christmas came and went without incident. Keely's cousin Lindsay, who was nine, received a Barbie dollhouse and a set of quint dolls with bottles.

One evening in early January, Lindsay and Keely were playing quietly together with their Christmas presents in the basement bedroom where Lindsay was staying. Both children saw two of the little doll bottles rise up from the carpet and float freely about in the air, about two feet off the floor. The tiny bottles hovered, moving horizontally in unison, for about thirty seconds before dropping softly back onto the carpet.

"It wasn't until the bottles fell down that it started to sink in, what had just happened," explained Keely. "We both made a dash for the stairs." When the tale of the amazing floating bottles was related to the adult members of the family, their reaction was viewed as less than adequate by the children. "The hard thing was that no one believed us, and we just had to live with that." Who, after all, would believe in floating toys?

None of the parents felt that there was anything unusual about the house, but the children began to have a most interesting time of it from then on, both together and separately.

One day Keely's cousins "sat in shock as a blanket hovered in the air, about four or five feet off the ground. Then it just fell to the floor. There was nothing under it, and there was no reason for it to float around like that."

Keely's oldest cousin, Ian, who was eleven, had his own unusual experience.

"Ian was home alone, watching television on the main floor, when he heard the back door slam shut with a loud bang. But when he went to check out who was there, he found that the door was still bolted shut from the inside. He could remember bolting it himself after the rest of us had gone out. He was very confused, so he went back into the room with the television set to just think about it for a while."

Then Ian heard the sound of heavy footsteps coming up the stairs from the lower level, directly towards him. He knew he was the only person in the house. Just then, the rest of the family arrived back home, and someone knocked loudly on the front door for him to let them in. Ian charged towards the front door, relief shining on his face. The sound of the footsteps ceased abruptly!

For the duration of the Osland family's stay in Riverdale, strange incidents continued to puzzle and irritate the children. Blinds that had been securely fastened suddenly shot up on their rollers. One after another, the youngsters developed a fear of going down to the lower level by themselves; they would generally wait until they had a companion in tow.

The Oslands have since moved away from their strange residence with its floating objects and scary stairway, and Keely is delighted. Puss and Chucky have settled into their new home with ease, relaxed and lazy again, and Chucky is overweight once more.

And the adults? They still don't believe any of this!

THE GHOST OF THE TRAPLINE

This story is an almost classic example of the supernatural illustrating "fetching," in which spirits appear at the moment of, or shortly after, death. It takes place in the western area of Canada, although most such occurrences have been reported in the eastern and Maritime provinces. Time and distance seem irrelevant to the recently departed.

Gordon Sculthorpe was about twenty-five at the time of his first and only encounter with the supernatural. It was the winter of 1933–34, and he was trapping to the north of Fort St. John, in British Columbia. Even today, there are great stretches of completely isolated country up in that area. In the thirties, the district comprised a world of its own.

The main village servicing the entire sector was made up of three trading outposts, the largest of them belonging to the Hudson's Bay Company. Around the three posts were various Indian encampments, some of them for Cree; but mostly Beaver Indians. From there the traplines ran outwards in all directions.

It was a harsh life, one that few city dwellers could even begin to understand. Before the onset of winter, all travelling was done by pack pony or saddle pony; four-wheel-drive jeeps and snowmobiles hadn't yet been invented. When the men were going out to their traplines, they would put packs weighing up to sixty-six kilograms right onto their dogs. In the depth of winter, supplies were hauled into the trading posts using horse-drawn sleighs. Maintaining the health of both humans and animals was a prime challenge and a requisite for survival.

Gordon Sculthorpe's trapline, unfortunately for him, was not one of the better ones. Those tended to be granted to the seasoned professionals, and Gordon was considered a novice in this hard land. He would have to earn the right to a more profitable line. His assignment started some eighty kilometres from the outposts. Five cabins were located along the line, each of them about three metres by four metres, erected with logs to a height of about 120 centimetres and topped with a sod roof.

The interiors of the cabins were excavated to a depth of a metre, so that they had an interior height of about a little over two metres. The excavated dirt was used in the construction of the roof and to bank up the exterior walls as added insulation. The exposed areas of the heavy log walls were chinked with a combination of mud and moss.

Each cabin had a cache, a small storehouse built up on the top of poles solidly dug into the ground. The poles had pieces of stove pipe tacked around them so that intruding animals could not climb up to get at the supplies and furs kept at the top. Gordon selected one cabin, a little larger than the other four, as his "home cabin." The others served as overnight stops along the trapline.

The cabins were located about twenty-five kilometres apart, and the trapper usually managed to move along his line from one to the next in a day. Sometimes, however, he was forced to spend the night with only spruce boughs as protection against temperatures of thirty or forty degrees below zero.

At that time, he had three brothers, one sister, his mother and father, and his maternal grandmother as family. It seems almost unnecessary to point out that Gordon didn't receive any mail from anyone for the entire winter. No newspapers, no deliveries, no telephone calls.

Gordon related his experience as follows:

"Late one clear, very cold night in mid-January, while I was sleeping in my home cabin, something startled me and I woke up. I was not just dreaming, I was really awake. Leaning onto my right elbow, I semi-rolled over and there was my grandmother, standing in the doorway to the cabin. I asked, 'What is the matter?' She stood there silently, smiled at me, and then slowly dissolved into the air.

"When I got back to civilization, the outposts, it was early

73

in April. There was a letter waiting for me, informing me that my grandmother had died on that very night in January when her spectral form appeared to me in the cabin."

There is written evidence of Gordon's spectral encounter: he scrawled his thoughts and recollections of his grandmother's strange visit to him that January night into a pocket diary. Similar incidents are often dismissed on the grounds that the person must have had prior knowledge of a forthcoming event. Yet this young man did not even know that his grandmother was ill, and he certainly had no way of knowing the specific date she would die. He had been totally isolated from any sources of information, and had had to rely upon the evidence of his own senses. The fact that the woman died on the very night that Gordon Sculthorpe saw her apparition in his cabin seems impossible to label as a coincidence.

Some interesting questions arise out of Gordon's experience. It is natural that the spirit wanted to reassure her absent grandson after she had died, but how was she able to locate him? How could she have travelled that far in such a short space of time? She was literally in two places at once. Given the choice of five equally isolated cabins on her grandson's trapline, this ghost went directly to the one in which Gordon had elected to spend the night.

THE MISSING PILOT

Even those who possess an innate psychic ability and strong mental self-control can encounter unexpected trouble when they resort to the use of a Ouija board in a quest for detailed information. One highly qualified and experienced individual in western Canada found herself embroiled in a thorough mess.

Lauretta Kitchen studied supernatural manifestations for many years and frequently served as a consultant to others doing research in this field. Up until the time of the incident I am about to relate, she considered herself to be virtually shockproof. Operating on the theory that experts know best, I shall tell the story in her own words as much as possible. The name of the ghost has been changed to provide some privacy for the other individuals who became involved.

"This was in the days when I would, if asked, fool around with the Ouija board. At that time there was an American pilot by the name of John Sherwood who was attempting to fly, nonstop, in a small plane from Alaska to the southern United States. He failed to make it and crashed somewhere north of Whitehorse, in the Yukon. The wreckage wasn't discovered until almost a year later.

"Everyone who could help was aiding in the search for the downed plane and its missing pilot. Since my family lived in the area then, we were very interested in what was happening, in whether the pilot might have survived. So one night, a couple of ladies who worked at the airport came over to our house. They knew that I had played around with the Ouija board before, and they asked me to try it again, with them. The idea was to see if I could locate the pilot, if he were dead, as so many people seemed to think. Nutty me, I agreed!

"Thereby began such a strange series of events, it finished me on the Ouija board for good. We got him loud and clear! He tried so very hard to describe to us where he had crashed, and every time it proved to be the wrong location.

"He first told us he had crashed near Canyon City, so in all earnestness we phoned the search-party base operating out of the flying field at Whitehorse, and told them what we had 'learned.' We also told them how we had come to receive this information. They were quite skeptical, as well you can imagine, but they nevertheless did make an effort to check out our information. But there was no sign of the missing pilot or his downed plane at that spot.

"Then we realized that, being an American, John Sherwood really didn't know that much about Canada. To him, it was just a large space lying between Alaska and his destination in the United States. So we came up with the bright idea of using an Alaska-Canada aerial map, and then we hit paydirt! We placed the little wooden planchette down on the map and John directed it right to the exact place where he was later found.

"We didn't report this finding, as we felt that we had dug deeply enough into the matter. The man's buddies were there taking part in the search, but they were too skeptical to try the 'medium bit.' There was no opportunity to hold a session to prove our findings for them. They eventually took off, back to Alaska. We figured that if they weren't sufficiently interested, then we weren't either."

Lauretta's attitude may seem cold-hearted, but after all it had already been determined that John Sherwood must be dead. Finding the downed plane at this late stage was of only academic interest. Since the man's friends were prepared to accept his loss, it would have been futile for them to remain indefinitely in the Yukon. And Lauretta, like most of those who have genuine psychic abilities, is most reluctant to force herself upon those who do not understand.

But the story doesn't end with the return of John Sherwood's friends to their homes in Alaska. Once summoned through the Ouija board, John refused to leave! Lauretta continued the tale as follows.

"Then we found that we couldn't get rid of this man. Talk about teleportation! Things would disappear like magic around the house, and I could always feel it when he was being a nuisance.

"One day I was all alone in the house, preparing to go to the store for some groceries. So I laid a ten-dollar bill on the dresser and went back to the kitchen for something. When I came back, in just a couple of moments, my money was gone! No sign of it. Out loud, I said, 'John, I know you're there. Put that money back.'

"No dice. He kept the money.

"A few days later, I was working at my sewing machine and discovered I needed some black elastic. I called to my oldest daughter to bring me some from her sewing kit. She complied, and placed it right on the machine in front of me. Then I dropped my needle and bent down for a fraction of a second to get it. When I sat up again, the elastic was gone. Again I repeated my order, to put it back — to no avail. He was always doing things like that! John always made quite sure that we knew he was in the house.

"Through the medium of the Ouija board, John Sherwood told us all about himself, his family, his girl-friend's name, all about his father. All of this information later proved to be true, when his friends calmed down enough to respond to our questions. It bothered them that we had all of this information."

At first, John seemed like an amusing and childlike visitor to the members of this Yukon family. Indeed, with Lauretta's background in the supernatural, he could not have selected a more tolerant and sympathetic group upon which to prac-tise his newly acquired talents and pranks.

But ghosts can be a bit like fresh fish — after a while, they start to go bad. John began to exceed his welcome and the limits of good taste. He interfered in important family matters, and became a general nuisance around the house. Now that he had received some attention, he began to demand all of it.

John proved to be quite capable of petty jealousy and, as he realized that the family was tiring of him, put up a stiff fight to be allowed to remain.

"He admitted to taking the money and the elastic and many, many other things, some of which we hadn't even missed yet. But he wouldn't tell us where he had hidden them. Instead he would just write, 'Ha! Ha!' across the board. He said he did it just for kicks and that we'd better get used to it!"

After this, then began the period when Lauretta and her family began seriously trying to rid themselves of John Sherwood's spirited ghost. The family attempted all manner of things to convince or persuade him to leave. They used various commonly recognized exorcism rites, and ordered him sternly to clear out. But Sherwood apparently liked it where he was; he clearly enjoyed the attention reluctantly given his antics by the Kitchen family, and strongly resisted. These people had this light-fingered ghost living with them for almost five years. John was finally ousted after the visit of a highly regarded medium with very potent psychic powers. This person was able to undermine the ghost's self-confidence by pointing out repeatedly that he was dead, and that he should remove his spirit to where it properly belonged. This he promptly did! The vanished articles, however, were never recovered.

4

GHOSTS ON GUARD

Many spirits are alleged to be in our world to protect things they had an interest in while alive — their wealth, home, possessions, etc. In coastal communities, ghostly figures stand on lonely guard to this very day over chests of buried pirate gold. These stoic guardians are generally members of the original group that stole and then concealed the treasure in the first place. Opinions vary as to whether the accidental discovery of their chest of gold and silver frees them from their long, solitary, silent task.

In the Maritime provinces, many complex formulas have evolved as to how to outwit and rob these spectral sentries. Silence, timing, and respect are believed to be three of the primary ingredients essential for a successful treasure-hunting expedition. Courage is another requisite, and the hunter should also be quick of mind and fleet of foot. If a digger is provoked into speech, as often happens, the guardian ghosts can exercise greater than usual power. The treasure-seeker may even bring about his or her own death, or sustain serious injury, from the wrath of the avenging spirit. And the treasure could simply vanish back into the depths of the wet sands forever.

Superstition holds that guardian ghosts cannot cross water. Although it seems irrational, a landsman thinks himself safe from the spirits of now-dead sailors if he has managed to place a body of water, however small, between himself and possible pursuers. Flight across a stream or into a small waiting boat are therefore considered to be among the best methods of escape from the pursuit of spectral guardians of buried pieces of eight, golden doubloons, and silver ingots.

⊕AK ISLAND

Oak Island, off the north shore of Nova Scotia, has been the site of many a treasure hunt. History has it that Blackbeard's treasure lies there beneath the shifting sands. Since that same fantastic hoard has also been reported as buried in untold other places, its imminent discovery at Oak Island seems unlikely. But there is definitely something hidden there, and so the search continues. But contending with ghostly apparitions in the damp sea air can unnerve the most diligent and committed fortune-seekers. The old belief that a treasure search must be conducted after dark never did much to add to the peace of mind of diggers; this notion has lately been abandoned in favour of daylight digging when the tides were right.

People have sought treasure on Oak Island since 1795, yet the legendary money-pit still eludes discovery. Some seekers simply ran out of time, money, and energy; others fled in total panic and disillusionment. Modern knowledge and heavy-duty excavating equipment have not made searching this area any more successful or enjoyable than in the eighteenth century. No one is even certain what, if anything, lies beneath the island's many layers of timber, sand, and mystery. As Kerry Ellard of Montreal, the public relations representative for one of the groups involved, said, "It is awfully difficult to say when it will end. We don't know what we're looking for. No one does. There is a terrific body of evidence which indicates that there is something there. But just what it is and how it got there we don't know."

Oak Island is the private property of David Tobias, a Montrealer, who is one of the major supporters of Triton Alliance Syndicate Limited. This group, formed in 1971, is a hard-nosed bunch of realistic individuals who are working with some very impressive financial support to find whatever treasure the island holds. More formidable than any of its predecessors, Triton uses the most modern scientific methods in its search and digging operations. You can also bet that the staff at Triton are mindful that six people have perished in modern attempts at solving the Oak Island puzzle.

There is no reason to believe that the six deaths were caused by the involvement of ghosts. Little is known about the first two fatalities. The other four men died in a single nasty accident in 1965. Robert Restall was working in a pit in Smith's Cove when he was overcome by carbon monoxide gas. His son and two other workmen rushed to his assistance, and all four perished.

Is Oak Island's puzzle called "the money pit" because of the nature of the treasure lying beneath its surface, perhaps old gold, or because of the vast resources of money and manpower that have been poured into its exploration?

In 1971, Triton lowered a submarine television system into a deep cavity. This system sent back pictures of three chests and a severed hand. But sea water eroded the banks of the shaft and these items were not recovered. Searchers did draw to the surface three links from a chain, a bit of parchment inscribed with a "V" and an "I" written by a quill pen, and a flat stone marked with symbols. The stone was examined by experts from local universities, who believed the symbols revealed that treasure worth two million pounds lay buried somewhere within the diggings.

In the early 1970s, Don Blankenship, who was then supervising the Triton operation, stated, "I have been involved with this damned island, in one way or another, since 1965, and I have learned a long time ago that it doesn't pay to look for simple solutions. We are now pressing ahead with new equipment, which might bring us final answers to the whole mystery in the next few months." The hunt still continues.

In the late summer of 1987, David Tobias announced that in the near future Triton would make a public share offering to undertake the "deepest and most expensive archaeological dig ever made in North America." Nothing newsworthy has occurred since his statement, however.

Oak Island is a great tourist attraction, partially because of the promise of its vast riches, but also because of the rumours of ghosts on the site. The treasure-seekers involved have not actually seen a ghost, but rather, they have "felt" that there must be an intelligence behind the events that continually foil their work. Perhaps the spirit of the man who designed this fantastic trap, probably a slightly insane genius, still guards it.

In a way, it would be a shame if the current crew of treasure-seekers could produce a logical and coherent explanation for all of the weird events that have occurred on or near the job site. Fortunately for mystery-lovers, it seems highly improbable that anyone will ever be able to destroy the reputation of Canada's most bizarre island.

Who created this incredible snare, and why? What happened to the workers who brought it into being? Were they Canadian or foreign pirates from faraway ports? Is this really a secret hiding place for a king's ransom or merely a marvellous joke to highlight man's cupidity?

A BROWN AND EGG-SHAPED THING

Does a ghost always have to represent a dead person? Is it possible that a human being who is still alive can project some portion of his or her spirit to haunt another physical location? This idea has been advanced as a possible explanation for a series of terrifying and unusual incidents in Etobicoke, a western suburb of Toronto, where the spirit of a still-living old woman may have been trying to "guard" her former home from its new inhabitants.

It was spring in the late 1960s, and two families were sharing a large, eighty-year-old farmhouse on Prince Edward Drive. (The names of the people involved, who were harassed by mobs of curious people when the story was first published in the Toronto newspapers, have been changed.)

Edward Craighill and his wife, Kirsten, rented the house for two hundred and fifty dollars a month. Living with them was their ten-year-old daughter, Anne. The second-floor apartment was sublet to the Craighills' twenty-seven-year-old married daughter, Diana, and her husband, John Bullen. The Bullens had two small daughters of their own. The Craighills also rented out the basement of the house to a bachelor schoolteacher. These arrangements suited everyone. The Craighills loved the old rambling house and had no intention of moving for the foreseeable future.

Life in this pleasant domestic situation took an ugly turn one warm May night. Diana Bullen, asleep in one of the second-floor bedrooms, awoke in the early hours of the morning to the sound of heavy muffled footsteps coming from the attic overhead. She recounts: "I heard the sounds, thump, thump, thump. Next I heard piercing, screeching laughter. It sounded like a middle-aged woman was right in the room with me."

She reached over and awakened John. At first they both lay in bed, listening to the strange sounds, absolutely terrified. Then they got up to check on the two little girls asleep in the adjoining bedroom. The noise stopped abruptly. Their daughters were sound asleep. The Craighills, too, were still asleep on the main floor, apparently undisturbed.

Early the next morning the family searched through the attic and found nothing that could account for the previous night's occurrences. Diana Bullen eventually went back to bed to try to make up for some of the sleep she had missed.

Lying in her bed, half-asleep, Mrs. Bullen suddenly sensed that someone was standing in the room, leaning towards her. She could see no one. She felt a sudden deep chill, "as if somebody had walked right through me," exclaimed the frightened young woman.

The next night the thumping sound began again. It

commenced at two in the morning, a slow, measured, confident step that continued until the light of early dawn.

The Bullens decided they needed a break, and spent the next night with friends. They returned in the morning. The following night was to be the worst yet.

At 12:30 a.m. the ominous sound of footsteps began, followed shortly thereafter by an almost maniacal screeching. John Bullen, feeling he had suffered enough, spoke up in a harsh, hoarse voice, commanding whatever was disrupting their sleep to keep quiet and leave them alone. Surprisingly, the noises ceased. After calming down, the Bullens managed to fall asleep.

But around four o'clock they were aroused again. On this occasion, Fluffy, the family cat, disturbed by all the activity, left the Bullens' bedroom, heading towards the door to the attic. This door was around a corner of the hallway and so out of the line of vision from the bedroom. The Bullens heard a sudden hollow thump, as if the cat had been kicked, and then Fluffy screeched out as if in terror or pain. This was immediately followed by a shrieking sound and then by a horrible roll of deep-throated laughter.

John Bullen eased himself gingerly out of bed. "Is the cat dead?" asked a panic-stricken Diana, a quaver in her voice.

John found the cat stunned and half-standing, leaning against a wall for support. Its long fur was standing erect, as if the animal had suffered an electric shock. Fluffy was staring wide-eyed at the door leading towards the attic.

The Bullens managed to go back to bed, but neither of them were able to sleep very well for the balance of that bizarre night. John called his wife several times during the following day from the factory where he worked. On one of these calls, Diana told him that since his last call she had heard the footsteps again, and that a strange light was seeping out from under the closed door to the attic. She had been so unsettled by the idea of an intruder that she had sought assistance from a neighbour, Ron Leyzack. He took his .22-calibre rifle and a hefty flashlight and stormed into the attic, but found nothing.

It was apparently one of the other neighbours, now aware of the problems in the Craighills' house, who telephoned one of the Toronto newspapers. Two reporters, John Downing and John Gault, were dispatched from the *Toronto Telegram*. Both were experienced men, and showed the usual skepticism of the press at such ghostly shenanigans.

Arriving late in the afternoon, the reporters searched the attic and found nothing. It was a fairly large room with a sloping roof. There were no openings that would allow an animal to get in from the outside. The footsteps and the strange sounds could not be explained as a result of their search, nor through the interviews they conducted with the families. The reporters asked permission to stay the night. Everyone was quite happy to have the two men remain and experience for themselves what had so disturbed the Bullens.

As a basic precaution against a hoax, the two reporters covered the attic floor with a fine dusting of flour. Their thinking was that if human feet were responsible for the thumping noises, the flour would be disturbed. Any footprints would help establish the size of the culprit.

At three-thirty in the morning, the reporters heard the heavy walking sounds. The cat began to cry out in fear. The two men climbed up into the attic and checked the flour-covered floor. They saw nothing; the flour was undisturbed.

The following day, while her husband was at work, Diana Bullen invited the Reverend Tom Bartlett of the Star of

Progress Spiritualistic Church to the house to investigate the mystery. He arrived with his wife, Pat, and both were fascinated by the challenge.

Reverend Bartlett climbed up into the attic alone. It was dusk and the attic was gloomy. He closed the door to the attic behind him and stood for a few minutes in the murky half-light, surrounded by silence and his thoughts. Glancing slightly to his left, Reverend Bartlett spied a brownish, egg-shaped form. It glowed with its own light in the now quickly darkening room.

He would later describe this form as about four feet by two feet in size. It moved slowly from his left side over to his right and then it seemed to hover there, close beside him. Reverend Bartlett called out for his wife to come up.

When Pat Bartlett's eyes had adjusted to the poorly lit room, she also saw the form, off to her left, but in the shape of a brownish yardstick, about two or three inches in width. At that instant, Pat Bartlett felt sharp pains in her stomach and chest and a couple of loud thumping sounds were heard.

Down below, just outside the closed attic door, there was also activity. Diana Bullen, standing anxiously with the two *Telegram* reporters, saw a strange light underneath the door. The reporters confirmed that they had also seen the light, and then all three people became aware of a sudden and intense sensation of an icy cold embrace.

The reporters cautiously joined the Bartletts in the attic to see the mysterious shape for themselves. But Diana Bullen turned on the light from the switch at the foot of the stairs, and the brown, glowing form could not be seen. Reverend and Mrs. Bartlett described it in detail, and said they thought that the shape was trying to direct their attention to a dusty dormer window overlooking the backyard.

Reverend Bartlett speculated that the egg-shaped apparition might be a thought form. Both Bartletts thought that the colour brown might signify that the spirit was still somehow attached to the earth, but that it was very ill.

The Bartletts performed an exorcism service and then everyone prepared to leave the house. At this point Diana Bullen became hysterical and fainted, remaining in a state of semi-consciousness for approximately half an hour. By four o'clock in the morning, the heavy thumping footsteps were heard once again. Mrs. Craighill noticed a light at the top of the stairs that led to the second-floor apartment. Could the spirit have left the attic and descended to the main part of the house? "We were all petrified now," Kirsten Craighill commented.

The following day, Edward Craighill telephoned his landlord and told him with great reluctance that they would be forced to give notice. When he explained the reason for this, the landlord's son volunteered to remain in the house overnight to determine for himself what all the fuss was about. He felt it would be a shame to lose such good tenants because of some floating thought form.

So once more there were guests in the old house. The two reporters, the landlord's skeptical son, and the Craighill and Bullen families all settled in for what might be a long wait. John Downing and John Gault, defeated with their flour trick, rigged up a complex network of fine, virtually invisible threads throughout the attic. They attached small bells to the ends of the threads, reasoning that if even a really strong draft blew through the attic, the bells would ring. If there was a human causing the disturbance, there would be no way that he or she could avoid the myriad of threads that crisscrossed the area. They also re-dusted the floor with flour.

Shortly after eleven that evening the footsteps began again. At two in the morning, a terrifying series of cold waves of air swept through the entire house. The two reporters estimated that they felt the temperature drop from the normal seventy degrees to a chilling forty degrees. With the temperature drop there came a sensation of dampness. Everyone scrambled to locate sweaters and coats. Kirsten Craighill smelled a strange fragrance in the hallway, a musty dank scent of apples that had lain too long in the barrel. A quick check of the attic revealed no disturbance to the fine coating of flour on the floor. None of the tiny bells ever rang.

In the face of all the excitement, and after the irregular sleep of the past few nights, ten-year-old Anne Craighill became hysterical. She was gathered up and taken away to stay at the home of an aunt. Kirsten Craighill also broke down and had to be sedated.

And now a new problem befell the unfortunate families. Their story appeared in the *Toronto Telegram* and the old house was besieged by curiosity seekers. The Bullens left the house, followed a few hours later by the Craighills, but the crowd outside continued to gather. It required four police officers to maintain order.

The newsmen, in an attempt to trace the history of the house, interviewed William Tomlinson, the present owner and landlord, whose great-grandfather had built it. Mr. Tomlinson said that his grandparents had lived in the house and that he himself had purchased it in 1942 and then converted it into apartments. He also confided that, for the last fifteen years of his grandfather's life, the upstairs of the house remained unoccupied. "I don't know why," Tomlinson declared, with a shrug and a small shake of his head.

The two reporters, having nothing further to add to the

stories already written, dropped the subject in frustration. The Craighills and the Bullens vacated the house for other accommodation. The throngs of people left, disappointed, and the furor died down.

Reverend Bartlett and his wife continued to maintain that the disturbances were caused by a thought form. It was discovered that an elderly lady, an expert in fortune-telling, had once lived in the house. This woman became rather peculiar in old age, and took to sitting by the dormer window in the attic, shouting out songs at passersby. Neighbours complained about the racket and the old woman was forced to move. She was still alive at the time of the Craighill haunting, living some miles from the Etobicoke house. She had some sort of idea, attendants at the retirement centre where she resided said, that she was "keeping the house for her son."

Reverend Bartlett concluded that there was nothing to fear from whatever had been active in the attic. "The poltergeistic activity in that old house was caused by the ghost form or thought form of a person not yet dead, located several miles away and thinking of past experiences which she wanted to relive."

He theorized that the old woman was able to project her thought form back into the house where she had once lived and that, in a sense, she had indeed returned to the building.

A BOWL OF HOLY WATER

In September of 1988, Jean and Karen Chappelle moved with their two sons, Greg and Larry, to a newly purchased home in a small village in central New Brunswick. To the

Chappelle family, the house seemed new and wonderful, even though it was about twelve years old. It was ideally situated, at the end of a small, almost rural lane in the tiny hamlet, nestled snugly among a number of birch, spruce, pine, and poplar trees, which gave it a degree of shelter.

When the Chappelles first moved in, Jean and Karen subjected the property to a thorough inspection and a solid general cleaning. They wanted to settle in and live there for some time. After several months, they decided to redecorate a few of the rooms, partly to make the house more their own. They discussed the matter and decided to start in the basement, tackling the laundry room first.

This dingy room felt slightly creepy. It was always damp, cold, and dark, and had a strong musty smell. It seemed to attract hordes of flies, large clusters of which were always stuck on the two small windows.

However hard the couple tried to rid the room of the flies, they were always there. No one could ascertain how they were getting into the house, or why they weren't congregating in any of the other rooms.

Discouraged by their initial lack of success, Jean and Karen decided to leave the laundry room for later. They turned their attention to the basement bathroom.

While the bathroom was being scrubbed down, Jean found a rusty old axe in the top of the linen closet. He was certain that it hadn't been there before. He stored it away in a safe place. By the time the couple had completed cleaning and disinfecting the bathroom, the basement area was beginning to make them both a little nervous. So they headed back upstairs to concentrate their efforts in the kitchen, which seemed harmless enough.

The plan was to paint the kitchen walls in a brighter

colour, and to use some wallpaper trim near the ceiling. Jean started washing down the walls, and Karen dealt with the cupboards, washing and wiping them thoroughly and installing drawer liners where they were needed. On the top shelf of one of the cupboards, she discovered an old recipe book filled with handwritten, detailed recipes for East Indian dishes. Judging by the various handwriting styles, the recipes were a family collection, with contributions from several different members.

The Chappelles knew the people who had originally built the house, and also those who had lived there most recently. None of them had been of East Indian descent. When asked, they all claimed not even to enjoy that style of cuisine. The book did not belong to any of them.

The discovery of the axe and the strange book of recipes made the Chappelles very uneasy. They had carefully gone through the house from top to bottom, including all the cupboards, when they had first moved in. No axe, no cookbook.

Still, these oddities faded as the house became more like a home for the family. During the second year of their residency, Karen started waking up almost every night screaming, and not knowing why. As far as she could tell, she had not been suffering from any nightmares that might have caused her to panic and scream out. Over time, she began to see a dark form in the master bedroom, usually in the gloom of the middle hours of the night. Initially, it had no face or discernible body, just a blurry shape. But Karen would awaken in the night and freeze, trembling with fear, to find the thing above her face.

The phantom form always disappeared whenever Jean awoke, either naturally or at the sound of his wife's screams.

He believed Karen's story, but she made it virtually impossible to get a good night's sleep.

Another year passed by. It was 1991, and the couple still had been unable to rid themselves of either the massed flies in the basement laundry room or the vague form that haunted their bedroom.

Then, for some bizarre reason, the shape developed into a face that was visible to both Karen and Jean. They would wake up in the middle of the night and see this vision floating in the air above their bed. It was the face of an old man, with thick, curly grey hair reaching almost down to his shoulders, and a greyish-white beard and mustache.

As the strange, disembodied face continued to appear before them regularly, the bewildered couple came to realize that the man meant them no harm. If he had, they concluded, something terrible would have already occurred.

The Chappelles never discussed the nocturnal intrusions in the presence of their two young sons. But in their third year in the house, the younger boy, Larry, aged eleven, awoke one night yelling for his parents to come immediately. When he had calmed down and they asked him what had been the trouble, he cried out, fearfully, "There was a man in my room!"

The disturbances in Larry's room went on for several nights while his distraught parents tried to figure out what to do. They were afraid to ask too many questions, and unwilling to confess their own experiences.

Finally, after much discussion (some of it conducted with the strange face hovering right over their bed), Jean and Karen decided to sit down with Larry one evening and ask him, quietly and calmly, to tell them all about the man in his room. The face that Larry described to his parents was identical to the one that they had been seeing with such regularity. When they explained to the youngster that they saw the same man, Larry seemed to feel a bit better. They explained their theory that the phantom figure was probably not evil.

Next, the Chappelles approached their other son, Greg, then a mature fifteen-year-old. They wanted to determine if he had ever been awakened during the night, or seen anything strange in the house.

Greg admitted that he often saw an older man with a greyish-white beard and mustache hovering over his bed during the night. He hadn't mentioned anything about this apparition to his parents because he had thought that it might be his maternal grandfather, who had passed away several years ago. Greg had not wanted to upset his mother.

The two boys had been questioned separately by their parents without the other knowing what it was that they wished to discuss. This way Jean and Karen hoped to at least obtain two independent stories.

The family's dog, Sport, had always slept in the boys' bedrooms, alternating between Larry and Greg so as to avoid hurt feelings. The family wondered why he never barked or whimpered during these nighttime visitations. Maybe Sport knew something about the old man that the others didn't.

The cat, Jingles, however, was quite a different case. Early on in their occupation of the house, Karen and Jean had feared for the cat's sanity. Every night Jingles would let out ear-piercing cries. Friends told the Chappelles that the cat must either have some Siamese traits in her breeding or be always in heat. The vet quashed both of these theories, however. The cat had absolutely no Siamese characteristics, and, as a spayed female, was certainly not in a state of continual heat.

Jingles's obvious distress increased as time went on. In addition to the nightly shrieking, she began to lose control of her bowel movements. The Chappelles were forced to seek another home for the cat, and were not too surprised to learn that with her new family she cried out no more and her bowel movements were back to normal. Obviously, the problem had been within the Chappelles' house, not with the cat.

The nightly intrusions were more than enough for the Chappelle family to deal with. When they started to hear footsteps in the house during the daytime and loud bangs from the basement, and had the feeling of always being watched and followed, Karen decided that they had to fight back. This was, after all, their home. It did not belong to an apparition, or to any one of a number of annoying sound effects.

When the Chappelles had moved in, the side windows by the front door had been covered with little religious stickers. None of the previous owners had known anything about them, and when the Chappelles had moved in, they had simply scraped them off. Remembering those stickers now, they decided to take a more serious, and yes, a more religious, approach to their problem. Things couldn't get much more out of hand or bizarre. Jean and Karen drove to a well-known shrine in New Brunswick and procured some holy water. Actually, quite a lot of holy water.

Karen and Jean sprinkled the holy water liberally all over the house, especially in the bedrooms and the basement laundry room. They left a good-sized bowl of it on a table sitting right inside the front door, and every now and then they would sprinkle some of it into the house as they entered.

Since the Chappelles brought in the holy water, there has been only one brief incident of a family member seeing the face of the old man. When that happened everyone panicked, thinking that their problems were going to be starting all over again. But Jean discovered that the bottle of holy water was empty and quickly remedied the situation.

The last appearance of the old man was in 1993. The Chappelle family has promised itself that, so long as they continue to make their home in this rather peculiar house, they will always have a large bowl of holy water about. One day, they hope to be able to solve the mystery of who their ghost was and if he is in some way connected with the old axe and the East Indian recipe book. They would like to know why he appeared to all of the family members and exactly what it was that he wanted from them.

But for now, Karen and Jean and their two sons are just thankful that they can once again sleep peacefully, and without disturbance, through the night.

5

PRAIRIE
PHENOMENA

THE RED PHEASANT AFFAIR

Red Pheasant was a post-office/general-store combination located about thirty kilometres south of North Battleford, in Saskatchewan. You probably would not be able to find it on a modern map.

The store was old, unpainted, rambling, flat-roofed, with two stories, and an additional storage area located in the basement. The property included a large barn and a quarter-section of land, which was alternately used as pasture or for crops. Most storekeepers of the day kept some cattle and poultry; some had horses.

There were a number of resident owner-operators over the years, but the ghostly duo living at Red Pheasant remained constant. The spirits at Red Pheasant came to be considered almost as family members by the living people whose home they shared. One of the owners confided that "pets" might have been a more accurate label, given that the spirited pair contributed nothing to the operation of the business.

At the beginning of this century, the store was operated by Eric and Daisy Lund and Eric's father, Jack. They all slept upstairs, Jack in the northeast corner room, later dubbed "their room," as most of the unusual activity seemed to centre there. Jack found that he had one roommate plus a second ghost that paid regular visits to his room. There was a male ghost, referred to as "Wilbur" and a female spirit nicknamed "Annie."

Presumably the room had once been occupied by Wilbur — his ghostly presence would glare fiercely at anyone sleeping in "his" bed. Once in a while, his sister, Annie, would look out the window, dust the furniture, or make up the bed. She was a busy soul, and seldom stayed for very long.

Jack Lund saw Wilbur more frequently than did his son and daughter-in-law. A big fellow, Wilbur would stand stolidly at the foot of the bed, feet astride and arms akimbo, just staring at Jack. Jack would keep right on reading, trying to ignore Wilbur.

One night Jack awoke suddenly, sensing that he wasn't alone in the room. Cautiously opening one eye, then the other, he saw an old lady standing by the window. She would look out into the dark, then at the bed, then at Jack, out the window again, then back to Jack. Though puzzled, he could tolerate this, but when she turned, advanced towards him, and then started to make up the bed with Jack still in it, he could contain himself no longer. He yelled!

Annie, the ghost, turned and walked out of the room.

Daisy Lund was in the next room, reading by a coal-oil lamp. Hearing her father-in-law's shout, Daisy grabbed her lamp and sped over to Jack's room. She reached the doorway just as Annie was leaving the room. Jack saw Annie walk right through her!

Jack was sitting upright in his bed, staring in utter disbelief at the doorway.

"Did you see that?"

Daisy hadn't. Nor had she felt an unusual sensation.

Jack spent the rest of the night sleeping downstairs on an old couch, muttering angrily that if they wanted the bed that badly, they could have the damn thing.

Daisy believed her father-in-law's weird story, but Eric, his son, did not. Not, that is, until he had his own bizarre experience.

One night, after supper, Eric headed out to do his final chores of the day. Part-way across the yard, he noticed a male figure following him and, in the the lowering dusk, he supposed it was Jack coming to lend a hand. He even called out a greeting, but there was no reply. Eric felt that his father was being rude, and wondered what was troubling him. He had seemed fine at supper.

Irritated, Eric started to feed the horses, expecting Jack to come and help. But he didn't. Once all the mangers had been filled, Eric grabbed a milk stool and proceeded to do the milking of the dairy cows. He was really angry by this time. His usual gentle touch for the milking was absent that evening.

When the pails had been emptied into the silver-coloured milk cans, and the cans stoppered, Eric stomped back to the house. There was Jack, engrossed in a book at the kitchen table. At the other end of the table, Daisy was sorting through a box of preserves from the storeroom.

It was then that Eric got a bad case of goose bumps. He realized that his silent, laggardly companion out at the barn must have been Wilbur.

On several occasions, a female scream echoed through the old structure. Annie and Wilbur did not appear when this happened; sometimes they would be absent for several days.

No one can remember when or why the Lunds had named their strange guests Annie and Wilbur. The names somehow made it easier to accept their presence. Later, they learned that about twenty years earlier, the store had been owned and managed by a brother-and-sister team called Walter and Annie. Annie, apparently, had been the manager, the brains behind the operation. Walter/Wilbur was a more unstable sort. A rumour indicated that the man's fiancée had died under mysterious circumstances, possibly drowned in a local pond. With his great bulk and his brooding, unpredictable behaviour, he was regarded as a bit of a loose cannon.

A picture of Annie in a local history book, taken when she was about thirty years old, revealed her as quite large, with dark hair wrapped tightly around her head. The Annie ghost had seemed old, quite small and bustling. Could this indicate that she had died as an older person?

The Wilbur spirit's formidability might indicate that he had died at a considerably younger age than his sister.

Both Wilbur and Annie would have been fairly simple people, and their ghosts bear this out. They were plainly clad, she in a cotton dress and apron, and he as a farmer in solid work-clothes. The fields and the animals would have been Wilbur's responsibility.

Given her brother's emotional imbalance, Annie probably bossed him around, while looking after him at the same time. She certainly kept his room clean. As a ghost, she continued to spend a part of her time making beds, dusting, and straightening the nightstand, alternating this activity with looking out the window and at whoever might be lying on the bed.

The Lunds, and probably all of the storekeepers before and after their tenure, stacked extra cans of produce in the dark, cool downstairs storeroom. This meant they could purchase bulk quantities of goods several times a year. Potatoes and apples, for instance, could be maintained there for long periods of time. The owners were occasionally startled by a loud crash, seemingly from that area, as though the stacks of canned goods had collapsed. The first few times this occurred, they went running down the stairs expecting to find a fearful mess. But everything was in order, the supplies undisturbed. Eventually each new group realized that the crashing sound was not related to any physical event in today's reality. There was also another noise, appearing to originate in the roof. The bang coming from the roof or basement was soon acknowledged as a sign that Annie and Wilbur were present, and was usually followed shortly by the sound of footsteps.

There were no attempts to remove Wilbur and Annie. Those who came to live in the house felt that the two ghosts had lived there first, indeed had not really left after they died. In those pre-television days, life could occasionally be dull, especially during the long, hard winter months. Annie and Wilbur added a bit of excitement, and were routinely accepted with even a tinge of friendliness. The residents of the house seemed happy to make room for an additional couple. After all, they didn't take up much space.

After the Lund family left the little community of Red

Pheasant, the management of the general store and post office was taken over by Fred and Ada Lendberg, together with Ada's brother and sister, George and Edith Caldwell. The Lendbergs had a young daughter, Joyce.

The new owners heard about their strange tenants from the departing Lunds — *after* the purchase and sale of the property had been concluded — and from neighbours and customers who gradually welcomed them into the community. They refused to allow themselves to become unduly disturbed.

They quickly learned that it was a waste of time to rush into the basement in response to a crashing sound. Like the Lunds before them, they reached a conclusion that satisfied their need for an explanation: they attributed the noise to Wilbur (Walter had never caught on as a name) having a temper tantrum. People who remembered that odd man were able to verify that when frustrated Wilbur used to sneak down into the storeroom and decimate the stacks of cans. But, back then, Annie was around and she used to make her rather clumsy brother restack the cans after she had managed to calm him down.

No one was able to explain how or why the crashing sound sometimes seemed to emanate from the roof, however.

One night, the Lendbergs were awakened by a woman's bloodcurdling screams — but no one was there. That was the only time that they heard this most unsettling sound, something for which they were most grateful. They wondered if it might have been the dying scream of Wilbur's fiancée, sinking in the pond. Were Wilbur and Annie perhaps involved in the unfortunate girl's death? There was no way to verify this.

Annie and her brother had owned a small dog. Once in a while, Ada Lendberg would hear a scratching noise at the door. She would go and open the door, letting something in or out. Not being able to see the creature, she never knew in which direction it was heading until she heard it pattering off across the linoleum, or running through the leaves outside on the front lawn.

Joyce Lendberg grew up aware of the ghostly inhabitants in her home, but it was mostly the adults who related unusual experiences. Sometimes supernatural events centre around a young girl, but that did not happen here. Joyce went away for her schooling and missed many of the incidents.

"I was only involved once," she recounted. "It was in the winter, about seven in the morning, after a heavy snowfall. I was sleeping upstairs, across the hall from 'their room' and my aunt Edith was kitty-corner from me, in the room next to 'theirs.'

"My sleep was disturbed by a loud BANG, followed by a long sliding sound. Still half-asleep, I assumed it was just some snow sliding off the roof. Then I heard someone making a bed. Aunt Edith usually didn't get up that early, but it was quite close to daylight, so I had no reason to be alarmed. But I was curious about my aunt's change in routine. We used to make jokes about how hard it was to get her up and out of bed. I listened carefully, deciding that if it wasn't the bed being made, I'd have to get up and go to investigate.

"No doubt about it — footsteps, those of a woman or a small man, then sheets tucked, blankets flipped, pillows fluffed, and then some more steps. The usual sounds of morning. I promptly went back to sleep.

"About an hour later, Mom, who slept downstairs, came up and started to talk with Aunt Edith. But, how could that be? Aunt Edith was already up, and must have gone downstairs by then. Or was she not up yet?

"I found my voice, and our disjointed conversation went something like this.

"Me — 'Aunt Edith! Are you there?'

"Aunt Edith — 'Joyce! Are you still there?'

"Me — 'But, I heard you making your bed an hour ago!'

"Aunt Edith — 'No! I heard you making your bed!'."

It appeared that Annie had been at it again!

"That afternoon, I was out skiing and turned around to look back and admire the sun shining on the store's flat, snow-covered roof. Flat? Snow-covered? What about my BANG?"

Joyce returned quickly to the house, where she demanded an explanation from her mother. Over coffee, she learned that when the Lendbergs had taken over the store operation, Daisy Lund had warned them to expect a loud bang, a sliding sound, and then footsteps. That, she had said, was an indication of "Annie landing." Joyce's parents, sleeping downstairs, seldom heard the bang, and Aunt Edith claimed never to have heard it.

It was not until a few nights after this experience, en route back to her school at Hudson Bay, that Joyce realized how much the antics of Annie and Wilbur, no matter how benign, had been spooking her. On the long journey, she had to spend one night in a Hotel. She awoke around midnight and heard footsteps out in the hall. She felt so warm and cozy and safe in the hotel bed, just knowing that if she should open the door at the sound of footsteps, she would actually see a living human being!

With the passage of time, the old general store at Red Pheasant was demolished, and part of the original barn was moved a kilometre away to where a new store was built. There are still rumours of people seeing Wilbur walking between the two sites. Maybe, maybe not. His room has vanished, so where could he go? Is he still searching for it?

Joyce comments on the experiences shared by her family and the Lunds:

"Why do such things happen? I haven't the slightest idea. I just know what happened, not the cause of it. Annie and Wilbur meant us no harm and, although I never met the original Walter and Annie, I have a warm feeling towards them, even now, and regard them almost like friends. For a while our paths crossed, and we lived, walked, and made up beds under the same roof.

"I also think that God intends us to live life to the fullest, and if He decides to spice it up a bit by allowing Wilbur or Annie to join us, we may as well enjoy it.

"Annie and Wilbur were gentle ghosts; they just didn't seem to know that they were spirits. Maybe they just wanted to come home for a visit and clean the place up a bit."

WET ADIDAS

Young Joyce Lendberg felt more secure in a hotel than in her own home. But, if she stayed at the Hotel Saskatchewan in Regina, she most likely had not been assigned to a room on the fourth floor, or her experience might have been quite different.

The Hotel Saskatchewan is a very old, stately, somewhat grand building, a survivor of the great railroading days of Western Canada. If its walls could only speak, what interesting stories would come forth to fascinate us?

Rumours about a suicide, or a bloody murder, on the fourth floor of the landmark hotel can be traced back to the

1930s, but there are no known facts to back them up. People simply seem to assume that no Canadian Pacific Railway hotel worth its reputation would be without at least one resident ghost!

Alan and Marilyn Moffat arrived at the Hotel Saskatchewan from Moose Jaw in the late afternoon one day in June 1992. Their advance booking was for a double room for just the one night. After completing the registration forms as required, the couple was shown up to Room 420.

The room was perfectly ordinary, quite spacious, clean and cheerful, with a well-supplied bathroom beside the closet.

The Moffats dined that evening in the large and friendly hotel dining room, admiring the wall panelling and other furnishings, and they lingered over their coffee, talking until it became quite late. Returning to their room, they prepared for bed, and secured the door to the hallway with a deadbolt. A notice on the back of the door assured guests that this precaution would prevent them from being unnecessarily disturbed by the housekeeping staff before they were ready to leave their room in the morning. Before turning out the light, Alan left his Adidas training shoes against the wall beside the television set.

In the morning, Alan was bemused to find the Adidas shoes on the floor in front of the room's only comfortable reading chair. When he went to slip them on, he discovered that they were filled with a clear liquid. It looked like water, but he wasn't sure. Calling Marilyn and explaining what was happening, he walked over to the bathroom, shoes in hand. Watched by Marilyn, Alan emptied the liquid from the shoes into the sink, having first set the stopper to prevent the stuff from running down the drain.

The liquid was water, just plain ordinary water. But where

had it come from? The Moffats found themselves faced with a puzzle that they have not, to this day, managed to solve.

There were no leaks in the ceiling. The windows and their frames were dry. The air conditioner had been turned off and there was no moisture leaking down from it. The floor around where the shoes had been found was perfectly dry except for the exact spot on which the Adidas had rested.

Thanks to the deadbolt, no one had had access to the Moffats' room. They had not brought with them or ordered to the room any beverages; neither ice nor ice bucket was in the room.

When it was suggested that the shoes could have been soaked with rainwater, Alan angrily asserted that he wasn't fool enough to have spent a day wearing wet shoes. In any case, the previous day had been hot and dry.

The Moffats, intrigued, cornered the room maid as she worked her way down the hall. They asked her whether anything unusual had ever happened before in Room 420.

The woman's reply was less than helpful, "No, not in Room 420."

Alan and Marilyn still don't know if she meant to imply that unusual things happened in other rooms. They do remember, however, that the maid showed no surprise at, or interest in, their query. Could it be that employees who work on the fourth floor of the Hotel Saskatchewan have become used to hearing that sort of question?

THE INVISIBLE MANAGER

Given that ghosts seem to thrive on locations where humans have come in large numbers and enacted their personal tragedies and comedies, it is not too surprising to find a spirit in an old theatre. The phantom of the Paris opera is a famous historic example; in Fort Macleod, Alberta, the restoration of an old theatre seems to have triggered a modern haunting.

Early in 1992, reports began to circulate that the eighty-year-old Empress Theatre had an employee not listed on the payroll. A number of people, some involved in the actual restoration work and some concerned with the daily operations claimed that there was something unnatural about the atmosphere in the Empress.

Jim Layton worked at the Empress. Late one night, he was in the basement when he heard strange noises coming from the area of the main stage. Layton had been quietly reading a book while waiting for wax he had just applied to the floor of the green room to become dry enough for buffing.

"It was kind of spooky," he recounted. "It's hard to explain. It was almost like someone was walking around, but there was no one else in the building because I had locked myself in."

Layton went upstairs to investigate. He turned on the house lights and looked around the theatre carefully, including up on the stage. There was nothing. Puzzled, and feeling uneasy, Layton finished work and went home.

The following night it was the lobby floor that was due to be polished. Layton placed his chair near that area to wait for the wax to dry.

Again the noises came, sounding this time like the wind. That really alarmed Layton. There were no windows open, the door was locked, and he knew that there was no wind blowing in Fort Macleod that evening. He left, and has since refused to work alone in the theatre.

Juran Greene, the theatre manager, firmly believes that something nonhuman inhabits the Empress Theatre.

He affirms, "I never ended up seeing it, but it always let me know it was there."

Greene began to suspect that something wasn't right when lights that had been turned off by him would be turned back on, either in the theatre itself or in the backstage hallway. He used to think somebody was playing tricks on him.

Then one night when Greene was working late on paperwork, he heard someone walking about upstairs. As was his custom, he leaned out of his basement office and shouted upstairs to let whoever it was know where he could be found.

There was no reply, and he went upstairs to discover a darkened theatre, just the way he left it. After checking the front door to ensure that it was locked, Greene went, very carefully, through the entire building to determine if an unauthorized entry had been made by anyone. He found no sign of this, nor did he find anything that could account for the sounds he had heard.

Convinced that he had, indeed, heard these footsteps, Greene quietly positioned himself in one of several large chairs and waited for whoever it was to walk along the hallway again.

A few minutes passed. Then Juran Greene became aware that he was being watched. Without giving the matter much thought, he started to speak to the presence that he felt in the room with him.

"I don't care who or what you are, you can try and scare me out, but I'm not leaving!"

As the last words left his mouth, a tall ladder left over from the restoration work came crashing down to the floor. Startled, Greene didn't know whether to get up and flee or to stay his ground. Choosing a mix of the two alternatives, he walked to the back of the theatre and addressed the invisible intruder.

"I mean it, I'm not leaving!"

Silence reigned. After waiting for several long minutes, Greene slowly returned to his office.

Juran Greene and Jim Layton were only two of the many people who had strange experiences in the Empress Theatre.

Wendy Rigaux was very uneasy while she was working in the old theatre, especially when her chores led her to the rear of the basement: "I always felt like I was being watched, and yet there was never anyone there. Still, there was something that made you sure you weren't by yourself."

Terry Veluw is the theatre's assistant manager. Initially skeptical, she has become a firm believer in the ghost.

"I've never seen anybody," she explained, "but I've felt it, heard it. You feel like someone's watching you. Quite spooky!"

At first, Terry dismissed as simple mistakes things like finding the lights on when she was certain that she had turned them off, until one night when the intercom system came on by itself. The noise that came over the intercom was just that, a noise. It wasn't a static sound or interference, but a noise as if someone had pressed the intercom button and was preparing to speak to her. There was no one else in the theatre that night.

Terry had also shrugged off the feeling of being under observation while she was in the back of the basement, rummaging for office supplies. Then, while working late one night, the feeling became stronger than it had ever been before.

Terry, who often works late in order to avoid interruptions, was in the downstairs office with the door half open. Something drew her attention to the opening, and then to the small strip of glass beside the door, as if someone was watching her through the windowpane.

Like Juran Greene before her, Terry felt compelled to talk. She informed the presence that she wasn't leaving.

She laughed about the scene later. "Here's me, all by myself at night talking very firmly — to it!"

Three weeks later, Terry lost a silver earring. The earring was particularly precious, having been a graduation gift from a maternal great-aunt who had worn them herself. Over the next few days, Terry and everyone else working in the theatre searched for the errant earring.

Then, one evening, after the Rose Bud Theatre Group had performed at the Empress, Terry and a number of other people were standing in the hallway between the lobby and the auditorium, talking about that evening's performance.

Terry happened to glance down, and there, by her feet, she saw her missing silver earring. Terry believes that the ghost must have found the earring for her and placed it at her feet. Had it been there all along, it would have been found by then, or damaged by people walking in the hallway. The hallway is a very heavy traffic area, and the carpeting there is vacuumed on a regular basis.

Employees are not the only people who have experienced a sensation of being watched at the Empress Theatre. Canadian singer Sarah McLachlan's band members, along with other visiting groups, have said that they could feel someone observing them, especially while walking up the backstage stairs. These comments from strangers are all the more interesting because the theatre's staff takes care not to mention their resident ghost.

Trent Moranz, the manager of the Empress Theatre, feels that he is under constant scrutiny. Like the majority of the employees, he says that he feels it most in the older part of the building.

As he described it, "You get the feeling — it's as if you were sitting in the room preoccupied and someone comes in very quietly, without making any noise whatsoever."

Moranz has also experienced lights and electrical switches being turned on, including the marquee strip, which he personally turns off before going home each night.

His strangest experience happened a few days after the McLachlan concert. Trent had to pass through a magnetic fire door on his way up to the stage. The door is located between the stage and the rear steps, and stays open unless the fire alarm goes off, when it automatically closes. As Moranz walked out onto the stage, the steel door slammed shut behind him.

"That's the first time that it's happened," he said. "I thought that perhaps I had brushed against it or kicked it or hooked it with the sleeve of my shirt."

However, after opening the door again, he tried pushing it and kicking at its base, but found "no way to physically cause the door to move."

Moranz has had the unnerving experience of having someone or something breathing cold air on him. While turning off the lights in the theatre one night, he felt a cool draft on the back of his neck; the direction of the draft was all wrong — it was coming from the stage area, not from out by the front door.

"The hair just went up on the back of my neck!" he exclaimed.

There is some controversy about who or what the invisible being at the Empress represents. Some say it must be the spirit of an actor or actress, while others believe that it may be a former caretaker or manager.

Terry Veluw has her own ideas. "This just doesn't have the feeling of an actor or performer — this is a very steady person. This is someone who was an organizer, someone who doesn't like disruption, someone who is pretty level-headed."

Trent Moranz has his money on longtime owner Dan Boyle, who purchased the building in 1937 and operated it until his death in 1963. He sometimes "feels a kinship with Dan Boyle" because they have the same job.

The renovations marked the beginning of these incidents. It seems clear that they disturbed the spirit, whoever it may be, that now wanders through the empty theatre throwing light switches and picking up misplaced silver earrings.

CHILD AT THE CROSSROADS

Elinor Tesky's family lived for a while in a small, closely knit farm community near Yorkton, Saskatchewan. It was a large extended family, effectively headed by her grandfather, a very religious individual who took his responsibilities seriously and was highly respected by all of the neighbours.

Strange things frequently happened at the crossroads near Elinor's home. Two of the more interesting and memorable occasions are described here.

One of the most common occurrences at the crossroads involved the spirit of a small girl, about three or four years of age. This child would appear, unattended and apparently unsupervised, along the side of the road. People used to worry about the little girl as she wandered about through the tall weeds and the wildflowers that grew there, all by herself. No one knew whose child she might be or where she had come from. She would vanish whenever the local residents tried to approach her.

As the years passed, the child kept returning to the edge of the road. She never seemed to grow any older. The people in the community came reluctantly to accept her presence. No explanation for the child's appearances, or suggestion of who she might have been, was ever discovered.

Another strange happening near the Yorkton Sideroads occurred one spring.

Every year, just before Easter, the local Greek Orthodox Church held a very special service. One member of each family, generally a senior male, took a bottle of water to the church to have it blessed. The holy water was later sprinkled about the homes in the area to prevent difficulties from occurring during the coming year. The water was also considered to possess curative powers, in times of sickness. Some felt that the holy water would also protect them from supernatural attacks.

During the year in which we are interested, the service for the blessing of the water was to be held quite late at night, because the minister had to visit several other small churches in the area first. Shortly before ten in the evening, men started to assemble at the crossroads. It was a natural meeting place for people coming from the various nearby farms, from which they would walk in small, friendly groups the two kilometres or so to the church.

Elinor's grandfather was with an old friend, and the two of them were just leaving the crossroads when her grandfather spotted what appeared to be a faint light off in the distance. He slowed his pace, saying, "That must be Arthur, late as usual. I rather thought he might join us this evening. Let's wait for him to catch up. There's plenty of time."

The two men stood quietly talking, waiting for their friend to overtake them. They were both carrying their water jars, and Elinor's grandfather lit his well-worn pipe as they chatted about the weather, crops, and local politics.

The light in the distance grew brighter as it approached them across the fields. One of the observers called out impatiently, "Hurry it up, Arthur! We don't want to be late, and we've quite a long walk ahead of us yet. Most of the others have already left, but we can all use the same lantern if you'll just move along there."

There was no answer, but neither of the men thought much about that at the time. Freshwater springs ran through the area, and they just assumed that the sound of Arthur's footsteps coupled with the gurgling sound of running water had prevented him from hearing them.

Nearer and nearer came the bobbing lantern. Elinor's grandfather and his friend prepared to greet the tardy Arthur. Then they both stopped abruptly in mid-sentence. The lantern came right up to where they were standing and passed between them. Nobody was carrying it! It was just bobbing along through the air at the correct carrying height, all by itself. Both men had viewed exactly the same thing.

The two friends stared in shocked and silent amazement as the strange lantern went off in the direction of the church. When it reached the first fence, they could hear the distinctive sound of barbed wire being forced open to allow someone passage through. The wires were spread wide enough to permit a grown adult to pass, and then the lantern appeared, still bobbing along in rhythm, on the other side of the fence.

The two men just stood there, utterly speechless, for a few uncomfortable minutes. They watched as the lantern's glow grew gradually fainter and fainter, and then faded away completely in the direction of the evening service. Then, temporarily forgetting about the annual blessing, and still clutching their water jugs, they made a dash for the nearest residence — Elinor's home.

Elinor met her grandfather and his friend at the door. The two older men were extremely pale and obviously shaken. At first, they refused to discuss what had happened, but they later told family members about the peculiar events out by the crossroads. Then, reminded of their responsibility to obtain the annual blessing of the water, the two men bravely resumed the long trek to the church.

The next day they learned that Arthur had, indeed, planned to walk along with the others to the evening service, but at the last minute he found himself unable to go — the vet was coming to check on an ailing calf. Arthur insisted that he had not been near the crossroads; indeed, never left his property that night.

THE CALGARY POLTERGUEST?

A residence on Beaver Dam Way in Calgary, Alberta, is providing more entertainment than they really want to a woman, her teenaged son, and her two smaller children. Since this is an ongoing situation, we'll call the boy Rick, and his mother Barbara Goodwin. The two younger children have not been involved.

The home, a duplex that feels like a detached house, was built in 1971. The Goodwins moved in on September 5, 1992, and ran into trouble almost immediately. Later, they felt that something had been lying in wait for them. The first and most powerful incident occurred on September 19. It was

11:55 p.m., five minutes short of Rick's seventeenth birthday.

Rick had his bedroom in the basement, which gave him a greater sense of freedom and independence from the rest of the family. His mother's bedroom was upstairs, where she could be closer to the two younger children.

That night Barbara was upstairs, finishing some unpacking that had been put off for too long. Suddenly she heard the loudest banging noise that she had ever encountered rising from the basement area. She headed downstairs to order Rick to stop the terrible hammering. Could he perhaps be hanging some pictures, or installing a shelf in his room? She was surprised that he would be so very loud at midnight, as he was generally a considerate boy.

The banging got louder and louder as Barbara moved down the stairs. Then it stopped. Barbara paused, debating whether or not to tackle Rick. Perhaps, she reasoned, he had just wanted to hang up a single item, and had now completed the task. Still, the noise had seemed louder than a hammer driving a nail into a wall. Deciding it wasn't worth an argument, Barbara turned away and began to ascend the stairs.

Since it was a cool, early fall evening, the furnace was on, and the interior of the house felt warm and comfortable. But just after the pounding noise stopped, the house grew icy cold.

Back on the main floor, Barbara checked the heat setting. Despite the fact that the thermostat was set to normal room temperature, the actual reading on the thermometer was as low as the dial was capable of indicating.

Then the noise began again, louder, if that was possible, and more persistent than before. Barbara lost her temper, flabbergasted that Rick could be so unaware of people trying to sleep, both in his own home and in the neighbouring unit. After all, they had just moved in. This was no way to make new friends.

Barbara angrily started down the stairs again. The noise stopped, as it had before, and she heard the door to Rick's room open. He came running up the stairs, with a look of terror on his face.

"Mom! Did you hear that banging? What the hell is going on here?"

Rick had been sitting on his bed at 11:55 p.m., talking to a friend on the phone. He was facing the closed door of his room when, all of a sudden, he heard a horrific pounding noise on the door. The door itself was vibrating and bending under some very strong force. The girl with whom Rick had been speaking heard the loud noises quite clearly at her end of the line.

Moments earlier, one of the family's two cats had been meowing outside Rick's door, wanting to get into the room and onto the bed, where it occasionally slept. Rick had been about to open the door for the animal when the noisy assault began. When Rick did manage to get out of his room, the cat was still there, shaking with fright and frozen in place. To this day, that cat refuses to enter Rick's room, although she seems to have no problem with the rest of the basement.

Rick and Barbara, shivering with cold, looked carefully at the door. There were no marks on it. If a hammer had pounded wood hard enough to make the noises they had heard, the wood would have been severely dented, or even splintered and broken.

The temperature in the house remained ridiculously cold for about an hour, all told, and then slowly returned to normal.

On September 22, just six days later, at a little after 11:30 p.m., the banging from the basement reoccured three separate times. This time, Rick was upstairs with his mother, and

CANADA GHOST TO GHOST

they waited the sound effects out. The temperature in the house remained stable.

Barbara was awakened at two in the morning of October 2 by a strange sound that she could not identify. She followed the direction of the noise and discovered that the windows in the basement had begun sliding back and forth. These windows were covered with dust and cobwebs on the outside, and clearly had not been opened for many years — maybe not since the house had been built. Loosening these windows had been one of the many chores on Barbara's list of things to do in the spring.

Another nocturnal event took place on October 14. Barbara had begun to note down the times when odd things occurred, hoping that this would help her to understand what was going on. At a few minutes before 3:00 a.m., a toy musical piano began to play in the living room. This was quite impossible, thought Barbara, staring at the little thing. There were no batteries in the piano.

The Goodwins braced themselves for Hallowe'en. They expected it to be very loud and icy cold. After all, on this night, by tradition, spirits are at their most vigorous. But they heard only a soft banging followed by light footsteps on the stairway. The smell of honeysuckle and mixed spices wafted through the dining room and into a bedroom that was located directly below. It was as if a gentle and kind being had replaced the loud and vulgar visitor that they had come to know.

Just before midnight on November 2, there was a loud, insistent tapping on Rick's bedroom window. Barbara could hear this sound from the dining room, which was located directly above. She looked out the window and discovered that the rear movement sensor had been activated.

Something or someone had crossed the alarm's light beam and should have been visible. But no one was there. As she watched in mounting concern and confusion, the back gate swung shut.

By November 15, the ghostly footsteps were at the back door. Then a discarded toy telephone began talking. The toy was in a drawer in the dresser in the upstairs hallway, its batteries useless, where it had lain since the younger children tired of it in the early fall. The speaker on the colourful toy phone played very, very loudly, over and over, "Have a nice day!" This was the first daytime occurrence; it took place shortly after noon.

The back and front doorbells began to ring at three in the afternoon on November 22. No one could be seen from any of the windows, although light clicking footsteps and the small smack of the front gate shutting could be heard.

There was a light snowfall during the afternoon of December 10. By six in the evening, no one had been in or out of the Goodwin's residence all day. It was pretty well dark, but the back-door light was on. The dining-room window was right beside the back door, so when the light was on, it was possible to see who was standing there. The Goodwins had adopted a secret doorbell ring — actually three separate, spaced rings — so that whoever was in the house would know that a member of the family was coming in.

That afternoon, the doorbell kept ringing three times, over and over again, just the way the toy phone had repeated itself. Barbara looked out the window right as the bell was ringing, but there was no one standing by the door. Nor could she see any footsteps in the blanket of newly fallen snow. She could, however, see a bluish light shining onto the snow by the patio area.

Throughout December, Barbara and Rick heard footsteps on the basement stairs. The locks on the back door opened noisily by themselves, and the sounds of other activity continued, usually followed by the clunk of the door closing.

Moisture and bits of plaster began to drop from the ceiling onto Rick's bed. A building contractor was called in, but could find no reason for this to occur; the plumbing ran across the other side of the basement. Barbara moved Rick out of the basement, and his departure from that area seemed to reduce the number of incidents.

Barbara sat down in frustration one evening and demanded evidence of the spirit's identity — something, anything, that would help her to comprehend what was happening. What she received was a gift! A pair of Indian-crafted earrings that she had lost shortly after the move to Beaver Dam Way mysteriously appeared on the kitchen table.

The new year brought the semblance of peace to the Goodwins. There was still some activity, but it was less frequent. Most people would have found this situation unacceptable, but after the unprecedented chaos of their first three months' residency, the Goodwins greeted the change with welcome relief.

It is now several years since the Goodwins moved into their new home in Calgary, and they still have an unknown presence operating at will in the house. Or perhaps two presences: one mischievous and brightly clever, linked to the return of the missing earrings, the activated battery-run toys, the scents of spice and honeysuckle, and the light footsteps; the second one, a potentially nasty piece of work, responsible for the mindless banging, the rebellious doorbell, the icy chill in the house, and the dripping ceiling.

Barbara and her family are unusual in their acceptance of what has happened to them. They do not talk of exorcism, or of moving elsewhere, now that the level of noise and disruption has lessened, although Barbara admits that during the early period she was feeling very frightened and persecuted.

6

UNREAL REAL ESTATE

Some property owners will hush up or deny outright the story of a haunting in order to protect the property value of the affected building. Others, for any number of reasons, actually desire the apparent invasion.

For one thing, some people have a strange obsession for notoriety in any form. For another, the value of a property or building can actually escalate if it is haunted. A colourful resident ghost, for example, may attract customers despite the indifferent cuisine of a chef in a restaurant or hotel. A roadside inn or a big-city hotel can benefit immeasurably from the accompanying publicity garnered when a supernatural incident is reported. The public's curiosity button is an excellent one to push when revenues slip a bit. Some people's overeager desire for an other-worldly connection is one reason investigators spend so much time attempting to verify the sites of reported hauntings.

Recently a professor from Montreal learned a bitter lesson on the subject of gullibility. Reuters News Agency related the story of this gentleman who purchased, in 1988, what was reported to be Britain's most haunted house. Banking, quite literally, on the public's fascination with the supernatural, Professor Trevor Kirkham planned to convert the historical residence into a tourist attraction. He felt that a skillful advertising campaign could attract interested parties from all over the world, and he could have a marvellous time entertaining visitors searching for ghosts.

To his dismay, Professor Kirkham discovered that he had been tricked. The seven-hundred-year-old house in Preston in the north of England was not haunted, nor had it ever been. The real estate agent who engineered the sale of the property was occupying it at the time, and created tales of multiple apparitions in an attempt to entice a foreign buyer. The only way for Professor Kirkham to operate a tourist attraction involving the supernatural would have been to perpetrate a hoax of his own on the unsuspecting customers.

The estate agent involved believed that he would be protected by the old credo "buyer beware," and that the sale of the misrepresented haunted house would be upheld. But he had not counted on the stubborn, angry, and very swindled Canadian. Professor Kirkham refused to fade into the woodwork in shame, and instead took the matter before the English courts. After a thorough investigation, a sympathetic high court justice in the city of Liverpool awarded Professor Kirkham $110,000(Cdn.) in damages. The judge's ruling included the right to evict the present occupant, the estate agent who had been responsible for the fraud. In handing down his decision, the judge referred to the case as "a classic example of estate agent licence" that could not be permitted to go unchallenged.

THE HIGH PARK GHOST

The original parcel of land known as High Park in the western part of Toronto consisted of 408 glorious hectares of woods and hills, with many small ponds and a large centrepiece known as Grenadier Pond. Only partially cultivated when it was deeded over to the city as parkland by John Howard in 1875, High Park came to Toronto with the understanding that Howard, an architect and town planner, would receive in return a lifetime annuity. As he lived for fifteen more years, the transaction was attacked as costing the city "a great deal." The total paid to John Howard was about $11,900 — not too shabby as the cost of West Toronto's huge playground.

Howard's house was built on a southern point of land with a view out over Lake Ontario. He and his wife, Jemina, created a unique home, called Colborne Lodge. The focal point was a beautifully shaped living room that ran across the entire southern face of the building. The wallpaper and carpeting were purchased in London. Meticulous care was taken in the construction and furnishing of the place, and the result was an elegant example of a prosperous and tasteful home of the period.

Jemina Howard died in 1877, thirteen years before her husband. The stated cause of death was breast cancer; she had been ill for several years. For the most part, she had secluded herself in a second-floor bedroom. When she did venture down to the main floor, which was rarely, her temper was unpredictable. Certainly Jemina resented any attempts on the part of her husband to entertain visitors. Even neighbouring children that he had invited for tea were treated to severe glares and icy silences.

After John Howard died in 1890, Colborne Lodge remained for nearly fifty years just as it had been on the day that his funeral procession departed for the cemetery. The elegant Empire sofas and chairs in the living room fell into shreds and tatters, torn and eaten by mice. China remained in haphazard settings on the dining-room table, nestled in baskets of cobwebs. Pots and pans, dust-encrusted and tarnished, still hung from their hooks in the kitchen. On the ground level, floors were sagging dangerously and the stairs to the bedroom area had become impassable. The neglect and decay that characterized Colborne Lodge could be seen in the carriage house, too. Rust, mould, and mice were ruining John Howard's irreplaceable vehicles from another era.

In the 1940s the first sightings of the ghost of Jemina Howard occurred. She was observed at a front window on the second floor of the house, looking out across Colborne Lodge Drive in the direction of the cemetery where she and her husband lie buried. It was as though she had somehow been left behind. Did Jemima decide to stay or did she find herself stuck there as a ghost?

Following the death of John Howard, Mr. and Mrs. Lightfoot were appointed caretakers for High Park, a very onerous assignment for two people. They lived in a small cottage where the Rose Gardens are located today. Delightful Cockneys, they were most concerned about everything that was involved in the care and upkeep of the vast park.

Throughout the Lightfoots' tenure, Jemina continued to

make her presence known. Although there were no lights in the abandoned house, people commented on her frequent appearances. Her shape seemed to glow, always at night in the same room, and always in the large master bedroom located at the front of the building.

The utter abandonment of Colborne Lodge finally drew the attention of several newspaper writers, who deplored the decay of one of the most generous gifts ever made to the city. This uproar acted as a spur to the conscience of several individuals who had an interest in the reputation of the city of Toronto, and who were able to combine their financial clout with their social influence to bring about positive measures to save the lodge. The Women's (Canadian) Historical Society undertook its initial restoration, a task since handed over directly to the city.

The house and its period furniture were renewed with loving attention to detail. Scraps of the original wallpaper and carpeting were sent back to England, along with swatches of fabric from the damaged sofas and chairs, so that the reproduction of the new materials would match perfectly with those originally ordered by the Howards.

All of the painstaking labour was done under the watchful eye of the quiet ghost of Jemina Howard: one can only hope it met with her approval. Over a period of several years her former residence was beautifully restored, and was then opened to visits by the public during the summer months.

But Jemina never did think much of visitors; she had preferred to be alone with John. Now her anxiety can be felt both in the master bedroom and, strangely, in a small room located on the top floor at the rear of the building. It has an odd kind of musty smell, of stuffiness and old bedding, illness and time-worn despair, that defies all attempts to remove it. And certain visitors can sense another's presence as they complete their tour of Colborne Lodge. In any case, no one lingers for very long in the territory that Jemina had once called her own.

THE HOPKINS SPIRIT

Jemina Howard is just one of any number of female ghosts who demonstrate a marked reluctance to leave a place where they felt safe and secure while alive. These women were frequently married to important and powerful men and, during their lives, tended to remain in the background. Only once they have shed their spouses, do these female spirits tend to move into the limelight.

Edward Nicholas Hopkins left his home in Ontario in 1882 to join the earliest settlers migrating west. After travelling the initial distance by train and the balance of the long overland trek by oxen-drawn wagon, he arrived in Moose Jaw, Saskatchewan, on July 21 of that year. His arrival marked the beginning of the town and the forging of a lasting relationship between the man and his chosen destination. He pioneered the agricultural concept of leaving some fields fallow, i.e. dormant, each year so as not to drain them of their natural nutritive elements. As the years went by, Edward Hopkins served on numerous boards, helped establish schools and churches, and supported the evolution of modern trade practices in this once-isolated wilderness. He was elected to the House of Commons, and was responsible for the creation of the Wild Animal Park. His energy, interests, and breadth of knowledge were legendary.

This astonishing man married Minnie Latham in 1890.

The couple, very taken with each other, immediately set about building a home and establishing a family. In due course they had three children, Earle, Marguerite, and Russel. Earle, a young man with great promise, drowned in the Moose Jaw River in 1907, several years after the completion of his family's spacious home. His death was a blow from which his parents never fully recovered.

While the Hopkins family lived a long time ago, the many benefits brought into the area by Edward Hopkins are still much appreciated by the Moose Jaw residents of today. The original house is the present location of the Hopkins Dining Parlour, a popular eatery — and, it would seem, Minnie Hopkins still acts as a hostess to people who come to her former home.

The restaurant is situated within the original hundred-year-old three-story house. In the early 1990s, an addition was built onto the rear of the building. The home is now owned by the Pierce family, among whom are Gladys and her son Rick. They find themselves forced to live and work around the ghost of Minnie Hopkins, who is far from content to stare quietly from an upper front-bedroom window.

Longtime employees at the Hopkins Dining Parlour are also convinced that they are accompanied during the performance of their duties by a friendly ghost, and that this happy spirit is the former Minnie Hopkins. The funeral for Mrs. Hopkins was held in what is now the downstairs dining room; that event may have drawn her back to and kept her in the house. Some people feel that, insofar as Minnie was a total abstainer from alcoholic beverages, she might find the presence of a lounge objectionable. But her presence has never been felt in the lounge, nor has anyone observed her wandering about the new addition, which consists of the gift shop, the banquet hall, and a large modern kitchen facility.

At about seven in the morning, the cook arrives to review the menus for the day and ensure that all the necessary supplies and fresh ingredients will be available. Part of this early morning ritual is to appear nonchalant and pretend that there isn't anything of a gauzy-white nature floating up the main staircase, a pale image impossible to ignore.

After putting in her early morning appearance, Minnie Hopkins proceeds to move slowly and with great dignity throughout her old home. A bewildered cook once saw the strange shape waft into one of the bathroom stalls in the main-floor ladies' room. The cook stood transfixed, trying to figure out what use a ghost would have for such a facility. No answer came, and the ghost did not re-emerge.

An employee of some ten years was in the same washroom one evening, drying her hands at the sink. Something caused her to turn her head and she saw a figure dressed entirely in white, wearing a white shawl over its head. The shape was an older woman of average height, not threatening in any way — just there! But obviously not a material presence, for the door to the washroom had not opened to admit her and the room had been previously unoccupied. Trying to remain calm, the waitress turned back towards the sink and washed her hands again, her mind a little befuddled. Suddenly she felt her body relax, and was fairly certain that the ghost had departed from the room. Before leaving the washroom, the waitress usually checked out her appearance in the mirror to ensure that everything was in place. But on this particular occasion she kept her head down, avoided the mirror, and left, still a little shaken.

Later during that same evening, the inside front door

opened and closed three times, by itself. No draft was felt and no one appeared anywhere near it.

Minnie Hopkins may have been an abstainer from alcoholic beverages while alive, but her spirit shows a strong and playful sense of humour. She indulges in pranks such as lighting the candles on the dining-room tables and turning the electric coffee makers on and off at inappropriate times. She releases balloons that casually float up the stairs, and on occasion plays the piano, not too loud but quite tunelessly. Last, but not least, after the lights have been turned off at the conclusion of the last sitting, she bangs loudly on the walls until she succeeds in frightening everyone upstairs to the point of distraction. On certain nights, the members of the staff are convinced that there is a wonderful ghostly party in progress after the last of that night's customers has left.

Is there any point in booking a table in the expectation of seeing the spirit of Minnie Hopkins float casually up the staircase? Not very likely. Sometimes Minnie is not seen or felt or heard for nights, weeks, and even months. Then some little thing must upset her and the staff know that she's back in operation.

At one point, some local people wanted to hold a séance to determine if the spirit that roams the old Hopkins house is truly that of Minnie. While those entrusted with the day-to-day operation of the dining room would like to know the answer to that question, they are reluctant to interfere. The ghost is a friendly one and has been thus for some fifteen years. Better to leave things be, rather than risk the possible ire of something that is not quite all there.

In general, a hands-off attitude towards an apparition is advisable, if its activities can be accommodated without danger or too much inconvenience. In the case of Minnie, only the lighting of the table candles calls for a note of caution. Spirits that freely indulge in activities employing fire or electrical wiring are entitled to a bit more respect than those that pass the years in the silence and solitude of a single room.

MACKENZIE HOUSE

The reactions of people encountering an apparition may vary in many ways, but the greatest cause for differing responses lies in the physical location of the haunting. If the place is a private residence, the owners or residents generally are quite upset and apprehensive. If, on the other hand, the site is a more public place, a tourist or commercial area such as a hotel, the owners' response may be far calmer, even welcoming. For to paraphrase W. P. Kinsella, "If you haunt it, they will come" — often in droves.

Mackenzie House, located on Bond Street in downtown Toronto, went through a period of caretaker-occupants, at a time when there was all manner of supernatural turmoil. It was then established as an untenanted historical tourist attraction, open to the public during specified hours each day. The stream of ghost stories dried up as soon as humans ceased spending nights in the house.

William Lyon Mackenzie, Toronto's famous rebel leader and first mayor, was a most patient ghost. He waited for over one hundred years before making things uncomfortable at his old home, which has become a popular tourist attraction operated by the William Lyon Mackenzie Homestead Foundation. This nonprofit group maintains the house in trust as an historic site.

Mackenzie himself was a scrappy little Scot, long a thorn in the side of the powerful ruling establishment of York (now Toronto). He founded a newspaper, the *Colonial Advocate*, which constantly attacked the government as being non-representative of the needs of the people. In 1828 he was elected to the Legislative Assembly of Upper Canada and in 1834 he became the first mayor of the city of York.

An old printing press in the house figures prominently in the tales of the Mackenzie hauntings, a machine purchased by the fiery William in the year 1825. Although it looks quaint and is somewhat fragile, it is still in working order according to its label. It is kept locked, however, so that it is impossible to turn the handle and activate the machinery.

The old house, located on what is now a cramped and fully built-up street, consists of two basement rooms, two rooms on the main floor, two bedrooms on the second floor, and a small flat on the attic level. At the time of the reported hauntings, the printing press was situated in one of the basement rooms. The piano, which also figures in the super-natural activities, was located in the main-floor parlour.

William Lyon Mackenzie died in this narrow, common-looking house in 1861. Since no reports about his ghost appeared until 1960, it can be assumed that he was in no great hurry to return to his old home. He died in a good deal of both physical pain and mental anguish — the basic ingre-dients for a classic ghost story.

Once the tale of late-night ghostly shenanigans broke, it caused a great wave of publicity and controversy. The hauntings were reported on at some length in the Toronto newspapers. Both believers and skeptics had a field day. Two different caretaker couples swore out affidavits concerning the spirits they had seen. These were followed by a denial from one of the couples. An exorcism service was held on the premises. Finally, the story died down and passed into legend.

Here follow quotations from three former residents of 82 Bond Street:

"We hadn't been there long when I heard the footsteps going up the stairs. I called to my husband. He wasn't there. There was no one else in the house. But I heard feet on the stairs." — Mrs. Alex Dobban, wife of the caretaker of Mackenzie House, June 1960.

"From the first day my husband and I went to stay at Mackenzie House we could hear footsteps on the stairway when there was nobody in the house. Nearly every day there were footsteps when there was no one there to make them." — Mrs. Charles Edmunds, wife of the caretaker of Mackenzie House from August 1956 to April 1960.

"You knew you weren't alone." — Mrs. Winnifred McCleary, caretaker at Mackenzie House, November 1966.

The story first broke in the *Toronto Telegram* when Mr. and Mrs. Alex Dobban had been working as caretakers in the house for a little over a month. They had moved into the house in April and, by June, had become so disturbed by the weird happenings that they handed in their notices to leave. The fact that they were willing to forfeit free accommodation gives their testimony even more weight.

Mr. Dobban was retired and on a pension from a maintenance job in a downtown Toronto office building. The caretakers' flat, though small, was comfortable and rent-free, and a reasonable salary went with the caretaking position. The work was not onerous, and Alex Dobban initially considered the entire arrangement to be quite a good package.

But in June, the Dobbans packed up their possessions and moved out of the flat to a rented apartment. They remained on the job at Mackenzie House until a replacement could be found, then resigned, although Alex Dobban had no other job prospect in sight.

It turned out that the disturbances they had encountered had not been restricted to footsteps, which the Dobbans had no problem with. It was the other incidents that forced them to leave.

One night Mrs. Dobban awoke to the sound of a grating, rumbling noise originating in the basement area of the old house. At first she took it to be the oil furnace starting up, but when Alex went to check he found that it was not even turned on. The noise they heard was coming from the printing press. It was supposedly locked, and yet the old printing press was running, by itself!

On another occasion, Mrs. Dobban clearly heard the piano playing in the parlour. The couple had been asleep in bed, the house was locked up for the night, and there was no one else in the old building.

"It wasn't a tune," Mrs. Dobban said at the time. "It was just as if someone was hitting the keys with closed fists, or possibly a child attempting to play the piano."

When asked if she believed in ghosts, Mrs. Dobban replied that she didn't know how else to explain the strange happenings.

The *Toronto Telegram* pursued the reports of supernatural incidents at Mackenzie House with great enthusiasm, sending veteran reporter Andrew MacFarlane to ferret out whatever lay at the bottom of the mystery. He discovered that the previous caretaking couple had experienced even more bizarre events than the newsworthy Dobbans. They had also resigned from the position, but had been reluctant to reveal their story to strangers at that time.

Now, Mr. and Mrs. Charles Edmunds explained that they had endured the uncomfortable situation for three long and harrowing years. During this time Mrs. Edmunds had lost forty pounds, due, she said, to the constant strain of knowing that there was someone else, invisible, present in the house with them.

"One night I woke up around midnight, though I am usually a sound sleeper," recounted Mrs. Edmunds to the fascinated *Telegram* reporter. "I saw a lady standing over my bed. She wasn't at my side but at the head of the bed, leaning over me. There was no room for anyone to stand where she was. The bed was pushed right up against the wall. She was hanging down over me like a shadow, but I could see her quite clearly. Something seemed to touch me on the shoulder and this woke me up. She had long hair hanging down in front of her shoulders. Not black or grey or white, but dark brown. She had a long narrow face."

About a year after this event, Mrs. Edmunds saw the same lady again. On this occasion the ghost reached out and struck her sharply in the eye. When she arose in the morning her left eye had a massive purple bruise, and the eye itself was bloodshot.

There was yet another ghost in Mackenzie House. Mrs. Edmunds sometimes saw a smallish, totally bald man in a frock coat in the vicinity of the second-floor bedrooms. (Pictures of William Lyon Mackenzie all show him sporting a red shock of hair. But that was a wig; he was completely bald, apparently the result of a fever.)

Mrs. Edmunds saw each of these spectral figures on eight or nine occasions.

There were other witnesses to the hauntings. The Edmunds's son, Robert, and his wife sometimes stayed overnight with their two young children. Each one of the group acquired an unusual tale to pass along. Robert heard the piano playing in the dark and, together with his father, went down into the parlour to investigate. They found nothing.

The children were startled and frightened one day by the intrusion of a strange lady into the bathroom. Susan was four at the time and Ronnie just three. They had gone together down to the second-floor bathroom, and Mrs. Edmunds, hearing them scream, had come running and found them huddled on the floor, crying and terrified. The children both said that a lady had startled them in the bathroom, but she had disappeared.

To add to the growing confusion, and to Mrs. Edmunds's consternation, someone or something had watered all the plants one night and left a track of mud on the curtains. The house was locked. The Edmunds could think of no reasonable explanations for these unnerving events, and finally decided to leave the job, although it suited them in every other respect.

The publishers of the *Toronto Telegram* were unwilling to simply accept every story and statement that they received or uncovered. They demanded sworn statements from those involved, and received them.

In his notarized affidavit, Edmunds stated, "Certain happenings during the three years and eight months we lived there have convinced me there is something peculiar about the place."

The wary *Telegram* published two stories about the haunting in June. The *Toronto Daily Star*, not even waiting for the second installment of the series, pounded upon the ghost story with a stern debunking. "The whole ghost business was a put-on," said the *Star* writer solemnly, "a dream from the over-heated imagination of a publicity writer." The article claimed that the Foundation wanted to draw attention to Mackenzie House to advance it as a tourist attraction, and this was their way of doing it.

According to the *Star*'s version, Alex Dobban had "huffily denied originating the tales of ghostly doings," and said there was "nothing to it." The fact that he had voluntarily moved out of the free accommodation provided with the job had nothing to do with ghosts, the *Star* contended.

Mr. Dobban failed to explain in the *Star*'s story why he would have consented to swear out an affidavit if he knew his story to be a lie. No mention was made of the Edmunds couple or their version of the haunting.

By the end of June, the *Toronto Telegram* had received a deluge of letters and telephone calls about supernatural experiences. Such a flood of stories is common in the days approaching Hallowe'en, but rare at the beginning of the school summer holidays when the days are long and busy.

Everyone had a ghost story to tell. One caller reported that the spirit of a murderer regularly tramped the steps of Gibraltar Point Light over on the Toronto Island. Another tale that had been floating around for a hundred years or so resurfaced, about a Rosedale ghost who actually killed a youth in a ravine mausoleum because the curious and ill-advised boy had dared to invade the family crypt.

Another caller insisted that he had once visited a haunted house (no location was given) where he observed a tray fully laden with a traditional afternoon tea rise from the table surface on which it sat, hover in the air for an instant, and then settle back down without even rattling one of the fine bone-china cups.

None of these stories added anything to the Mackenzie House mystery, but they demonstrated that people were extremely interested in ghosts, foreshadowing the crowds that would soon gather at 82 Bond Street.

Meanwhile, the *Star* was not idle. While the *Telegram* published a report of its readers' reactions, the *Star* set about organizing a séance. In retrospect, this ploy sounds even odder than the publicity scheme of which the *Star* had accused the Homestead Foundation in the first place.

Unfortunately, the *Star* was unable to keep its séance a secret. Somehow the word got out, and a crowd was waiting outside expectantly when seven spiritualists gathered around the Mackenzie dining-room table one night. From its central position on one wall, a large oil painting of William Lyon Mackenzie looked down on the assemblage. The seven, one of whom was a newsman, placed their hands palm-down upon the oak table and waited for Mackenzie, or one of his relatives, to make an appearance.

Mackenzie didn't appear. Neither did the spirits of any other individuals. Although bodies vibrated and a disorganized series of Morse-code-like rappings was heard, one of those present dismissed the action as unimportant. "That's nothing," he said. "After all, with seven spiritualists in a room you're bound to get some sort of reaction."

Harold Hilton, one of the mediums present, said, "This definitely proves that Mackenzie House isn't haunted. After all, if William Lyon Mackenzie was coming back he would certainly communicate with those who understand him."

To anyone who has read much about spirit manifestation, Mr. Hilton does not sound as if he would understand much about Mackenzie's problems. In fact, he sounds quite arrogant. No ghost is compelled to show up at a given place or time just because seven spiritualists happen to be gathered together. There is no literature to support Harold Hilton's stand that Mackenzie's failure to appear on that particular occasion meant that he was "definitely" not present in the old house.

Aside from lack of interest in the seven spiritualists, there is another plausible reason why no sensible ghost would have materialized that night. Outside Mackenzie House, chaos reigned. Dozens of young people roamed the grounds during the séance, yelling, laughing, shining lights in through windows, leaping over hedges, and opening doors. Police were finally called in to break up a raucous mob scene around midnight. The rear door of the house was forced open and a fire extinguisher was emptied of its foaming contents in the narrow hallway. A concrete birdbath was broken and flower pots smashed; earth, plants, and broken potshards littered the entranceway.

"This is a house of calm," said Mr. Hilton, ignoring or maybe not wishing to hear the noise and destruction that was occurring outside. "A place of great tranquillity. There are no spirit influences here."

A little more cautious in his pronouncements, but still firmly on the side of the debunkers, Reverend W. C. Partridge of Springdale Spiritualist Church, another of the participants that evening, told the assembled press, "We're sensitive people and there are always some spirit bodies present. But we are sure that there is no evil spirit or ghost at the Mackenzie Homestead."

Despite the conclusions of the spiritualists, it seemed impossible to let the matter rest. An appeal was made to the clergy of the city of Toronto to assist with an exorcism service.

Exorcism is defined as the expulsion of malign spirits from an object, person, or habitation by ritual means. At what point someone had reached the decision that the ghost of Mackenzie had been malevolent we cannot know. Certainly the only scary element of the reported incident had been the rather nasty ghostly woman who struck Mrs. Edmunds. The Mackenzie spirit had been only tentatively linked to the mysterious piano playing, the operation of the locked printing press, and perhaps to the echoing footsteps.

Nevertheless, an exorcism was requested, and Archdeacon John Frank of Holy Trinity Anglican Church offered to perform the service. On July 2, accompanied by a single reporter and certain representatives of the Homestead Foundation, the Archdeacon toured the residence, stopping to pray in each room. In his spoken prayers, he asked that disturbing spirits should leave the Homestead henceforth and forever. He also asked God to visit the besieged dwelling-place and drive from it all torment, unhappiness, and fear. He prayed for Mackenzie and added another prayer that "this house may stand long as a monument to those who pioneered in this country."

For two years nothing more was heard about ghostly activity in Mackenzie House. Press coverage died down, and life returned to normal around the previously beleaguered residence. Caretakers came in by the day and the upstairs flat was closed off. Anyone who requested permission to remain in the house overnight was given a firm and negative response.

Then in 1962, while some renovation work was being undertaken in the old building, another report of unexplained events surfaced. This time it came from the workmen who, eleven in number, went in each morning and left together late each afternoon, locking up the house behind them.

The foreman, Pat Ryan, reported that things had been moved during the night. "Dropsheets that had covered the old printing press were pulled back," Ryan said. "And a sawhorse and a length of rope had been moved."

Mackenzie House had been locked tight, and there was no sign of a break-in. Following the initial report, though, the old house was broken into and an electric bandsaw was taken from the site. The ghostly antics were being imitated by human mischief.

Murdo MacDonald, one of the workmen, came in one morning to find a hangman's noose draped over the stairway. He didn't know how it got there. He couldn't tie an authentic hangman's noose himself, he said, nor did he know of anyone who could, certainly none of the work crew.

Another worker said that he wouldn't spend a night in the house if someone dared him, even for money. Nobody offered, so he didn't have to consider the daunting prospect seriously. And nothing more untoward happened for a time.

When it ceased to employ live-in caretakers, the Mackenzie Homestead Foundation returned the house in a sense to whatever spirits might be calling it home, who are free to perform at night without notice or interruption. Very few stories about strange occurrences have surfaced since then, although in November of 1966 a new caretaker, Mrs. Winnifred McCleary, said that the ghost was still present and would occasionally put its arms around her. Possibly the haunting is over.

Authorities on supernatural manifestations say that eventually a ghost will disappear through lack of energy, if for no other reason. Perhaps Mackenzie's ghost grew tired, or even bored, or maybe he was satisfied that he had drawn sufficient attention to his former home and to himself. Or perhaps this site of the unexplainable will be the source of new reports of mysterious happenings in the future. As tourists studying the early days of Upper Canada and Muddy York find their way through Mackenzie House, the notion that it might be furnished with a period ghost or two adds a zesty tang to the history lesson.

7

ONTARIO APPARITIONS

FROM THE BEGINNING

The town of Stratford, Ontario, is best known as the home of the Stratford Festival, a drawing card for artists and patrons of the theatre from around the world. It is also a perfectly lovely little town, complete with scenic shops, a winding river, and ghosts.

One fascinating house in Stratford has a history linking the building to the earth on which it stands and to entities that were there well before the town was even established. This residence was erected near water and surrounded by a grove of trees. Several streams flow underground to the nearby river, making the spot a sacred place to the early inhabitants of this area. The builders of the house would have been well advised to take some of the history of the immediate surroundings into account when construction commenced.

The first residents of the house faced a number of financial problems, and were forced to sell the property during the Depression years. The next owners, one of whom still lives in the house, had far more interesting experiences.

Martin and Margaret Chalice (not their real names) moved into the house with their young daughter Laina sometime in the 1930s. Margaret was of Irish heritage and extremely superstitious; she disliked the place from the beginning. There was a section of the attic into which no one would venture. Nor was the big cement cistern in the basement, which provided plenty of soft, clear water, a place to linger.

Margaret used to have violent headaches that kept her in bed for days on end. During these times, she often felt threatened. At one point, she was convinced that someone had drowned in the cistern. Martin was unable to establish this for a fact, but he felt that such an incident could have occurred and he agreed to have the cistern removed. Even today that area, now the laundry room, can be highly uncomfortable on occasion.

There was no doubt it was a strange house, but no one yet realized how very strange.

While Martin and Laina tended to avoid the basement and the one uncomfortable portion of the attic, they did not fear for their personal safety. They both loved the house and its marvellous location.

The years passed, and Laina left home to marry Stan Crannock. She became a successful art teacher and lived with her husband in an apartment on the other side of Stratford.

Margaret developed Alzheimer's disease. Today we can speculate that the culprit might have been her zinc and aluminum cooking pots, but Margaret was convinced that the house was causing her condition.

She died, and not too long afterwards Martin also passed away. Laina could not afford to live in her parents' house, but she was determined to retain it until she could afford to live in it once more. In most places such an arrangement would be difficult, but Laina was able to rent the house to the Stratford Festival as one of the residences available to visiting artists. Meanwhile, living nearby, she was able to keep an eye on her family home.

A friend, Glenn Fenton, volunteered to help with the task of preparing to turn the house over to the Festival: making some minor repairs, painting, and packing up boxes of the Chalices' belongings. He worked whenever he was free from his regular job, which meant that he was often in the house at odd hours.

During the renovations, Glenn felt the presence of someone watching his progress. He was fairly certain that it was Martin Chalice, so he began speaking to his invisible companion, discussing the work he was doing. Somehow Glenn felt that he was receiving his unseen observer's approval for the work.

But Glenn began to feel there were others watching who did not approve of what was going on. He would work straight through a night rather than go to bed when he felt these presences around him. A passive and approving Martin Chalice was just fine — Glenn had known and liked him in life — but these other beings made the renovator feel somehow threatened.

As a condition of the rental contract, the Festival agreed not to use the attic, which Laina and Glenn used to store many household items she might want in the future. A solid lock was placed on the door to the attic, together with a sign explaining that this area was out of bounds and not included in the rental agreement.

Well-known Canadian actor Douglas Campbell was one of the first tenants of the house. One evening, Mr. Campbell and a friend were relaxing in the living room, together with Campbell's dog. Presumably drinks were being enjoyed, but neither of the two men had consumed an excess, nor, of course, had the dog. Suddenly an angry male figure appeared in the doorway, glaring at the two men. No words were spoken, but the message of anger was abundantly clear. The apparition was extremely unhappy about something.

Determining that the apparition must have been the home's previous master, Martin Chalice, the perplexed Douglas Campbell contacted Laina to try to ascertain what the problem might be. He liked the house and wanted to remain there during the Festival season. She was easily able to explain her father's reaction. Martin Chalice loved dogs, but they had had their own place within the family, and the living room had always been off-limits to household pets. Laina was amused, but not alarmed, that her dad was still trying to enforce his old house rules.

Some years later, the people who were then staying in the house decided to break the lock on the attic door in order to turn that area into a rehearsal room for guitarists. Not long after this breach of the lease, the radiators froze and a flood of water ran down from the attic into the second floor of the house. Laina, who left most of the dealings concerning the house up to the Festival management, was fairly certain that the unauthorized entry into the attic area was connected with the frozen pipes. In all the years her family had owned the house, they had never had trouble with pipes freezing.

Another Festival tenant had an extremely embarrassing experience. Ian was a very small actor who was not used to dogs and felt quite uneasy in their presence. An old school friend of Laina's, Clark Scofield, was staying in the house with his two large farm dogs at the same time as Ian. When Clark went off to work each day, he locked the animals on the third floor so that Ian would not be bothered by them. The dogs were secured behind one firmly closed door and another that was locked with a key.

Ian, who had been up until quite late the previous night, got up at the tail end of the morning, donned his bright red bathing trunks, and went out into the garden for some sun. Somehow, the two doors that were supposed to be securely closed were opened, and the dogs thundered down the stairs onto the main floor. They refused to allow Ian back into the house. They were large and aggressive although not the least bit vicious and Ian was petrified of them. The stand-off continued for some time, the dogs inside and the actor outside. Ian became increasingly desperate; a rehearsal was approaching and he had to retrieve his clothes from inside the house. Skimpily clad though he was, he went to the neighbours and asked for assistance. They, in turn, called the Festival offices.

The bemused accommodations manager hopped into her car and went to track down Clark Scofield, who returned to the house and sorted out the problem. But Ian was furious at the sustained and uncontrollable laughter his situation had evoked, and soon left for more accommodating lodgings where the only house pets were two goldfish.

*

Stan Crannock died suddenly and mysteriously while in Europe, leaving Laina completely on her own. She allowed the Festival to continue to rent the old house and moved into a smaller apartment. The rental income was a substantial supplement to her regular teaching salary.

In the fall of 1989, Laina reclaimed her family home. After its years of temporary occupants, the place required a great deal of renovation and repair. It was while this work was going on that the very weird events began to occur.

Laina started out sleeping on the third floor while the other areas were being cleared out and renovated. Plans to get the place back into shape were speeded up when she decided to marry Clark Scofield, her childhood companion who had recently returned to Stratford after a long absence. The nights seemed remarkably long, and she often heard the sounds of breathing, footsteps, and groaning. Laina was frightened by these unexplained noises, but she felt that a lot of what she heard might be due to the oddity of moving back home after so many years, and her imagination.

Soon Laina and Clark moved their belongings into the big house. She also had some possessions from her dead husband, and Clark was in the process of tidying up his mother's estate, so there were plenty of items to be allocated their appropriate space in the residence.

The house seemed to take on an unfriendly attitude towards the addition of the strange items and furnishings, and to the two new residents themselves. Soon after the wedding, Clark confessed that he thought he and Laina should move out. He felt extremely uncomfortable in that house, and suspected his unease resulted from Martin Chalice expressing opposition to the wedding. But Martin had always liked Clark. The two men had gotten along well, and

Martin had once assisted Clark in the purchase of a farm-house. Why would he be causing trouble for his daughter and her new husband?

Nothing seemed to go right. The couple laboured mightily but were unable to get their boxes unpacked or sorted. The possessions of Stan Crannock and of Clark's mother proved particularly difficult to deal with; the house seemed to be rejecting them! All the improvements to the house had to be done over at least once, sometimes several times. The new carpeting had stains from some rusty water that leaked out of a radiator. The locksmith, a man with many years of experience, inadvertently hacked at two wooden doors while installing new locks, and the tradesmen sent to repair the damage made the situation even worse. Doorbells rang when no one was there, and fuses short-circuited constantly. Some indoor-outdoor carpeting laid on the verandah developed a quarter-sized hole in it the first night after it had been installed. A friend of the couple suggested that this was the contribution of a woodpecker. But at night?

The house was clearly under siege. If Martin Chalice's spirit was not the cause, who or what could be responsible? Laina felt that Stan Crannock's possessions might be at the root of the matter. But Clark cast his ballot for the spirit of his recently deceased mother. Never a pleasant person, she had been referred to by some members of the family as "the broom-pilot," and had spent the latter portion of her life in an institution. As it turned out, both Laina and Clark were partially correct.

It all came to a head one gloomy and rainy morning. Laina had purposely left the side door unlatched so that she could bring the dogs in that way after taking them for a walk. When she returned with the dogs, the door was locked.

Clark was half-heartedly stacking books in the library. When Laina came storming in the back door trailing wet dogs and angry words, he announced that the situation had become impossible. They would either have to get some help or move out.

In desperation, Laina called upon the services of an old friend now living in England. She knew this lady had dealt with the supernatural in the past. Laina was barely into her description of their varied experiences when the woman cut her off abruptly. She told Laina that they were not dealing with a single entity, but a whole collection of spirits that had been stirred up by their arrival back into the house. The couple had brought upheaval with them when they installed the personal and highly charged possessions of Clark's weird mother and those of Stan Crannock. The woman gave Laina the number of a friend in a nearby town who could assess the situation. She advised the couple to go into a room where they both felt secure, to light candles and incense, and to remain there until the friend, Jimmy, arrived.

The frightened couple quickly retreated into the library and called Jimmy. He said that he hadn't much experience with such matters but that his mother most certainly had. She could join him and they would both come up to Stratford on Saturday. But it was only Wednesday! Jimmy mentioned that the intensity of happenings would vary and that they should, as the earlier psychic had suggested, retreat to a safer area when they felt cold or if things seemed to be closing in on them.

Laina and Clark readily agreed to make the trip to collect Jimmy and his mother early Saturday morning. They wrote down the directions to his house carefully. Both of them knew well the small town where he lived.

Thursday was a quiet period, strange in its almost sullen silence. But Friday was quite a different story. After supper the dogs grew restless and padded off to the den, with Laina and Clark following along behind. Through the doorway of the den they could see a thick, murky fog that seemed to swirl about the room. The air suddenly became icy and the hairs on the back of everyone's neck stood upright. And this in the room where they had hoped to feel safe and secure.

Without warning, something hit Laina sharply on the arm, and she recoiled in pain and shock. Clark said that it looked as if Laina was struck by another woman. Laina was terrified, and her arm stung from the blow. She had been through recent neck surgery and that, added to the growing tension in the house, was almost more than she could bear. Clark suggested that Laina go upstairs and take a warm shower to fight off the chill — but not alone. He would stay with her.

As Laina stood under the soothing warm water, she suddenly turned icy cold again, and once again she was struck. Clark, standing just beyond the shower itself, felt the cold and saw the second blow land. They both dressed as quickly as possible, secured the dogs and the house, and bundled into the car to drive to the nearby town for assistance. They had tried telephoning Jimmy's house but had been unable to get a reply. (This in itself was strange, for they learned later that there was seldom a time when there was no one at Jimmy's place.) They were determined to find him, even if they had to spend a part of the night asleep in their car in his driveway.

The couple had travelled that road many, many times before, but became terribly lost. They found themselves on an incredible, surreal road beside a twisting, frothy, rocky river, saved from an accident only by timber strewn on the steep bank. Clark slowed the car to a crawl and they picked their way to safety through the strange terrain.

When they arrived at the nearby town, there was a bed and hot tea waiting — Jimmy had sensed that they were coming. The young man lived upstairs over his mother's apartment. His psychic abilities seemed to help Laina and Clark, and the two of them unwound and relaxed. The threat appeared to have been left behind.

The next morning the trio collected Jimmy's mother, Martha, and they headed back towards Stratford. No strange roads or rivers were encountered this time. As they entered the driveway to Laina's family home, Martha suggested that she would enter the house first. The troublesome entities were all waiting at the front door — she could see them clearly. Laina and Clark were told to collect the dogs and take them for a long walk, far from the house. They were to have no further contact with the troublemakers; she and Jimmy would take over.

Jimmy and Martha started in the attic and worked their way down through the house, sprinkling holy water as they went, moving the unwanted guests ahead of them. The room on the third floor in which Laina had tried to stay on her initial return had been their gathering place and haven.

Martha described one of the spirits as being a woman of medium height with a long single braid down her back. There were four others, two of them so aged that they stooped like gnomes. All had been peaceful until their little spirit world had been invaded by the auras of Clark's violent mother and Laina's first husband, both of which had accompanied their physical possessions into the house.

When Laina and Stan Crannock had been in Texas for a holiday many years before, Stan had purchased a set of long-horns in which he took inordinate pride. These had remained with Laina, and she had been about to hang them in the den. Martha told them that the vibrations emanating from these horns was incredible, and she treated them generously with oil, from the tips to their bases. Leaving nothing to chance, Laina put out the set of long-horns with the next garbage collection. Before the garbage could be picked up, the horns were "rescued" by a neighbour. Laina and Clark, watching from behind the curtains as he tiptoed up and walked away with them, silently wished good luck to the garbage-picker and his family.

During the following several days, everything in the house that wasn't specifically owned by Clark, Laina, and her parents was disposed of. Her old wedding ring went, as did a large and bizarre collection of dolls that had belonged to Clark's mother.

Martha assured Laina that her father was not among the ousted spirits. He was, she reported, still there in the house, but had been unable to withstand the onslaught of other spirits. He was very interested in what was happening, however.

One member of the old clan who was not removed took refuge at the bottom of the garden, where he now dwells peacefully. This refugee from the distant past has since become a gardening companion of sorts, becoming noticeably friendlier whenever there is talk of the care and cultivation of plants and flowers.

Peace has finally come to the house in Stratford, and Laina and Clark Scofield are both very relieved. When they were looking after a neighbour's house a few summers ago, they encountered some of the very nasty spirits from their old place dwelling in a basement washroom of that house.

They seemed to have settled comfortably into this new home and were not causing any trouble.

What exactly transpired at this Stratford home? It appears as though the location on which Laina's house had been erected had been a very special gathering place for spirits far back into Canadian history. As these people passed on, the spirits of some managed to remain. They made their presence known just often enough to give the house a strange atmosphere, one that upset Margaret Chalice and may have contributed to her illness. When Martin Chalice passed away, he retained enough energy to remain in his well-loved home. His appearances were rare but effective. Then Laina and Clark moved in, both carrying physical baggage with a highly negative psychic charge. When Stan Crannock had died far from home, his spirit was on the loose for a long time. And Clark's mother had been a problem even when she was in her physical form. The combination of these two spirits seeking their own ways, both a threat to the marriage of Clark and Laina, stirred up the ancient occupants of the house. Like little time capsules, they exploded, ruining the atmosphere of the residence until they were driven away.

Yet all sorts of questions remain unanswered. How was Margaret affected by the history of the land upon which her house had been built? Who or what loosed the dogs on poor little Ian? Do woodpeckers attack newly laid carpeting, and do they perform at night? Who hit Laina and why? And how does one explain that strange and surreal road that suddenly appeared between Stratford and a nearby town? And, possibly of greatest interest, what happened to the family who took Stan Crannock's long-horns?

THE CAT IN THE STORM

It couldn't have happened, but it did. Readers of science fiction and followers of *Star Trek* are familiar with the theory that spirits can transfer into new bodies after death, and that the new bodies need not necessarily be of the same shape, type, or even sex as the old ones. This next story adds an additional twist to this concept, and it is not the work of a science fiction writer. It really did happen as reported.

Just beyond the town of Haliburton in north-central Ontario, a road twists, turns, and rambles its way through the overgrown brush of the countryside. Only five houses have so far been built on this road. The residences are not clustered together, as one might expect, but are separated by a kilometre or two.

Mr. and Mrs. Barry Neilson were an older, retired couple who lived in one of these five isolated houses. They had little contact with the outside world, except for a trip into town every so often for supplies, or perhaps a visit to the doctor or dentist. They did, however, have a much-beloved dog, their only companion in an otherwise lonely existence. Bentley, an amusing mixture of poodle and spaniel, had his own special bed and always received extra bits of meat at the conclusion of the evening meal.

It was early summer when the elderly dog died, leaving the Neilsons desolate and even lonelier than before. They hesitated to get a replacement for Bentley. Both of them felt that nothing could replace their former pet and fill the emptiness that his departure had brought to their lives. Besides, they didn't feel capable of going through the tedious process of training a new puppy, and their limited daily quota of exercise would be insufficient for an active creature.

Winter arrived, and with it a nasty ice and sleet storm that raged for more than twenty-four hours. But the Neilsons were snug and safe in their little house. Just before sitting down to supper, the couple were interrupted by the familiar sound of loud scratching at the front door. It sounded very much like the noise Bentley used to make when he was anxious to get into the house in a hurry.

But when they went to the door, the bedraggled animal crouching there, wet and covered with sleet, was not a dog but a large, green-eyed cat.

The startled pair let the cat in and carefully towelled the icy water from its tawny fur. They had no idea how it had managed to reach the sanctuary of their house, as all the access roads were closed by the severity of the storm and the nearest neighbour was more than a couple of kilometres away.

The cat sauntered over to the corner of the dining room where Bentley's bowl had once stood. One would have expected the cat to go into the warmer and more inviting kitchen where the evening meal had been recently prepared.

After feeding the strange animal with a portion of their own beef stew and a small bowl of milk, Mr. and Mrs. Neilson ate their evening meal. They took their time, lingering over their coffee, but were soon distracted by the cat's activities.

The animal proceeded into the kitchen from the dining room and scratched on the wall beside the sink. This was an exact repetition of the actions frequently taken by Bentley when the Neilsons tarried too long before fixing his after-dinner treats. The scratch marks left by the dog were still visible on the wall.

Then Mrs. Neilson came up with a bizarre idea. She walked towards the kitchen and stood quietly in the door-way. In a low and deliberately even voice, she began to recite a list of different names. There was no reaction from the cat until she reached the eighth name. Sure enough, as soon as Mrs. Neilson uttered "Bentley," the cat ceased its scratching by the sink and walked over to her, where it rubbed up against her leg.

The couple were not given much time to recover from their surprise. Directly after finishing off the last of the table scraps, the cat sauntered over to the cupboard in the entrance hallway and stood there, as if challenging the elderly couple to make the next move.

For a few long moments, the Neilsons remained riveted in place, absolutely speechless, staring at their strange visitor. Both were remembering that Bentley had always slept in a padded bed just inside the cupboard door, which had always been left ajar while he was alive. The bed was still there, just inside the cupboard, although neither of the Neilsons had thought about it much since the past summer.

Finally, Barry Neilson bestirred himself and went to the cupboard. Glancing up slowly and meeting his wife's frightened eyes, he slowly opened the door. Without hesitation or any examination whatsoever, the cat walked through the door, turned slowly around a few times, and then settled down to sleep in Bentley's old bed.

After puzzling over the cat's behaviour, the Neilsons washed their dishes and locked the house in preparation for bed. But first they peeked into the hall cupboard. Their feline visitor was still sleeping peacefully, the storm clearly forgotten, as if it didn't have a care in the world.

The next morning the cat was gone. A careful search of the small house failed to uncover any sign of the animal, and the elderly couple were unable to determine how the cat left the building. They checked further afield. None of their neighbours had lost a cat, and no one was able to account for the strange appearance of the tawny feline in the midst of such a fierce ice storm.

When asked about their reaction to this most bizarre experience, the Neilsons replied that they were both awfully surprised and more than a little frightened. However, after reflecting on the incident and discussing it in detail, their general feeling turned out to be one of delight. At their advanced age of life, they took some consolation in the events as a possible indicator of an existence after death.

INDIAN LAND

Comparing the vast tracts of productive land once controlled by Indian bands with the current extent of reserves, often on inferior land, can be a depressing exercise. However, in the case about to be related, the Indians involved registered their objections to this state of affairs in a most unusual way.

It was springtime in the town of Mississauga, just west of Toronto. Two young boys, one eleven and the other thirteen, approached their mother complaining they were unable to sleep at night. According to the boys a bright light shone into their bedroom, apparently originating in the far corner of their backyard.

The skeptical parents investigated, suspecting a prank of some sort. To their surprise, they discovered that the boys had been telling the truth. A strange light shone out from that very corner of the yard.

The father explained to his sons that he thought perhaps rotting stumps left when the land was originally cleared by developers might be the cause of the strange light. In any event, the matter was, for the time being, forgotten.

One day not much later, however, the two boys ran screaming in a panic to their parents. An Indian man was peering in the window at them! The boys insisted that their story was true, and no amount of parental coaxing could overcome their absolute refusal to sleep in the bedroom that looked out onto the backyard. Their mother decided that she needed help in dealing with this unprecedented situation. A friend urged her to contact a local woman living in nearby Port Credit. This woman was a psychic and medium with a wealth of experience in various types of hauntings.

The psychic, intrigued by the story, arrived the next morning. In broad daylight she was able to "see" what had frightened the two youngsters. There, in the middle of the suburban backyard, stood a tall Indian man. His face was painted and he was wearing only a loincloth and a simple headdress.

The woman headed for the Town Hall to do some research into the previous owners and uses of the land. She discovered that the backyard of the boys' house just touched the edge of a burial ground once used by the Mississauga Indians. From that information, she surmised that the lone Indian figure might have been a witch doctor defending, even after death, the hallowed ground of his former tribe.

Using a crystal ball and automatic writing, two useful tools in knowledgeable hands, the psychic was able to convince the Indian to leave the property. It was no easy task. The woman assured the Indian spirit that no harm or disrespect was intended towards his ancestors, and she persuaded him that he could honourably end his long period of guard duty.

The boys were able to return to their room and no further incidents were reported.

Several days later, the Port Credit psychic received another request for help. She found herself in the same neighbourhood, but with a very important difference. The residence to which she had been summoned did not just abut the Indian burial ground; over half of its total area was within the boundary of the ancient cemetery.

Upon entering the second house, the psychic immediately felt a dense and heavy pressure upon her chest. Breathing was difficult. The unhappy and very frightened people living in the house were constantly plagued by what several local physicians had dismissed as psychosomatic illnesses.

The young wife and lady of the family was afraid that she might be losing her mind, and her marriage was on the verge of collapse. Everyone who entered the house experienced sudden and severe blasts of icy cold air, fits of bad temper, and feelings of nausea or dizziness. The once-beautiful hardwood floors that were laid throughout the house had become water-spotted and mildewed, and the atmosphere within the house was dank and very depressing. Family members squabbled among themselves and blamed each other for any number of perceived slights. Even the dog had turned nasty, whining and barking for lengthy periods.

The psychic admitted that she was unable to deal successfully with this situation — a true psychic doesn't hesitate to confess to weakness or lack of ability. A witch was called in to assist, and together the two women were able to remove a number of spirits from the troubled house. The witch employed ancient rites, handed down within her family for generations, for this difficult exorcism. She refused to discuss her methods in any detail, concerned that they could be misused by others.

At least four Indian spirits were living in the besieged residence. There were men and women, as well as a small child that cried constantly. Naturally enough, the Indians were reluctant to leave the burial ground; they felt that the area was rightfully theirs, and historically it had once been their home. Only after several long and tiring nights of incantations did this group of spirits from a bygone era agree to leave.

Since the exorcism, the resident family has been in excellent health. The blasts of frigid air have ceased and the hardwood floors are gradually responding to treatment, the stains fading slowly away. Domestic relations within the family have improved immensely and the family is hopeful that the last of the Mississauga Indians are finally resting in peace. Since many houses touch or encroach upon this gravesite, and construction of new ones continues, it is quite possible that other cases involving Indian spirits will occur in the neighbourhood.

I asked the psychic who was involved in this experience to explain how the Mississauga Indians were capable of understanding her communications in English. She spoke of her belief that a learning period of sorts takes place after death. During this interval, which varies in length, long-dead spirits teach those newly arrived the various methods of communicating with the world of the living, a kind of English School of Spirits. This theory would also explain why there is often a delay between the time of a person's passing and his or her first appearance as a ghost.

BEATRICE, A DETERMINED SPIRIT

Can a very determined lady who is officially dead return to her childhood home and take over its management? In the case of Beatrice Simms, a pious spinster who died in 1967, it seems the answer is yes.

Beatrice lived in a three-story house on Colborne Street in London, Ontario. Beatrice loved the house and wanted to live there for the rest of her life, but in 1943 she was forced to sell the property because of financial problems. Her parents had both died and her brother had left home. Beatrice could no longer maintain the large house by herself. She needed money; the house had to go. But she had vowed to her friends that she would return to the London house. In fact, she was a bit of a bore on the subject of her very special house.

The ownership of the house changed several times during Beatrice's lifetime. None of the owners noticed anything the least bit psychic or unusual about the building then; it was just another large and comfortable house to them. But when Beatrice died, years later in Toronto, the trouble began.

Late in the summer of 1967, Richard Saunders' family occupied the Simms' old house. (The name of this family has been changed, but all other names, dates, and times are factual.)

Mr. and Mrs. Saunders were a sensible and practical couple. At that time, they knew nothing whatever about ghosts; nor were they much interested in the subject. You would not have found their names on the membership lists of any spiritualist organizations. They had never heard of Beatrice Simms and had no complaints about the neighbourhood or the house itself. But during September that year, Mr. and Mrs. Saunders began to hear and sense strange things. Doors creaked for no apparent reason, and the sound of light footsteps echoed throughout the house. Mrs. Saunders was the first to comment on the changes.

At first, Mr. Saunders was skeptical. He thought that his

wife was suffering from nervous exhaustion; she was after all a woman with a new baby and two other small children, enough to tire anyone. (The three Saunders children were all under four years of age; far too young to be held responsible for the strange occurrences.) But his attitude underwent an abrupt about-face one day when, alone in the house, he clearly heard someone calling his name. There was no one in the house or yard, or playing in the street beyond.

From that day, the sounds and sensations gradually increased. Disembodied voices would call out unexpectedly from unoccupied rooms in the old house. Mr. and Mrs. Saunders became sure that they felt another presence in the house with them. While uncertain about exactly what was going on, they were positive that something unnatural was happening. The mood of their home was actually being altered by someone or something that the Saunders could not see.

The family dog, a German shepherd named Chimo, also began to act in a most peculiar way. He would stand motionless, a picture of frozen terror, at the head of the main stairway. A well-behaved, friendly, and dependable animal for years, Chimo now refused to respond when the family called him. He would just stand there staring out into empty space.

On Hallowe'en night, the dog vanished completely. No trace of him was ever found. Dogs in London are required to wear licences on their collars; if Chimo had been involved in a traffic accident, surely the Saunders family would have received some sort of notification. It seems more likely that the poor animal simply could not endure the dreadful atmosphere any longer. He was quite literally scared away from his home. Could he perhaps have seen something that was invisible to his human family?

Next the budgie and two goldfish died for no apparent

reason. Mr. and Mrs. Saunders were becoming extremely concerned about the safety of their three small children. Something or somebody was obviously infesting their home. It seemed too much of a coincidence to lose all of their household pets within such a short period of time. They became fearful of what might happen next.

The footsteps became increasingly frequent. They usually sounded as if some person were slowly and deliberately ascending the central staircase of the house. The sounds would cease just before the invisible climber would normally have crossed into the hearer's line of sight.

One day during that memorable winter, a visitor to the Saunders house listened in disbelief to those strange footsteps as she stood at the head of the stairs. She could see the entire stairway stretched out below her, and could hear the footsteps growing louder as they approached her position. There was no one there. She hid with the three small children under the nearest bed.

Voices continued to call out at night and even during the daytime. Sometimes they sounded like those of adults, but occasionally they were childlike. Neighbours recall being clearly told, "Come right on in," when Mrs. Saunders, occupied elsewhere in the large house, insisted that she had not even heard a knock at the front door. At times such as this, it seemed as though someone other than Mrs. Saunders had assumed complete control of the household — a most disconcerting thought.

On New Year's Eve, Richard Saunders and his wife decided to go out. They wanted to get away from the house in order to greet 1968 in a proper frame of mind. By that time, Mrs. Saunders was very much in need of an evening away from the endless confusion that now marked her days at home.

The Saunders's regular daytime baby-sitter and another local girl reluctantly agreed to stay with the children that evening. Perhaps they hoped that there might be some security in numbers; the haunted Saunders house was not after all an average baby-sitting assignment.

When Mr. and Mrs. Saunders left, they carefully shut the front door after themselves and locked it. The wary teenagers checked the door from the inside just to reassure themselves that everything was secured and in order.

One of the girls went upstairs to check on the children. Her friend remained in the living room. They both heard the front door open and close, although they knew that such a thing was impossible. Knowing how frightened the girls were, Mr. and Mrs. Saunders would have rung the doorbell or knocked if they had forgotten something and had to return. No one else was supposed to have a key.

The baby-sitters stayed silently where they were, one upstairs and one down. They listened intently. Someone walked slowly and firmly across the front entrance hall, through to the back, and then entered the little back shed used for storage.

Then the young girls were astonished to hear the sound of a rocking chair in motion. *Creak, creak, creak, creak . . .* But when they tried to get into the shed, the door was still so securely latched that the combined weight of the two baby-sitters was unable to force it open. Nor was there any way for them to have known that Mrs. Saunders had placed an old rocking chair out in the shed just the day before.

After that unnerving experience, the two girls refused to return, even in the daytime. They had no desire to chance any further spooky incidents.

Mrs. Saunders began to get increasingly frightened and nervous. Several times she felt a strong compulsion to simply run outside with the children. And she would suddenly feel a very cold sensation right up against her back or following her about as she worked in the kitchen.

No logical explanations could be found for any of the strange happenings. Whatever had invaded the Saunders home seemed determined to force them to move away. And the intruder was almost successful.

At this point, Mr. and Mrs. Saunders finally learned about the late Beatrice Simms and her intense desire to return to her former home. After some searching, they found books and papers bearing Beatrice's name secreted in a remote corner of the attic. They considered the matter carefully and concluded that the old rocking chair in the shed might once have belonged to Beatrice. It had been one of a number of bits of furniture left in the house when it was sold.

"After that, I sort of took a friendly attitude towards this whatever-it-was in our house," said Mrs. Saunders. She began to talk calmly to the ghost each time that she felt its presence near her.

"You could feel something watching. You just knew something was standing there by the railing at the top of the stairs."

A number of times, she asked if the visitor might be the spirit or ghost of Beatrice Simms. There was no noticeable response to her questions.

As far as she can recall, Mrs. Saunders never actually went so far as to officially order the ghost to leave her home, although she might have suggested this on one of the many occasions when the thing got on her nerves.

Perhaps the spirit might have taken offence when, on one

occasion, she "got real mad and may have told it to get out." No one conducted a séance or tried to exorcise the spirit; the Saunders family had no experience with such matters. Whatever the reason, things began to settle back to normal in February of 1968.

"The house felt different, and we could sense it wasn't there any more. But I was very nearly a nervous wreck!" Mrs. Saunders recalls.

So maybe Beatrice did get her own way in the end. Perhaps she did manage to return after all those years of hoping and planning, only to find herself highly unwelcome in her old house, and her old room occupied by a new baby. How disappointed she must have been.

But she possessed enormous staying power, remaining in the old house causing voices, footsteps, and creaking doors regularly, several times each week, for a period of five months. Failing to frighten off these strangers who were living in her old home, the spirit of this very determined woman must have finally decided not to stay where she was unwelcome.

The Saunders family seems unchanged by their experience; they still look for natural explanations for what happened. In discussing the various incidents with reporters, they do not say that they believe in ghosts. Nor do they claim, as one might expect, that their house was actually haunted for a specific period of time. They will only say that these highly unusual things really did happen, and that the events coincided with the period just after Beatrice Simms's death in Toronto.

Of course, we do not know for certain that the spirit in the Saunders house was that of Beatrice Simms. But given the story of her single-mindedness, and the coincidence of her death and the beginning of the disturbances in the London house, it seems a reasonable guess that Beatrice came home to fulfill her vow.

MESSING ABOUT IN SCARBOROUGH

Only fairly recently have people begun to accept the fact that ghosts can appear without requiring a "traditional" background, such as a decaying castle possessing a sinister history complete with a cast of gnarled, obsequious retainers, stalwart lords, and lewd ladies. Ghosts can, and often do, turn up anywhere. They can actually be drawn to a specific location by living human beings experimenting with the occult. To their lasting regret, Bob and Edith Hall discovered this unpleasant reality. They really bit off more than they could chew.

The Halls were not a frivolous couple; they had a reason for becoming interested in spiritualism. They hoped to establish contact with their nine-year-old daughter, who had left the couple very lonely since her sudden and unexpected death. Bob and Edith decided that they should at least attempt to establish whether she had perhaps survived in another form beyond their understanding.

The Halls were in their early thirties. They were both regular churchgoers. Neither of them had any previous experience in dealing with matters of the occult, and if they had not missed their child so very much, they in all likelihood would not have become involved with it at all.

One evening, Bob and Edith set about constructing a makeshift Ouija board. The letters were taken from their game of Scrabble, and a large, glass-bottomed tray served as their board. Instead of the regulation pointer, they used a light-weight shot glass which moved easily across the surface of the tray. Their Ouija board was as modern as their bungalow in Scarborough.

At first, things appeared to be progressing smoothly. Contact appeared to have been made with the little girl, Becky, and she was able to identify herself to her parents' satisfaction. Becky indicated contentment with her present situation, but seemed unable to explain where she was or how she had gotten there.

Bob and Edith were quite willing to stop at this point. Their main question had been answered. The child seemed happy. By mutual agreement the Halls decided to leave the board. They had both noticed a deep chill in the room and were growing worried and very uncomfortable at the table.

But a Ouija board is something like an old telephone party line; if only one party terminates the conversation by hanging up, another can step in and carry on with the communication. Ideally, both parties should disconnect simultaneously to prevent outside interference from another source.

The situation in the Halls' living room was not ideal! Far from it. When the couple decided to quit their experiment, the "line" was still open at the other end just long enough for something quite extraordinary and unexpected to happen. Becky had gone, and Bob and Edith suddenly found themselves in contact with someone or something quite different.

The shot glass began to move in an agitated fashion, almost bouncing across the surface of the tray, moving rapidly from letter to letter. The resulting message indicated that the new "party on the line" was a seemingly unrepentant man guilty of several grisly child murders that had occurred many years ago in London, Ontario! (Disease, not murder, had claimed the Hall child.)

Quickly the Halls dismantled their makeshift board, but they were very much afraid that they had delayed too long. Whatever they had made contact with was loose in their home, and it was already starting to poison the atmosphere. The air temperature had dropped noticeably, and there was a sense of foreboding, that strange calm one sometimes feels before a thunderstorm.

Bob and Edith finished putting everything away and sat quietly in their living room. They shivered from the unnatural chill, and shook slightly with apprehension. Suddenly, throughout the entire residence, there rang an ear-shattering peal of maniacal laughter. The Halls were stunned and very badly frightened.

For the next several months, Bob and Edith Hall were besieged by an unwelcome intruder. The electrical system in the house went haywire; frigid air flowed through the house, accompanied by the smell of decay and loud bangs and cracks during the nights.

Slowly, with the passage of time, the effects lessened, until one day Bob felt that their Scarborough bungalow was back to what it had been. At least, it felt that way. Bob sent Edith out of town and remained alone in the house. He admits to feeling that the horrible laughter was "still hanging in the air," waiting for the opportunity to dominate whenever Bob's resistance felt low.

During that period on his own, Bob Hall slept badly. He came to dread the nights. In order to overcome the long, ominously quiet periods before sleep, he developed a system of defence. Every evening just before going to bed, Bob carefully placed ten long-play recordings onto his stereo system. That way, he could be well off to sleep before the music ran its course.

The maniacal laughter itself has never reoccurred, but the Halls had truly learned their lesson. There is no way you could get either of them to use a Ouija board again. They finally moved from Scarborough with a great feeling of release and relief. Still, Bob sometimes finds himself wondering what happened to "that thing" that he and Edith somehow accidentally turned loose. He's afraid that, once awakened, it might now be able to plague others.

8

POLTERGEISTS

"The ordinary ghost, although often inconsiderate, clumsy, noisy and frightening, is generally considered to be inoffensive, and even friendly and well-disposed to the living persons who occupy its place of haunting."

This definition from Frank Usher's *Fifty Great Ghost Stories* is quite acceptable if one keeps firmly in mind that the entity being described is an "ordinary" ghost. It is always dangerous to generalize with respect to either the motivational or behavioural patterns of ghosts. We simply don't know enough about them. Certainly there are some friendly, cooperative, and playful spirits, although even the best of them can upset a family group just by its presence. There are also ghosts who are complete stinkers and cause nothing but trouble. Not too many Canadian families would go so far as to actually welcome a ghost as a permanent, non-paying house guest.

And there are other unnatural things besides ghosts. Some completely malevolent forces seem to exist for no other reason than to cause chaos, embarrassment, and damage. These spirits create the most concern in the minds of investigators of the supernatural.

We refer to these entities as "poltergeists." They are very different from ordinary ghosts, and there is nothing the least bit funny about a visit from one. The violence of such infestations can reach a point where even the bravest and most stubborn individuals will seek some sort of assistance. Sometimes they will do anything, try anything, in order to get relief.

In a famous and well-documented case, the Amherst mystery of Nova Scotia, a spirit was held responsible for physical illnesses and mental breakdowns. It caused severe injuries to people and animals. The primary target of this entity was a young woman who was quite literally chased about the district from one hiding spot to the next. The Amherst poltergeist was even blamed for a rash of large fires that suddenly broke out in the vicinity of the haunting. The vicious pranks were all of a very serious nature.

It is this difference between mischievousness, stupidness, or carelessness and serious, unadulterated hatefulness, that separates the average ghost from the poltergeist.

GUYLAINE

A bizarre occurrence took place in Acton Vale, Quebec, about a hundred kilometres from Montreal, in 1969. It demonstrates the mixed results that the attempted exorcism of an unfriendly supernatural manifestation can have. It also illustrates quite clearly the emotional confusion that can afflict people who suddenly find themselves involved in such unnatural incidents.

The series of events took place one day in January in the home of the Saint-Onges family. Guylaine, a six-year-old child boarding at the Saint-Onges residence, became the centre of a most unusual performance, along with assorted religious and personal objects.

A sacred painting started things off. Although securely attached to the wall, it suddenly flew down the length of the room to the doorknob. Then it jumped to a nearby dresser and down onto the floor, where it began to enact a weird sort of rhythmic dancing pattern.

The Saint-Onges family watched in speechless horror.

Beds were stripped of their linen and torn apart by something that no one could see or control. Mattresses were tossed about the house as if by a powerful and utterly insane force. The Saint-Onges stubbornly laboured to remake their beds, which promptly and defiantly flew apart again.

Little Guylaine seemed to be the focal point of this frightening and violent turmoil. A frail child, she was trying in vain to dress for her morning classes. Her clothes danced around her. An array of rosaries, ashtrays, and vases filled the air in her vicinity. Mrs. Saint-Onges handed a rosary to the embattled child, hoping that this religious artifact might stop or at least reduce the commotion. But Guylaine was unable to hold on to the rosary; something unseen snatched it right out of her small hands.

Help was obviously needed. Three priests, Abbé Claude Léveillé, Abbé Normand Bernier, and Abbé Wilfred Bérard, were called in. They watched the activity for a while and promised to try to aid the besieged family.

The clergymen commenced by sprinkling holy water liberally about the room that seemed to them most critically affected. Next they tried to exorcise the spirit. Initially, the exorcism appeared to be effective. But the lull turned out to be just temporary. The thing had no intention of being removed so easily. A table and two religious statues were smashed in the new upsurge of violence.

Several long hours later, peace was restored. Whether or not this was a result of the exorcism is a matter of debate. Perhaps the rite required time to work; or perhaps the spirit left for some other reason. In any case, the three priests left, promising to issue a detailed statement to the press explaining their interpretation of the peculiar incident.

The trio of clergymen took well over a week before issuing their statement. Perhaps they were considering the matter; perhaps they needed to consult with their superiors, or with someone who had experience in exorcism. Finally they issued a statement that read in part: "It is the case of a diabolical phenomenon . . . he always attacks holy things and seems to fear their use against him . . . the first thing to do was search for possible natural causes but it was quickly established that there was no vibration on the walls, there was no draft and no one was touching the articles . . . those who were in the house began to pray and things quieted down."

The priests concluded: "We believe that the message God wanted to transmit to Acton Vale was transmitted. The supernatural exists, even if our scientific spirit leads us to doubt it, and we are invited to better observe our faith and to pray more and more for sinners."

No further incidents were reported by the Saint-Onges family.

It is interesting to speculate how this particular trouble-making spirit might react if it knew the reasons that had been attributed to its destructive performance! It seems unlikely that its initial aim, if indeed there was one, was to increase prayer and church attendance within the community. Unfortunately, communication with this sort of entity is almost impossible, so there is no way of knowing for sure.

Guylaine's parents took her away. Completely ignoring the verdict of the priests, they claimed that the child's vivid imagination was responsible for the incident. The Saint-Onges, with whom Guylaine had lived since she was a baby, disagreed. It was, and still is, their belief that the little girl was a victim of some sort of devilish force.

A similar episode in another small Quebec town in the 1960s did not have such a clear-cut ending. A poltergeist had driven an entire family of seven out of their home when the noise of banging cupboard doors and smashing china simply became too much to endure. The desperate family asked the local church to help.

The parish priest who attempted the exorcism in this case was relatively new at his work. He had never performed an exorcism before and was afraid of his invisible antagonist. This fear and vulnerability must have showed.

In the middle of the exorcism rite an unexpected interruption broke the concentration of all involved. The angry and clearly unrepentant spirit threw an orange directly at the unfortunate clergyman, who received a nasty black eye. For more than a week, he had to walk about the town with the mark of his battle clearly printed upon his face.

The poltergeist left the house about a week after the family members had been forced to leave, and two days after the exorcism. We cannot know if the clergyman was the cause of its departure or if the thing just missed an appreciative audience for its antics.

NOT A QUIET APPARITION

A quiet apparition might possibly be accepted by a broad-minded family with a sense of humour. If the ghost did not cause much trouble, some might prefer to live with it than to confide in neighbours or the local authorities. They might even feel a little superior about having a very special secret. In such a case the ghost-hunter is at a severe disadvantage, as the haunting is kept under wraps from all except the immediate family members and a few trusted friends.

A poltergeist, on the other hand, is considered fair game for investigation. It can cause sufficient damage to justify a full-scale inquiry. For the immediate sanity of those involved, it is usually customary to begin by checking with utility experts to officially eliminate the possibility that the trouble could be the result of natural causes. If no land faults, plumbing failures, or overloaded circuits turn up, the next step is often to consult representatives of the clergy, who may attempt to exorcise the visiting spirit. Utility repairmen and clerics, therefore, are often the sources of stories of poltergeists that find their way through the press and grapevine to a fascinated public.

Poltergeists, the most unpleasant of all psychic phenomena, often appear unconcerned or angered at the showing of the cross and the recitation of exorcism rites. They are seldom identified with a specific deceased person, or even considered to have a gender. Most people refer to all poltergeists as if they were asexual or masculine. Reports will read, "He then threw things around the room," or, "It makes awful banging noises and keeps us awake during the night."

Some people contend that poltergeists are the spirits of persons who died in a weakened condition and are thereby unable to express themselves through the more acceptable modes of communication. This theory has not been verified. One point against it is that it does not account for the violence and nastiness found in so many of the poltergeistic case histories.

The manifestation of a poltergeist is comparable to a sudden, explosive energy discharge by a disagreeable intelligence. Innocent individuals, often children, have been persecuted and sometimes severely injured by these malevolent spirits. A poltergeist is capable of following its unwilling victim from one place to another. Whereas most ghosts are generally associated with a particular area or dwelling, poltergeists attach themselves like leeches to specific persons or families. Only on rare occasions do they settle upon a limited area of operations.

Poltergeists are extremely powerful. They can transport a body or article through the air with apparent ease regardless of its weight, size, or shape. Chairs can be elevated despite the fact that someone quite solid might be sitting in them at the time. Cupboard doors bang. Windows open and shut at odd and usually inappropriate moments.

At one time it was believed that such forces could operate only when there were children, particularly little girls, in the area to serve as mediums or energy sources. This theory has been discarded, but it is true children are often involved, directly or indirectly, in poltergeistic hauntings. The child, usually small and physically weak, is often blamed at first for the destruction.

It would appear that some children can, unconsciously, increase the level of activity of certain poltergeists. They serve as unwilling assistants through which the entity gains additional power. But adults have also served as highly reluctant mediums and power cables.

One of the more recent theories about poltergeists suggested by psychic investigators is that all poltergeistic phenomena have, at their base, a source of energy in the form of repressed human sexual feelings. According to this claim, in every home where poltergeists occur, there must be at least one individual who is struggling with extreme sexual repression. This is a convenient way of thinking; all one would have to do to end the problem would be to locate that particular person and relieve those inner tensions. Of course, this is easier said than done, and even more to the point, this theory is easier to expound than to prove.

If the theory connecting sexual repression and poltergeists is true, the implications are disturbing. Every human being suffers from some degree of sexual repression during a lifetime; this could mean that we are all candidates for poltergeistic attack.

A poltergeist is quite simply a nightmare come true. Anyone who asks you if he or she has a poltergeist operating at home should probably be answered in the negative. If there was one, he or she would know it — no need to ask around the neighbourhood! A person posing that sort of question is more apt to have an ordinary, everyday ghost on his or her hands — and should be very glad indeed.

9

GHOSTS OF QUEBEC

Quebec is best known among those who follow supernatural phenomena for its poltergeists and religious apparitions. Perhaps because of the strong historical influences of the Church, more religious manifestations occur in Quebec than elsewhere in the country, and the province has seen some awesome poltergeistic displays. But Quebec is also home to many other types of supernatural activity.

MARY GALLAGHER'S MISSING HEAD

Montreal has a ghost that is said to return every seven years to prowl about the area of William and Murray streets. The next of these cyclic appearances is slated for June of 1998, which would bring the total number of sightings to sixteen.

Mary Gallagher, aged thirty-eight, and her best friend, Susan Kennedy, who was only twenty-three, were "ladies of the night," and sometimes "of the afternoon" as well. They worked the streets and bars of Montreal in 1879, using Susan's residence as a base.

A nineteenth-century writer described the two hookers as "dissipated characters who are in the habit of having friends in to see them and carrying on the most disgusting orgies." The Kennedy house was labelled "a carnival of vice."

One Friday afternoon in June, over a century ago, Mary and Susan wandered over to Bonsecours Market, looking for a bit of excitement. After the women had shared two bottles of whiskey, Mary Gallagher struck up a conversation with a young man, Michael Flanagan. After a time, the three of them went back to Susan's William Street house, where they continued drinking heavily.

At some point during the late afternoon and early evening, Michael passed out on the floor. Susan, who had spent the past few hours steaming with jealousy over her older friend's success in attracting such a handsome young man, erupted into violence. In a fit of intoxicated rage, Susan knocked Mary senseless, mutilated her with a hand-axe, and then, for good measure, chopped off Mary's head and threw it into a water pail sitting next to the kitchen stove.

Both Michael Flanagan and Susan Kennedy were charged with the gruesome murder of Mary Gallagher. But it soon became apparent that only the young woman could have been responsible. Only her clothing was caked with blood, and the hatchet that had been used was found hidden in her bedroom.

Susan Kennedy produced two alibis for the investigating authorities. She claimed first that a stranger had come into the house just before seven in the morning, and it was he who had slain Mary Gallagher. When asked why she had failed to report the brutal and bloody murder, she replied that she was giving the killer time to make good his escape, because "he was such a good-looking man." Next, Susan said that she had left the house for an hour to buy some more whiskey, and when she returned, Gallagher was dead, slain by an unknown killer.

At the trial, a downstairs neighbour in the Kennedy house testified that, at approximately 12:15 a.m., she had heard the noise of "a heavy body falling to the floor, so heavy that some of the plaster fell from the ceiling. This was followed by a loud chopping sound that lasted ten minutes at least."

The witness had not called the police because there were always late, loud parties in that place, she said, and she had given up trying to stop them.

A police witness, Constable William Craig, who had arrested Susan Kennedy on numerous occasions, testified that sometimes "she was so violent with drink that it took two men to hold her, and she had to be put into a woodcart to be taken to the station."

The defence attempted to prove insanity, but they were only able to persuade the young hooker's grocer to say that he "always considered that she was a little silly."

Throughout the proceedings, she sat in the prisoner's box with what was termed a "listless, indifferent air." The jury acquitted Michael Flanagan, but found Susan Kennedy guilty of Mary Gallagher's murder. The jury also made a recommendation for mercy.

The judge rejected the jury's recommendation for mercy, and sentenced Susan Kennedy to hang on December 5, 1880, saying, "You and only you butchered and mutilated your friend on the very spot where you had been carousing up to the moment of the murder." But Prime Minister John A. Macdonald commuted the sentence, and the convicted woman spent sixteen years in prison. She later died in 1916.

There was no disposition report for Mary Gallagher's body. Considering her lack of funds and family, and her wanton way of life, it is possible that her remains were dealt with casually or even incompetently. Most of the attention was centred upon the murderess rather than the victim.

Over the years, however, legend gradually grew up around the story of this murder. The headless form of Mary Gallagher is said to wander about the district in which she had once lived, returning every seven years to search for the head that was severed from her body in 1879. She arrives not around the Hallowe'en season but in June, the month in which she was so brutally murdered.

The last documented sighting of Mary Gallagher was made in 1928, shortly before the Griffintown neighbourhood was razed to make room for the O'Keefe Breweries. But someone sees Mary every seven years and the story continues. The haunting area is now a vacant lot on the southeast corner of William and Murray streets.

There have been no reported sightings of Susan Kennedy.

THE DEER HUNT

You might think that when humans go hunting, in large groups with the latest in equipment, it is only the animals that need to take care. But sometimes there is reason for the humans to be wary, despite all of the proper equipment and expertise.

Gene Doucet and three other young men in their late teens set out on their annual deer-hunting trip. It was well into fall, late in October or perhaps early in November; Gene isn't sure of the exact date, but he is positive that it was still while deer season was open.

The four men had spent the day tracking deer along trails between Georgeville and Fitch Bay in Quebec. It was hard and painstaking labour, working along the tree lines and crouching among the bushes, hoping for a glimpse of the elusive animals. The hunters were getting tired and frustrated.

Gene and two of his friends met up at an old, abandoned farmhouse and decided to go in and wait for the return of the final member of the party, who was still off somewhere in the woods.

The trio met with little resistance when they shoved open the front door of the old building. They found the deserted wooden structure to be still in fairly good condition, and it puzzled them that it should be standing empty. The windows were still intact, without a single broken pane. There were no signs of vandalism.

On the main floor was an old wood stove and a wooden kitchen table, obviously well-used over the years. A set of box-springs was pushed into a corner of one of the adjacent rooms.

At first, Gene and his friends paid no attention to the upstairs area. He recalled: "We were sitting with our feet up on the old stove, probably smoking and telling stories. Then we heard what sounded like someone or something walking across the floors of the upstairs. Really heavy footsteps. In the beginning, we thought it was our buddy, who we were waiting for, trying to scare us. We figured he could have gone from the shed roof up and through one of the upstairs windows."

Then there was silence for a long time. The three young men eyed each other uncomfortably, each waiting for another to take the initiative.

"There was sort of a group decision to all go upstairs and check out this weird place. Two of us went up the stairs first, with the third following, we later said cowardly, behind."

The door at the top of the stairs stood ajar. The upstairs consisted of one large empty room. There was more hesitation: no one wanted to be the person to pass first through the door and really look around. The impasse was solved, as are so many involving young people, by "peer pressure."

"So, the guy at the top, Jimmy, he had to be the guinea pig. He was also the smallest." Jimmy was unceremoniously shoved into the room. When nothing attacked him, the other two ventured beyond the doorway and looked around.

There was nothing to be seen. No animal, no person, nothing — just cobwebs. The windows were all intact and shut. There was absolutely no furniture that could have been moved to create the noise that had been heard from below, just a stone chimney going up in the middle of that one big room.

One of the young men checked out the chimney to ensure that there was no animal trapped inside that could be responsible for the sound effects. After that brief investigation, the decision to vacate the premises was unanimous. "Boy, we got out of there in a hurry! We were terrified! None of us would have dared to go back in. We waited outside for our missing buddy to show up."

The fourth member of the hunting party emerged from the woods just as it was getting really dark, about an hour later. He was astonished at the pleasure the others expressed when they saw him.

The three young men were reluctant to tell anyone about their experience, for fear that they might be laughed at or accused of cowardice. By listening carefully to local tales, and by asking subtle questions, they were able to learn that there was a strange story involving the man who had built the house and the manner in which he had met his death. However, whenever they tried to elicit details, they were met with blank stares. No one was able to explain why a perfectly good farmhouse was standing empty.

And as for the hunting expedition? Let us say that the deer population had a very good day!

JOHANNE

A child will often accept evidence of the supernatural while the adults around her are excited or skeptical. Johanne Allison, an eight-year-old living in Lower Town, Quebec, reported one day that she had seen a vision of her late mother. Johanne found to her surprise that this simple statement evoked an almost hysterical reaction from her friends and relatives.

On September 18, 1967, Johanne visited Notre-Dame-de-Grâce church in Lower Town, Quebec. There was nothing unusual about this; she had done the same thing many times before. After leaving the main church buildings, Johanne entered the small grotto behind the central structure. There she claims to have made three wishes, all of them quite typical of an eight-year-old. She wished for a chance to see her mother again, for a bicycle of her very own, and for her father to become a wealthy man.

Just after this, Johanne saw a vision of her late mother, who had died about a year and a half prior to the incident.

According to Alexandre Allison, the girl's father, Johanne had been praying regularly in the grotto since the death of her mother.

Johanne claims that the face of her mother appeared beside a statue of the Virgin Mary in the grotto.

The child's pleased and eager report to her friends and family caused great excitement, which eventually spread throughout the entire neighbourhood. Her young classmates misinterpreted her statement, thinking she was claiming to have seen the Virgin Mary.

The following weekend, September 25, the road leading to the grotto was blocked by people. Many fainted and had to be treated for hysteria and heat prostration. Alexandre Allison, an employee of the Canadian National Railways, was forced to move his family out of the district to escape the commotion engendered by Johanne's misinterpreted statement.

Although subjected to many detailed questions by the local clerical authorities and by members of her own immediate family, the bewildered girl held her ground. Johanne maintained that her mother had appeared as if in response to her wish. She was not afraid, and could not understand why all the adults were so angry and upset.

The instincts of children and animals are fairly dependable. Openness and trust may lead to other experiences related to the supernatural for the same reason. Johanne probably made it easy for her mother to return because of her uncomplicated receptiveness to the idea.

The only widely publicized clerical commentary on the Allison incident came from Reverend Raymond Lavoie, the priest at a neighbouring parish. (Most of the other church representatives were unwilling to commit themselves.) Reverend Lavoie stated that "God usually manifests Himself by supernatural signs such as apparitions in areas where faith has become feeble and decadent. In this region, I believe that the level of faith is sufficiently feeble, but one must be prudent about saying that there had been an apparition."

⊕N THE VERCHÈRES R⊕AD

Colin Clarke's father grew up on Ash Avenue in Point St. Charles, and his mother was from Montreal. They moved to Halifax as his father was starting a career with the Canadian Navy, and spent most of their lives in Nova Scotia, except for three years in British Columbia and one year in Sorel, Quebec.

Colin's uncle lived in Springfield Park, Quebec, and he worked for the Foundation Company of Canada. When Colin was nineteen, his uncle got him a job on the DEW Line. So, ahead of the Labour Day weekend, Colin and his parents drove to Springfield Park from Halifax, they for a visit, and Colin in preparation for catching a train in Montreal on Sunday evening.

During the few days he spent at Springfield Park, Colin decided to visit friends with whom he had gone to school while living in Sorel. Most of them had moved away, but he ran into one, Robert Miller, and that Saturday evening they went to a movie.

The show was over by eleven. Colin dropped Bob off at his home, and started back towards Springfield Park.

Like most nineteen-year-olds, Colin was driving the family car a little too fast, especially for the old river road. He raced through Verchères a little carelessly, having just passed through the area where the buildings are quite close to the road. The young man's head was filled with thoughts about graduation and his challenging new job in the North.

About a quarter of a kilometre from Verchères on the upriver side, something caught Colin's eye. The hair on the back of his head stood out and he jammed on the brakes of his car.

Crossing the road, about forty-five metres in front of the car, was an apparition about eight metres tall. It resembled a human-shaped heavy mist or fog, grey in colour. It moved slowly from right to left and out of the car's headlights. The road ahead was perfectly clear, and there was no sign of mist or ground fog. He, she, or it appeared to be wearing some sort of robe or loose dress, its head covered by a hood.

Colin sat motionless, clutching the steering wheel, and waited for the shock to ease off. Then he continued with great care, expecting something to happen at any time. There was no traffic on the road. Colin turned off around Boucherville and headed for Springfield Park. He became especially apprehensive while driving along by the air-force base CFB Saint-Hubert. The car radio was off and the driver's window was open.

The main line of the CNR runs along the side of the air-force base. This land had been elevated because of repeated flooding in the area.

Colin stopped his car just as the front bumper was on the first rail. He was afraid to cross the railway tracks. The headlights of the car were pointing slightly upwards and, on the other side of the tracks, he could see the railway crossing arm dropping. Colin jammed the car into reverse and, looking out the rear window, he could see in the reverse lights that the other CNR arm was dropping behind the vehicle.

The terrified young man backed his car so that the arm

behind him was resting against the rear window, just as a train rushed by on its way east, inches away from the front of the car.

Colin claimed he never saw any flashing lights until after the arms were all the way down. The interior of his vehicle was never illuminated by the train's headlights as it approached the crossing.

After the train had passed, he drove on to his uncle's home, completely drained. Mrs. Clarke asked her son what was the matter with him. He must have looked more than a little strange. He replied, "Nothing, just a little tired, I guess."

Colin kept quiet about his experience for about ten years. When he did finally begin to discuss what had happened, he was met with disbelief or polite, bland smiles. But he believes that it might be important to tell others about the large hooded figure on the road that night.

"I myself have always felt that Madeleine de Verchères was warning me of the danger ahead. I did see something marvellous that night; maybe others have experienced the same sighting."

Colin wrote a letter to the mayor and town council of Verchères in 1993, relating the events of that Labour Day weekend. He was hoping that a local historical group might have records of this sort of thing happening in the past. Colin never received a reply.

10

JUST PASSING THROUGH

MESSAGES FROM BEYOND

Ghosts have numerous ways of communicating with humans, especially those who possess an abnormal awareness or a highly developed psychic sense. Sometimes mortals make deliberate use of a Ouija board or séance. Other times it is the spectre, not the human, who takes the initiative. Spirits employ automatic writing, disembodied voices, tapping codes, thought transference, and simple dream messages. Sometimes they use a blend of the techniques to create a desired effect.

None of the systems is foolproof. Still, all have occasionally been successful with capable individuals who refuse to be frightened or disconcerted when contact is made. Through these and other, more personalized methods, some rather nasty hauntings have been cleared up.

The main problem of any haunting is usually in determining the purpose, if any, of the visitation. What does the ghost want? Some spirits just want to be recognized, a simple admission on our part that there really is a world beyond the one in which we now dwell. Other ghosts need to relate or dramatize the tale of an ancient wrong. Some require reassurance that an important personal matter has finally been settled to their satisfaction and they can now depart in peace. Still others seem lost and in desperate need of guidance. These latter ones simply have to be told firmly and repeatedly that they are no longer required on this particular plane.

An accomplished seer or medium, of which there are far too few, can sometimes intercept critical communications from spirits that an average person may find difficult to interpret. But connecting the living and the dead is never an easy task, and should not be undertaken lightly or without a real need. Someone who knows nothing about communication with ghosts should not attempt to act as a casual interpreter of their messages. Errors can have unpleasant results, and might actually hinder, rather than aid, troubled spirits. To increase their confusion, even unintentionally, would be cruel and pointless.

If the matter is approached rationally and calmly, communication links can be effectively established between the living and the dead. There are many recorded incidents of assistance or warning being passed on to the living by those now dwelling "on the other side." Such messages should be heeded whenever possible; they can be very important.

A relative or close friend may see someone's spirit at the exact moment of, or shortly after, that person's physical death in another, often distant, location. Frequently the visit by the apparition is accompanied by unexpected assistance or instruction. Some ghosts appear solely to protect friends or relatives from unseen or potential danger, others merely wish to reassure those who have been left behind. Some reveal crucial information, such as a hiding place where, while alive, they secreted away emergency money that is required for the support of the remaining family members.

Often spirits choose to contact friends or family still on earth, but one can be contacted by a ghost who is a perfect stranger. Spectres have appeared and come to the aid of complete strangers who apparently were in need of their gift of foreknowledge.

WHO WILL SEE A GHOST?

There can be little doubt that some people are more susceptible than others to sensations, sightings, and messages from the past and the future. They are simply more aware of what is going on around them. Naturally enough, their heightened awareness has led to the label of "sensitives."

These receptive individuals are sometimes said to possess a sixth sense, or second sight. We refer to them as "psychics." Occasionally they can act as intermediaries between the world of the living and that of the dead. Where a less acute individual may feel uneasy about a specific house or area, feeling, "There is something wrong; something's the matter with the place," a person with a highly developed psychic sense may be able to locate the source of the difficulty and actually eliminate it through communication with the spirit causing the trouble.

A psychic may well see ghosts and be able to understand them. But such interaction is a risky business at best. The psychical phenomena of mediumship are known to impose a heavy strain on both mind and body. Even under medically and scientifically controlled conditions at the most modern testing centres, electrocardiogram and electroencephalogram results change markedly when a person slips into a psychic trance of any depth. When an unknown spirit guide takes control of a human body in order to facilitate communication, the human involved even demonstrates a variation in responses to pretested drugs. In short, the physical body is no longer totally that of the medium. For a brief period it is being controlled by a different being.

The effect of these major physical alterations is difficult to determine or measure, but one thing is clear. An untrained or nervous individual would be ill-advised, if not downright foolish, to experiment with those special skills that enable a medium to treat successfully the supernatural.

There is in fact a school that trains people's psychic abilities. The School for Mediums in London, England, is available to those who feel that they simply must use their special sensitivity. The curriculum is a demanding one. People who are naturally psychic or receptive are taught what has been learned to date about communicating with the active spirits around them. These students develop their psychic powers and are taught to practise extreme self-control. They strengthen the kinds of thought transference that will enable them to work efficiently, effectively, and safely with most of the supernatural elements that they are likely to encounter during their lifetime; this course could be interpreted as one of mental self-defence.

Animals often have a far greater sensitivity to the presence of ghosts than the average human. Most people are not surprised to learn this. For years, dogs have been used to track and find items that people are unable to locate with their limited senses. We have long been aware that their abilities to hear and smell are more highly tuned than our own. Their other senses may also differ in some less evident, but equally important, manner.

Animals will often see or sense the presence of an apparition well before a human feels anything unusual. Horses refuse to pass certain areas, especially at night. Dogs will cringe or suddenly begin to wail dismally for reasons that are not apparent to us. The alertness and uneasy mannerisms of dogs, cats, and horses have frequently been the first indications of what turned out to be supernatural manifestations. Their purely instinctive actions and reactions can scarcely be blamed on prior knowledge of the unusual or tragic history of a specific house, building, or place. Humans are definitely susceptible to such suggestions; animals are not.

Cats have been associated with the supernatural for generations in many different countries and cultures. Egyptian royalty pampered these animals as good-luck charms or spirits. They went so far as to mummify feline corpses to accompany and stand guard over their human owners in the tomb. Right here in Canada, not so very long ago, it was believed that cats acted as messengers and companions to the practitioners of witchcraft. Some people continue to regard quite ordinary domestic cats with an awe and respect to which they are not truly entitled. It is true that there is something peculiarly admirable about their independence, but this characteristic has little to do with psychic phenomena.

Children, also, are frequently credited with an innate ability to contact spiritual beings. Perhaps this is because they are less skeptical than their parents and more willing to accept things at face value. Small children have been known to see ghosts and speak quite calmly to them. Apparently they notice nothing frightening or unusual about these incidents. Often parents describe how their children have "invented" invisible playmates with whom they spend long and enjoyable hours. It is just possible that some of these imaginary playmates are small, lonely spirits, readily seen and accepted by the innocence of our children, invisible and mute to our adult sophistication.

There is one supernatural phenomenon that may be experienced by just about anyone. Fetching, that astonishing and fleeting gesture made by the newly dead to those still alive, is a classic, almost commonplace occurrence. It can take many forms, and is generally recognized and acknowledged by those for whom it is intended.

BEST FRIENDS

In the mid-1970s young Beth Diamond married Bill Grant, exchanging her teaching career for the life of a prairie farmer's wife. Bill owned a section of land near Kindersley, Saskatchewan, and the two set to work to make a success of it.

To keep Beth company during the long hours when he was forced to be absent from the house, Bill purchased a puppy for his wife. It was love at first sight, and the tall young woman and her new pet became constant companions. They even had certain obvious similarities — both had outgoing, lively dispositions and an abundance of wavy auburn hair.

Rusty and Beth shared many happy times over the years, and occasionally commiserated with each other during periods of sadness and grief. When Beth's baby died, she confided her innermost thoughts to Rusty, and the pain seemed to ease a bit. Rusty had the misfortune of suffering a miscarriage and she would come to Beth and place her large head in her mistress's lap, comforted by the soft words spoken lovingly in her ear. With the passage of time, the friendship between woman and dog continued to grow and deepen.

In early 1993, Beth was rushed to the hospital so quickly that she didn't have an opportunity to say good-bye to Rusty. They had never been separated for more than a day or so. A long, anxious week passed, and during that time Rusty died. Beth was still so ill that Bill thought it wiser not to tell her. As it turned out, he didn't have to.

Their conversation on the following day went like this:

"Hello, Beth, dear."

"How's Rusty?"

"Okay."

"She died last night, at about 10:00 o'clock, didn't she?"

"Damn! Who told you?"

"She did. She came to say good-bye. I heard her coming down the hallway. She came right to my bed, stayed for a few minutes, then left. I heard her come, Bill, but there was no sound when she walked away. I didn't actually see her, but she came. You're right, though. She is okay."

AU REVOIR

Emma Service and her husband, Matteu, live in South Stukely, Quebec. On the night of November 23, 1981, the two of them went to bed as usual, after locking up their house and giving a few treats to their cat.

Emma suddenly awoke from a sound sleep and sat straight upright in her bed. Through sleep-blurred eyes she squinted at her bedside clock: it was five minutes past midnight. Puzzled, she just sat there mutely, alert but not knowing what to expect.

A few moments later, Emma both heard and felt a single chilling blast of air enter through the open bedroom door, pass across the room, and exit right through the tightly closed window on the opposite side of the room. She saw nothing.

While feeling a little disconcerted, Emma had not been at all frightened by the odd event, and she settled back down in her bed and was soon fast asleep once more.

The following morning, quite early, the Services received a telephone call from Emma's sister-in-law in Calgary, telling them that her husband, Emma's brother, Allan Pembroke, had died earlier that morning.

The mystery of the midnight incident was solved. Allan's spirit had visited her on its way out of this world.

THE HAMBLY HOUSE INTRUDER

Graham Donleavy moved into a large, rambling old farmhouse on the north shore of Hay Bay in North Fredericksburg Township in central Ontario. The place was referred to by the locals as "the Hambly house," even though many years had passed since any members of the Hambly family had actually resided there.

The Hambly house was in need of substantial repairs. One of the main drawbacks of the property was an old well that tended to run dry by the midpoint of the summer. But Graham was convinced that whatever work would be required to refurbish the place was more than offset by the magnificant setting of the house. The rambling white clapboard building was located on a rise of land overlooking the swampy eastern margin of Hay Bay. Graham could look out on the glistening waters of the bay from the upstairs windows facing west, and the sunsets were truly magnificent.

The old place revealed marvellous whispers of the past in every corner. In an upstairs bedroom, Graham found an ancient Indian grinding stone that had been used to prop open the window a notch or two. While digging up an abandoned and weed-filled flower bed, he discovered a 1913 silver dime. Later, a bank passbook from the year 1926, with a thirty-dollar balance, was unearthed from beneath the old linoleum on the main-floor landing just before the stairs began their ascent. One discovery Graham found more than a little disconcerting. Someone had scrawled in paint on the door to the summer kitchen the words "It is better to go out with a bang than to simply fade away." Graham found the message troubling and lost no time in erasing it with a few thick strokes of his paintbrush.

As autumn set in during 1985, early evenings were chilly. Graham had taken to setting a fire in the living-room fireplace, and the attendant friendly flickers of the flames cast a cheery glow on everything. One evening he was sitting in the comfortable room, reading the local newspaper, when he noticed that the wind had come up. He heard the sound through the fireplace flue and saw the flames jump to double their previous height.

Suddenly, his attention was diverted from the *Whig-Standard* by the sound of a tapping coming from a corner of the kitchen. Gradually the tapping increased in volume and made its way across the kitchen ceiling, or so it seemed.

Then it turned towards the living-room door. Graham thought it sounded like the snapping of electricity when something is shorting out. The snapping, tapping sound descended to the doorjamb on the right, turned to cross the south wall of the living room, and then proceeded towards Graham along the westerly wall of the room. He sat back deeply in his chair and twitched nervously. Whatever it was, it seemed to involve a tremendous amount of energy. It was a force to be taken seriously.

Graham's two cats, Sam and Maxine, jumped up onto the sofa, very excited. It looked as if they were attempting to pursue the invisible intruder, suggesting to their owner that they could see something he couldn't.

When the sound reached Graham's chair, it veered suddenly and climbed to the open vent in the ceiling above him, where an old stove-pipe passed through to the second floor. As the strange sound reached the vent, Graham could see the round metal interior turn, strain, and finally stretch as if something were squeezing through the painfully tight opening. The tapping continued, rising through the exhaust vent, until it finally found release into the night sky.

Sam and Maxine sat beneath the vent, gazing upwards in silence, the room once again still. Graham forced himself to bring a kitchen chair into the living room and check the interior of the vent, to determine whether or not it was loose. Try as he might, it would not budge.

After this bizarre and somewhat frightening visitation, Graham decided to do some research into the history of the old house. He learned that several years prior to his purchase of the property, a young man had lived in the place with his widowed mother. Apparently the youth was a hemophiliac; it was to him that the neighbours attributed the grim yet colourful little saying that Graham had painted over on the kitchen door. There were also stories about the manner in which the young man had died, and Graham felt inclined to credit his spirit as having been the late-night visitor. It was as if an exodus had taken place from the house, and somehow Graham, hidden behind the pages of the *Whig-Standard*, had been allowed to witness this passage. He found himself hoping that what had travelled through his living room in such an extraordinary manner was safely on its way to another place where it could find peace.

SWING ⊕ F FAREWELL

Ted Komisko's uncle, Arthur, died in the spring of 1993. He had farmed the same grain-land in Saskatchewan for over sixty years, through times of plenty and times of drought. Only once during that period had he left for a short and certainly well-deserved vacation.

During the summer of that same year, a group of the surviving family members gathered for a barbecue at Arthur's old, weathered farmhouse near Esterhazy, about two hundred kilometres east of Regina.

During his lifetime, Ted's uncle had built a swing for the many grandchildren in the family to use whenever they came to visit. Arthur had often sat upon it himself when he and his wife spent quiet, soothing summer evenings together on their shaded patio.

The day of the family gathering was particularly hot, and the horizon was a blur of faded blue mixed with the colour of suspended dust that the trucks travelling along the distant highway threw into the air. It was approaching thirty-five degrees; the heat was rising in waves from the surrounding fields of wheat. There was no wind, not even a breath of a breeze. Suddenly, before the eyes of the assembled family members, the vacant swing began to move, very gently. It continued its motion, increasing in momentum, moving rhythmically so that the stunned watchers could almost swear that someone was sitting on the swing, riding it.

At that point Ted's aunt moved slowly, but without hesitation, towards the moving swing. She asked gently, "Arthur, dear, is that you?"

The swing came to a silent, gradual halt. Ted's aunt assured her late husband that he was welcome to return to the farm anytime. She stood for a few poignant minutes beside the swing, comforted by the knowledge that Arthur had returned in spirit to bid farewell to his family, gathered there in his memory.

RADIANCE REMEMBERED

Rosemary Ward lived in Williams Lake, British Columbia, a small town in the province's scenic interior noted for its logging and cattle ranching. It straddles the highway that runs north to the frontier at Dawson Creek where the Alaska highway begins.

It was shortly after the beginning of a new year. Some six months earlier, Rosemary had given birth to her second daughter. Very suddenly, after only a short illness, her beloved father died.

Rosemary was totally unprepared for this event. Her life had been fulfilled and happy; now, even weeks after the funeral, she remained depressed and unconsolable, unable to carry out even the simplest of her daily tasks. Since both she and her husband, Michael, held jobs in addition to caring for the children, her loss was having a great impact on the entire family's situation. Michael took over more and more of Rosemary's responsibilities at home, and the depressed young woman took to lying in her darkened bedroom, the draperies tightly shut.

After more than a month and a half of this situation, Michael finally contacted the family's physician one day to check if there was someone in the area who offered a grief counselling service. He was told that there was a long waiting list; perhaps Rosemary should be taken to a specialist in Vancouver.

Later that bitterly cold winter evening, Rosemary was in her accustomed position, curled fetus-like on her side of the large oak bed that dominated the master bedroom. Alternately dozing and waking, she was trying not to think at all. From the kitchen she could hear the voices of her family, distant and unreal, as they went about their supper chores. It seemed impossible, but she simply didn't care about them any more. She lacked the strength of either will or body to get up and join them.

Suddenly, Rosemary felt the presence of someone there in the room with her. She thought perhaps her elder daughter was checking to see if she was awake. But no sound came, and she slowly turned her head towards the door to see who it was.

Standing close to the bed, near its foot, was her father, but not as she had seen him in life. He was a young man, filled with the strength and confidence of youth, with a radiance that almost filled the entire room. Rosemary was astonished, but not afraid. Her father was silent: he just stood there in the darkened room and smiled gently down upon her. After what seemed like several minutes, during which the two just stared at each other, the visitor simply disappeared.

The room seemed somehow lighter than before and Rosemary felt less weak. She carefully sat up and swung her feet over the side of the bed. Her head felt clearer, and the periodic tremors and cold chills she had been experiencing seemed to have passed. With great care, she slowly made her way down the hallway to the stairs, and descended, step by step.

Rosemary was ready to rejoin her family.

THE FAITHFUL COFFEE-MAKER

Most people are familiar with the old song about the grandfather clock that toiled for ninety years and then stopped suddenly when its owner died. Grandfather clocks are still with us, but they are far less common than they used to be. There are, however, modern equivalents to this story.

In the autumn of 1985, shortly after Jack and Cindy Brisson were married, Jack's father, Mark, gave them his old coffee-maker. It still functioned well, but the senior Brissons had just acquired a new, more efficient unit for themselves, and knew that the newlyweds would certainly put the old unit to good use. Jack and Cindy appreciated the gift as they were unable to afford the luxury of purchasing a new one.

Jack explained, "That machine still worked as well as it did the day it came off the assembly line. It went on to serve us for almost two years, never failing in any manner. In fact, it also provided an adequate night-light as well, since the digital time display frequently helped to steer us through the kitchen if either of us had to get up in the middle of the night."

In May of 1987, Mark Brisson was diagnosed as having

cancer. From his home in Chapeau, Quebec, he was first taken to the hospital in Pembroke, Ontario, for treatment, and ultimately was moved to the Ottawa Civic Hospital where he spent the remaining six weeks of his life. By early July, it became evident that he wouldn't be with his family for much longer.

Jack continued the story. "Back in Toronto, on the night of July 20, Cindy and I went to bed shortly after midnight. During the night, I made my customary trip to the bathroom, and on my way past the kitchen noted the time on the coffee-maker. It was 3:56 a.m. I went back to bed, fell asleep and the next thing I knew it was 5:50 a.m. and Cindy was shaking me awake. My brother, Paul, wanted me on the phone. I'll never forget a single word of that call."

The family had been prepared for news of Mark's death for several weeks; Jack anticipated the nature of the call even before he got to the phone. It was nevertheless a jarring moment for the young man.

"When I picked up the receiver, Paul said, 'This is that phone call in the middle of the night that you never want to get.' Then after a pause, 'Dad died.'"

All Jack could thing of by way of a response was, "When? Last night?"

"No," Paul replied. "At 5:15 this morning."

After setting the receiver back down in the cradle, Jack just sat there at the kitchen table for a while, staring vacantly straight ahead.

"And then it hit me. The red digits on the coffee-maker were not lit up. Puzzled, I got up and checked the counter behind the machine and found that it was still plugged in. I even checked the circuit-breaker, but found that it, too, was as it should be."

The Brissons' old coffee-maker never told the time again. Nor did it ever brew another cup of coffee.

"The coffee-maker had been in perfect working condition for some seven or eight years in total, but it quit working completely between 3:56 a.m. and 5:50 a.m. today, the same brief stretch of time during which Dad passed away.

"I have suspected since that morning — and always will — that, had I been sitting there at the kitchen table, as I so often did, I would have seen that coffee-maker blink off for the last time at exactly 5:15 a.m. I think it was Dad saying good-bye."

II

MARITIME MANIFESTATIONS

The Maritime provinces are particularly noted for their interest in and acceptance of different aspects of the supernatural. In this unique part of the country, stories of the supernatural have long been taken seriously and are well researched. Many have been handed down from generation to generation.

The grand matriarch of Maritime Canadian "ghostliana" was Dr. Helen Creighton. She intertwined the history and folklore of Nova Scotia in a manner that made the rest of the country pay attention. Her stories — the fiery return of the "Young Teazer," the Amherst mystery, the tales of guardian ghosts — are as compelling today as they were when she first set them down on paper to intrigue those interested in psychic phenomena.

These well-documented Maritime experiences form an important foundation of examples of various forms of ghostly manifestation that can be used for comparison with incidents in other times and places.

On the East Coast, Helen Creighton's work has paved the way for books on the legends of Newfoundland and Labrador, the spirited myths of Prince Edward Island, and the ghostly tales from New Brunswick. In the rest of the country, her work preceded efforts by Eileen Sonin and myself, as well as books on West Coast ghosts, and those from Alberta. Right now, someone is working on the supernatural phenomena in Saskatchewan, when for many years there seemed to be no ghosts in the prairie provinces. The important thing about Helen's stewardship was her unselfish willingness to take time out to encourage other writers in her field. This is both very unusual and most appreciated by those whom she touched.

THE WEIRD HAIRPIN

A relaxed or undefended mind may be more receptive to supernatural experiences than an active, highly analytical one. Perhaps for this reason, hindsight may occur in a dreamlike form to the very young, or the truly innocent, as happened in this rural Nova Scotian tale.

A small girl awoke very early one morning and rushed out of her bed in bare feet to arouse her parents and tell them about a strange "dream" that she had experienced during the night. In it, she remembered having seen an extremely old lady standing on the little oval carpet just inside her bedroom door.

The child was able to describe her nocturnal visitor to her

bemused mother and father in surprisingly clear detail for such a youngster. She even recalled that the peculiar old woman wore her hair braided and tied into a knotlike arrangement, held in place with a large hairpin in mother-of-pearl and enamel. To her parents' surprise, they found she had given an exceedingly accurate and detailed description of her great-grandmother.

Rosie, the little girl, had never met the old woman; nor had she ever seen a photograph of her. There had been no family discussions concerning the unusual hairpin that had figured so prominently in the girl's description. The older members of the family would have accepted that particular hair arrangement as normal, common to the lady and her time, and would probably not have bothered to even mention it. Such a hairpin would only have caught the notice of someone unfamiliar with that method of skewering hair into position, like young Rosie.

In a concerted effort to find a reasonable explanation for the little girl's dream, if it was a dream, all of the adult members of the family dug out their old photos from long-abandoned albums and scrapbooks. Pages of family history were carefully scrutinized and photographs closely examined. Eventually Rosie recognized the lady in her dream in a photo of her great-grandmother from a picture taken at the woman's fiftieth wedding anniversary. But not a single photo-graph in the entire family collection displayed the old woman's distinctive hairpin; the back of the head, after all, is seldom considered an appropriate subject for posterity. There was no possible natural explanation.

Rosie may have had a simple visit from the spirit of the old lady, or she could have been involved in an incident of hindsight, taking her back to the days when her great-grandmother had occupied the room in which she now slept. The two phenomena are closely related.

Rosie simply assumed that her visitor's appearance in the doorway of her bedroom belonged in the context of a dream. She was not upset or afraid. What sets this experience apart from an ordinary dream is the almost perfect detail with which the little girl was able to recall the incident the following morning.

TIPS ON THE STOCK MARKET

The tale of a great-grandmother paying an unexpected visit to one of her descendants is a gentle ghost story, a lullaby at bedtime, as it were. Sometimes, however, having a dead relative stop by for a call can leave a bitter taste in the mouths of all those who come under the influence of the spirit. There may even be a strong suspicion that malice was first and foremost in the mind of the visitor.

In September of 1993, Debbi Huff of Newcastle, New Brunswick, invested rather heavily in the stock of a new computer/electronics company; it had been very highly recommended to her by several sources she believed to be reliable. Debbi was assured that the stock purchase was a good and prudent investment on her part, and that the fledgling company could look forward to a bright future on the stock market. As a holder of the company's common stock she felt she would be on the front line of modern technology and its wondrous advances. While Debbi was unable to fully comprehend the specific procedures the company used, she was convinced that her move had been adventuresome without being risky.

During March of 1994, Debbi began to have a series of dreams that involved her deceased uncle, Herb Waller. Herb had been a chartered accountant, and he had served as the family's financial advisor for years prior to his death. Debbi could recall her mother making many positive comments about the man's extremely conservative policy towards investing, about how he was never one to take a risk.

The dreams were all alike. Herb was urging Debbi to sell any shares she was holding immediately! She wasn't to ask any questions, just unload the share holdings as fast as she reasonably could.

Initially, Debbi dug in her heels and resisted Herb's urgings. This advice was, after all, being tendered by a dead relative through the medium of dreams — hardly the most reliable of circumstances. Herb had been dead for twelve years at this point: how could he have any specialized knowledge of a recent high-technology development, or of a company that had not even existed while he had been alive? Or even of the current financial climate?

But Debbi began to tire of the recurring dreams, and decided that she should at least check to see if Uncle Herb knew what he was talking about. She placed a call to her broker to check on her recently purchased stock. Debbi owned no other shares; her only other investments consisted of a bank savings account, two Canada Savings Bonds, and one Treasury Bill that came due for renewal every six months.

The broker assured her that all was well. Her money was safely invested and she need have no worries. The company in which she had invested was "viable," healthy, and poised for new developments and products in the very near future. Basically, he belittled her financial anxieties, and made her feel that what seemed like a great deal of money to her was scarcely worth his time.

As things turned out, to Debbi's misfortune, the broker was totally wrong. The highly touted company went into receivership not long after her conversation with the broker, and Debbi's stock holdings were virtually wiped out.

Debbi Huff is still rather disgusted with her dead uncle Herb. If he knew enough to warn her after she purchased the stock, why in heaven's name didn't he come calling in the middle of the night *before* she had done so? She often wonders about his motivation. The ghostly financial advisor has not appeared since the electronics company folded, but Debbi is forced to admit that she will never again ignore warnings of this kind if they should ever occur in the future.

And the optimistic broker? He apparently had invested a goodly portion of his own money in the failed venture, as well as the funds of several other naïve clients. He too lost heavily in the market, and when last seen was taking a course in trading in conservative government bonds.

THE VIOLIN THAT WOULDN'T QUIT

Sometimes, with hindsight, a ghostly warning, known as a forerunner, can be so clear and distinct that, looking back, people are unable to understand how they failed to heed it. Then they are struck by the possibility that, even if they had comprehended the message and acted upon the information, nothing could have been done to prevent the eventual fulfillment of the predicted catastrophe.

One old story concerns such an incident that occurred in an isolated logging camp near Alma, New Brunswick. The camp was located in an area that has subsequently been allocated for use as a national park.

One evening, a group of loggers gathered at the campsite after a hard day. They sat around in several groups, played cards, exchanged the usual tall tales and jokes, and listened to the several fiddlers in the camp who provided musical entertainment.

Nothing untoward happened until one of the more highly regarded fiddlers decided to take a brief break from his music making. The man completed the lively tune he was playing and laid the violin down beside him on top of its case. The music should, of course, have ceased at this point. But it continued to fill the evening air without interruption.

Issuing forth from the strings of the instrument were three clear and distinct notes: one high, one low and vibrant, and another high one. Then a brief, bright flash of light illuminated the stunned faces of the gathering as they stared transfixed at the now-silent violin, which lay in the exact position on its case where it had been placed by the musician. There was no explanation for the trio of notes or for the sudden flash of light — no natural explanation, at any rate.

The men, greatly unsettled by the incident, gradually disbanded and trooped off to prepare for bed. They all realized that something was very wrong; they were uneasy, suspicious, and more than a little afraid.

The next morning dawned under low, grey, humid skies. The sounds of thunder rumbled menacingly off in the distance as the men moved out towards the stands of trees awaiting their attention. Some of the men later admitted that they were reluctant to go out into the woods to work that morning.

A few minutes before noon, with the ominously rolling thunder now right overhead, a bolt of lightning came hurtling to earth striking a tall spruce tree. The tree fell and the helpless logger who had been astride its upper limbs, one of those present at the strange events of the previous evening, died instantly.

Coincidence? It may have been just that, but the men who had heard the keening violin, then the next day witnessed a brilliant flash of light kill one of their comrades, never forgot that dreadful incident. Many of them passed the tale on to their children: this version originates with the daughter of the man whose violin was the vehicle of the forerunner. Fatalities were not all that unusual in the rough-and-tumble logging camps, but this bizarre incident had a lasting impact on all those connected with it.

THE OLD WOMAN WHO WASN'T THERE

The tale of the Alma loggers, while sad, seems somehow simple and neat. Some forerunners are a lot more difficult to understand; indeed it sometimes appears as if they are sent just to engender astonishment.

Darren Parrish had a close friend, Harold Manning, who was employed at the United States Naval Base in Argentia, Newfoundland, a few years back. Every second week, when Harold had enough time off from work at the base, the two men would pile into Harold's old car and head for St. John's to let off some steam. They never got into any real trouble, and their trips served as a welcome break from routine, something that they both enjoyed immensely.

One weekend, Harold's work shift was changed without any advance notice. He couldn't make the trip to St. John's;

instead he asked Darren to take the car and drop it off at a garage where he had arranged to have some much-needed repair work done. Of course, Darren was disappointed having to drive into the city all alone, but he agreed.

The night that Darren picked up Harold's car for the trip, conditions were poor for nighttime driving. It was drizzling lightly, and there was a thick, textured fog, a particular specialty of Newfoundland weather. Nevertheless, Darren set out promptly, as he was anxious to complete the two-hour journey as soon as possible.

For some reason, Darren felt chilled to the bone that evening. He turned the car's heater to its highest setting, but it made no discernible difference: he made a mental note to have the mechanic check this when he was going over the list of other repairs.

Darren had travelled approximately thirty kilometres or so when he had the distinct impression that someone or something was present in the car with him. Imagine his shock and horror when, glancing in the rear-view mirror, he beheld the image of an old woman sitting in the back seat, directly behind him. She was dressed in a shapeless, dirty-looking grey dress, and wrapped about her head was a dark shawl. With her bony fingers she formed a stiff triangle in front of her face, and she seemed to be staring intently at the terrified driver.

As Darren jammed on the brakes, he nearly lost control of the vehicle, and later considered himself extremely fortunate to have missed plunging over the embankment. Slowly regaining his composure by the side of the road, Darren turned on the interior dome light of the car. The woman was gone. He searched every inch of the back seat. There was nothing there except for a few gum wrappers and some loose change. Why, he pondered, am I having this hallucination?

Reluctantly, Darren got back into the car. He drove the balance of the journey with the interior light turned on. So what if the police stopped him! By now he was nearly to the city limit of St. John's. And then suddenly he was no longer alone. Once again, the frightening apparition of the grey-garbed old woman was in the rear seat, her aged, bony fingers forming a triangle in the gloomy light of the car's interior.

Darren had no idea what the apparition might mean, who the dreadful old crone was, or why she was riding with him.

The image of the old woman remained in the mirror for the rest of the trip, and Darren was certain that drivers in other vehicles must have seen her, illuminated as she was by the interior lights. She vanished when he stopped the car at a railway crossing. Darren navigated his way through St. John's, located the garage, and left the car there; he didn't care if he never saw that particular vehicle again. He was so upset that he forgot to mention the faulty heater to the man on duty at the shop.

But while he recovered his composure, Darren's curiosity was aroused. He began to do some quiet investigating about his unwelcome passenger. Unwilling to reveal what had occurred on the trip to St. John's, Darren asked Harold where, when, and how he had come to acquire his vehicle.

Harold's car turned out to be what most purchasers are careful to avoid, an accident rebuild. Although the vehicle had not sustained serious structural damage, two people had died in the accident in which it had been involved. Harold had dismissed this particular piece of past history; the price had been right and he wasn't superstitious. And besides, for the past year and a half, there had been no problems.

Mulling over this information, Darren was struck by the

notion that perhaps the old woman had been one of the fatalities in the automobile accident. Maybe he himself was fated to become number three, completing the triangle that she had formed behind his head. He vowed to avoid any further travel in Harold's car; he might, he thought, even invest in a vehicle of his own.

The following weekend, Harold caught a bus into St. John's and picked up his car from the garage. The repairs had all been completed, and the mechanic issued a cheerful report on its condition. Good for many more kilometres, he asserted.

Harold Manning was killed in a head-on collision while he was driving back to the base at Argentia. The car was completely destroyed.

GH◉ST SHIP

Skeptics often feel that incidents involving phantom ships are merely indicative of the very vivid imaginations of some maritime enthusiasts. Others charge that mass hypnosis and unusual cloud formations on the horizon are responsible. One man who would have heartily agreed with these theories was Bert Wood. He had lived all of his life in the Maritimes and had frequently scoffed openly at stories of flaming vessels returning from the past. Tourist nonsense, he asserted.

But one day, after all those years of scorn, something happened to change Mr. Wood's mind.

The Wood family home was in Stonehaven, New Brunswick, about thirty kilometres from Bathurst. The night of September 9 was unusually stormy for that area. The wind was gusting at speeds of sixty to one hundred kilometres an hour, and in some spots telephone poles were being felled.

The hydro poles seemed to be holding their own.

After an otherwise uneventful evening spent in front of the television set, Mr. Wood and his son headed upstairs to get ready for bed as usual. Mrs. Wood remained downstairs for a few minutes longer to finish tidying up and set the table for tomorrow's breakfast.

As she puttered around, Mrs. Wood happened to glance out across the Bay of Chaleur. Startled, she quickly called out to her husband and son to come and watch. A flaming tanker seemed to be steaming slowly up the bay — an incredible disaster for those involved, both on land and on board the ship.

Young Hadley Wood, who worked at Consolidated-Bathurst Limited, was the first of the three to notice anything unusual. He couldn't quite accept what he saw from the window; somehow it didn't feel right.

"I told Mom it had to be a phantom ship. It was a glowing mass of light from one end to the other. It was illuminated far too brightly for any tanker that I had ever seen."

Bert Wood later described the remainder of the evening to some local reporters as follows:

"The lights would flare up like a house burning, and within ten minutes or so, all would die down again until you only seemed to see bright lights in the bow and stern areas of the ship, but even these were far brighter than normal lights. They were sparkling bright, like a star, and far brighter than those we could see along the ship's water line.

"Then suddenly they'd roll up again. There were big flames, like those put out by a burning building. The flames would flare for a while, and then would fade away to the point where the ship itself almost seemed to disappear. Then, about fifteen minutes later, the flames would erupt again, flaring so brilliantly that you could see her whole out-line from one end to another."

Imagination? Cloud effects? Hypnosis? Bert Wood's description is quite a graphic one for an individual who is supposed to be unimaginative and realistic. The Woods had spent a goodly portion of their lives watching ships traverse the Bay of Chaleur. They were not the sort of people who are easily impressed or misled. They were completely and knowledgeably familiar with the normal running lights of various vessels, and the usual nautical speeds maintained by tankers and cargo ships that frequented their area. No strange boats passed through that stretch of water on September 9; the recorded traffic was in keeping with ship-ping patterns for that time of evening. The Wood family had seen a vessel that simply wasn't there.

Reluctantly, Mr. Wood continued the unusual story of that strange night, specifically commenting on the speed of the phantom ship.

"Vessels travel about twelve to fourteen knots at the most around here, but this one was covering that distance in what seemed to be between five and ten minutes. At first the ship was running fast up the bay, just off Stonehaven, and next she was off to the left, around the Janeville and Clifton area. It was going so fast I figured it couldn't be an ordinary ship. She seemed to be no more than a mile away at times, work-ing inshore and then out as she dimmed and blazed."

The Wood family watched the ship from the past in awe until after midnight. They awoke their young daughter, Betty, so that she could have an opportunity to watch the mystery craft with them for a while. They felt, perhaps correctly, that such an occurrence might never happen again. It seemed well worth the sacrifice of a few hours' sleep to see, out on the Bay of Chaleur, a world of mystery, and a part of the province's maritime past.

Attempts by the Woods to contact neighbours sharing a view of the bay were frustrated since the storm had brought down the telephone lines throughout the entire district. The sight of the blazing ship was the experience of a lifetime, but they were unable to share it with their friends.

When Bert Wood spoke with fascinated reporters, he confessed that he wouldn't be laughing any more when people talked jokingly about the Phantom Ship of the Bay of Chaleur. He had seen it with his own eyes, in the presence of other witnesses.

Even if it were possible that the entire Wood family was mistaken, what were they watching for such a long time on that long, dark, and stormy night? There were too many lights on the phantom ship for it to have been a tanker. And, more to the point, no vessels of any kind were reported lost in flames that night. A modern vessel would have had no need to tack against the windswept, stormy seas, but the phantom was described as working "inshore and out again," a tacking manoeuvre using the direction of the prevailing winds for advancement.

The vessel seen by the Woods in the Bay of Chaleur that storm-tossed evening certainly had no business being there. It belonged in Canada's maritime history. Where did it come from? Why was it visible on that particular night? And finally, where did it go?

SHIP OF FLAMES

Beverley Cook is a natural medium, a woman who has had many strange things happen to her during the past forty years. One experience that made a lasting impression on her was her first glimpse of a phantom ship afire.

Bev was visiting relatives in a small Maritime town called Saint Martin's, really more of a village than a town, located about forty-six kilometres from Saint John, New Brunswick. In this quiet and relaxing place, Beverley Cook was patiently awaiting the birth of her third child.

Late one autumn evening, someone wandering along the edge of the small Saint Martin's harbour spotted a flaming ship. The word spread rapidly; villagers telephoned one another and ran to alert cottagers without telephones. From past experience they knew that they had a minimum of two hours of excitement ahead of them. Sometimes, the fiery vessel had been observed for a full four hours.

Attracted by the noisy enthusiasm, Bev joined a group of people clustered on the top of a small nearby hill. To her astonishment, she could see the burning ship moving slowly up the bay just beyond the harbour. It was a masted schooner, something she had never seen other than in history-book pictures.

The ship moved with majestic grace up the Bay of Fundy and diagonally across the harbour mouth. The fascinated observers could see all three of its masts blazing fiercely, chunks falling off into the sea. Through binoculars, the view was even more impressive, quelling any lingering suspicions that the sight was actually a large school of herring or some other natural phenomenon. There was absolutely no doubt left in the minds of those who watched from the small hill-top that they were seeing a disaster that had occurred many years before.

Gradually the ship passed from view, her masts now gone, only the hull glowing in the distance.

Many people saw the mysterious fire ship that night. The villagers reported that the same flaming vessel often appears, always in the autumn, usually September or October, although some years it has not been seen at all.

Some New Brunswickers have claimed that this ship is the same one that has been sighted in the Bay of Chaleur. But local fishermen point out an interesting difference. The St. Martin's ship of flames moves much more slowly, covering the eight or ten kilometres during which it is clearly visible at a leisurely speed, while the Bay of Chaleur ship moves much more quickly.

THE DUNGARVEN WHOOPER

A collection of Maritime psychic events would be incomplete if the fascinating saga of the Dungarven Whooper were omitted. This strange tale varies depending upon the narrator and his degree of sobriety at the time of telling. There does seem to be some factual basis to the story although it may have been somewhat embellished over the years.

I have been able to trace one version of the story to Father William, a versatile individual who worked during his youth in a Maritime lumbering camp. Later he studied to be a doctor and eventually became a well-known and widely respected Roman Catholic priest. Father William designed and executed the Christ King flag that represents the Vatican around the world.

One of the major problems facing lumber camps is the ever-present threat that logjams will form on the river, thereby preventing the safe, prompt delivery of the freshly cut timber. These jams are quite frightening: once one starts, more and more logs pile up, increasing the degree of block-age. Tangled spars jut dangerously out into the air for many metres. A serious logjam keeps increasing in size until it actually prevents the water from following its natural course downstream. Water pressure behind the jam builds until the logs burst free in a sudden, explosive instant of release.

Just this sort of complex logjam formed on one of the branches of the northwest Miramichi River in New Brunswick. For days on end, the exhausted loggers struggled to free the trapped logs, but the pile-up became increasingly large and dangerous. And because the logs were already long overdue at the sawmill downriver, this jam also repre-sented a loss of revenue for all involved. There was no point in cutting and hauling additional timber from the forest until this huge batch could be freed and sent on its way.

Early one morning, a logger by the name of Dungarven jumped to his feet after breakfast and boldly announced that he was going to tackle the problem single-handed. He was quite determined, perhaps even a little crazy, and he told the other men to stand back and watch while he employed his consummate skill in manipulating his log pole, or prod.

"I'll break that jam, or breakfast next in Hell!" Dungarven vowed.

He strode out onto the tangled logs while his fellow lumberjacks watched in silent horror and amazement from the safety of the shoreline. After much hopping about, Dungarven managed to release a few strategic logs, and with a creaking, groaning sound the entire mass slowly began to move. The mad logger let out a triumphant whoop of joy as he sensed the success of his mission.

Then the logjam broke completely with a thunderous roar. The timbers seemed to sail in every direction through the air before heading downstream. The break-up was so fast, and the water pressure behind the jam so great, that there was no time for Dungarven to clamber back to the riverbank. He was carried off with the logs by the great mass of water that had been held captive behind them.

Shortly after Dungarven's sudden and violent death, teamsters and lumbermen alike, when passing along the logging road beside that branch of the Miramichi, began to report hearing strange whooping noises coming from the direction of the river. At first no one paid any attention to these tales, but with the passage of time a consistent pattern in their details began to emerge. The woodsmen had all heard the same peculiar sound, at almost exactly the same spot. The incidents always occurred at the same early morning hour when Dungarven had perished in the mighty cascade of timber and white water.

Dungarven had accomplished his aim. He had single-handedly broken up the massive logjam, so perhaps he didn't take his next breakfast in Hell after all. He or his spirit may still be celebrating his victory near the old logging camp, startling more recent passersby.

Each year, during the height of the logging season along the Miramichi, the tale of the Dungarven Whooper is related, with relish and a little bit of quizzical envy. Some people claim that when conditions are right the joyous whooping sound can still be heard at dawn along the bank of the Miramichi.

THE FACE IN THE WELL

Eleven-year-old Jamie Sayles lived in Manuels, Conception Bay, in Newfoundland, in the early 1940s, with his widower father and older sister. One of his assigned daily chores was to keep the water containers inside the house filled, and the outside water barrel topped up. This responsibility demanded a fair amount of grit and determination. Out on the back porch of the house was an old hand pump, which grudgingly drew water up from the shallow well in the sub-basement of the house. From time to time the pump would fail, and Jamie would have to take a bucket and crawl into the small area beneath the house where the well was. This task was young Jamie's particular burden. His father was too large a man to traverse the limited crawl space and his sister, Donna, would have refused point-blank any suggestion that she even try. Besides, she had her own house keeping chores. Jamie dreaded crawling down to the well, but he had done it many times without incident.

Jamie's father called one night to say that he would be working late. Donna — the teenager in the family — was getting ready to go out on a date when she discovered that the outside water barrel was empty. As always seemed the case when she was in a hurry, the old pump refused to cooperate. Jamie had no choice but to take a flashlight and his trusty bucket and crawl through the narrow entrance door to the well. How he hated going down there! And this was the first time that he had been forced to do so at night.

The area in which the old well was located was cold, damp, and musty, and home to a large colony of smelly mice. Jamie gritted his teeth and proceeded about the messy business. Crouching down and taking great care not to bump his head on the low overhanging wooden beams, he slowly, reluctantly, inched his way through the thick cobwebs towards the heavy wooden well cover.

At that point, the batteries in the flashlight died!

Not being too far from the well-head, Jamie decided to try to draw a bucket of water in the dark. He figured that this was preferable to returning for new batteries and starting all over again. Besides, Donna was not known for her patience and understanding.

Reaching out into the inky-black darkness that surrounded him, Jamie located a corner of the well cover. With a great effort, he shoved the heavy thing off to one side. As he did this, he was horrified to see, glimmering on the surface of the water below, the illuminated face of a young woman. Her fraying blond hair streamed about her face and her eyes, open wide, stared up at Jamie vacantly. Her lips were twisted in a contemptuous sneer.

Jamie's throat constricted and his mouth went dry as he lurched up with a start, striking his head sharply on a wooden beam. He turned and propelled himself out as fast as his arms would pull his body, scared out of his young wits.

Jamie never told his father or Donna about the frightening episode. He was quite certain that they would not believe him, and that both would just tell him that it was his active imagination running away with his common sense. Still shaking like a leaf, safely back in the house clutching his empty pail, he was very relieved to discover that the hand pump was again in service. After Donna left for the evening, he collapsed onto a couch in the living room and remained there for a long while, praying that he would never again have to visit the old well at night. He vowed to himself to keep all of the water containers topped up at all times, if only he could be allowed to do this chore during daylight hours only.

Several years later, while visiting a relative in Harbour Grace, Jamie noticed a faded photograph in a silver frame on the living-room mantelpiece. Fascinated, he asked his great-aunt who the lady in the picture might be. Jamie was told that she was a distant relative of the family who had drowned herself after her intended had run off with another and left her standing alone at the altar.

The face in the photo was the same one that Jamie had seen glowing in the well water in his basement that fearful night in his childhood. To this day, he wonders why this poor, distressed, and tragic young woman chose to reveal herself to him in such a strange and bizarre fashion.

A LITTLE GLASS B⊕TTLE

A very long time ago, there was an old grist mill located on the hollow at Emyvale on Prince Edward Island. It was operated in a most efficient manner by a singular gentleman named Dollar. He was the only Protestant in the entire district.

Dollar found himself under increasing pressure to convert to Roman Catholicism. His neighbours were always after him on the subject, and even his best friend, Pat McCardle, was a proper pest about the situation.

"Here you are getting all of the grinding business in this area from all of us who are your friends, and still you're the only Protestant."

This badgering just about drove Dollar to distraction. He conducted his business dealings in an honourable fashion; that should have been enough for them. One day the matter came to a head. No other topic, it seemed, could be discussed without the subject being raised, and Dollar finally offered a compromise.

"No, I'll not convert in my lifetime, but I'll die a Catholic!"

As time passed, the local populace maintained an increasingly attentive watch on the old man's health. This was worse than before! All he had to do was to sneeze or rub a sore shoulder and his neighbours were running off to get the parish priest!

When it became clear one day that Dollar was indeed truly sick, and apparently on his deathbed, Dr. Henderson, the local physician, informed the surrounding neighbours that there might only be a few more hours before Dollar's death would be at hand.

Pat McCardle, ever solicitous, hovered nearby constantly, on hand to ensure that the bargain was fulfilled. Standing impatiently beside his old friend, McCardle volunteered to go to Kinkora, some thirty kilometres away, to fetch Father Duffy. Father Duffy's parish at that time included Kinkora, Kelly's Cross, and Emyvale.

Dollar agreed that Pat should fetch the priest. He didn't feel that he had much choice, after all.

McCardle possessed one of the fastest horses in the county and he drove the poor animal hard in the pursuit of old Dollar's soul. But he and Father Duffy were still half a mile away from Dollar's home when the cleric said that there was no longer any need for haste.

"You may ease up, Pat. He's gone."

Pat McCardle was left wondering if Dollar had somehow planned things like this from the very beginning. Could he have conspired to keep his milling business and his soul?

The old grist mill was purchased from the Dollar estate by Jim McClosky, and it wasn't long after that until strange things began to occur on the property.

The grist mill was powered by a water wheel that had to be opened and turned on to start the action, and then closed and turned off to shut the system down. But the wheel began to start up on its own, for no discernible reason, usually at about 10:30 in the evening. By that late hour most of the work of the day had usually been done.

Jim McClosky's daughter-in-law clambered up into the barn loft one evening to throw down some hay. Neighbours would be coming by the following day to plow, and she didn't want them to have to perform this additional chore when they returned from the fields with their teams of draft animals.

The young lady loosened the hay stored in the mow of the barn, but she was unable to get it to move down through the hatch when she prodded it from ground level.

"It was as though someone or something was holding it back, pulling against me when I tugged at a forkful."

When the men returned from their labours in the fields and learned of her experience, they began to exchange stories in which the ghost of old man Dollar was being blamed for all sorts of incidents bordering on sabotage.

"Dollar was up there. He was holding back the hay!" was the consensus. "We'll never be at peace until we appease his spirit, and possibly he'll never be at peace because he didn't die a Catholic."

The local population seemed to be trying to placate itself for the escape of old man Dollar's soul. Why after all should Dollar be accused of making it difficult to bring down the hay for the horses, or upsetting the mechanism of the water wheel itself?

The McCloskys and their anxious neighbours took what they perceived to be a string of problems to the parish priest, Father Duffy. The priest had never had an opportunity to deal with Dollar during his lifetime; he more than made up for it now. He agreed to attempt an exorcism of sorts, and set a time to meet with the group of concerned members of the community in Emyvale.

After the routing of Dollar's spirit from the old grist mill, if indeed it was there, those who were in attendance claimed to have "taken Dollar and put him into a smallish bottle, wherein he was stoppered."

We are not told exactly what type of bottle was used for the spirit's prison. Who or what was the source of this miraculous container, and had it been filled with alcohol at one stage?

To dispose of the spirit-filled bottle, a fitting site had to be selected. Father Duffy, together with some of the other more prominent members of the group, chose a place just across the river from the old grist mill. They believed that there was some significance in the fact that a large black dog had been seen running freely, alternately barking, sniffing, and then whimpering in a plaintive voice near the spot at night.

The bottle was duly blessed and eased into a small hole in the ground.

The strange dog was never seen again, and the old grist mill never again started grinding in the middle of the night. The relieved neighbours experienced no more trouble with the restless spirit of their lone Protestant.

LONG-DISTANCE FRIENDSHIP

Michael Grobin, Sandy Snow, David Jones, and Rex Stirling were the best of boyhood friends. They attended the same elementary school, went everywhere together, and shared similar interests. In many ways, they were closer than brothers.

Rex Stirling's family and that of young Michael Grobin socialized a lot. Michael's family had come out to

Newfoundland shortly before the outbreak of the Second World War, when his father was transferred from Devonshire, England, to St. John's. There he was attached to the British Customs Office. Of all the boys, Michael and Rex seemed to have the most in common. Rex was part English, his mother having been born in Salisbury.

Michael would tell the other three boys such stories as he remembered of his early life in England. Rex developed a desire to visit his mother's birthplace, a fantasy that he wasn't able to realize for many years.

One morning in class, Michael was overly excited, incapable of listening to the teacher and bouncing about nervously in his seat. During the recess break, he told his friends that he and his family were returning to England for a visit after school closed for the summer vacation. Rex was very happy for Michael's sake, and secretly wished he could go along with the Grobins.

There was a general sadness on the morning when the boys waved good-bye to Michael, walking with his parents towards their waiting plane. From the moment of their departure, Rex felt an uneasiness he couldn't explain. The nagging worry cast a shadow over his holidays.

In those days trans-Atlantic mail service left a lot to be desired; sometimes mail simply vanished. The telephone connections to Britain were even worse, frustrating and often full of static interference. About two weeks after the Grobins' departure, Rex was getting ready to go over to the ball park to play in a softball game between the home-team Tigers and the visiting Blackhawks, when the telephone rang.

The crisp, English-accented voice was unmistakable. No interference, no static. It was Michael. He said that he was fine, and that his friend was not to worry about him. He reiterated twice that he was very happy. Before Rex could respond, the line went dead.

Rex thought it rather strange that Mr. Grobin, who was noted for his thrifty ways, would allow Michael to make an expensive overseas call to one of his classmates, however friendly the relationship.

When Rex reached the ball field, David and Sandy came running towards him, breathing hard with exertion and excitement. They both gasped out together, "You'll never guess who we just got a telephone call from!"

"Michael Grobin?" Rex asked.

Sandy and David stared at him, utterly amazed and somewhat disappointed. "Yeah, but how did you know?"

"Because I got one too."

"You did? When?" the two boys asked.

"No more than twenty minutes ago . . . let's see . . . at 6:30 p.m.," Rex answered.

"That can't be," David protested. "That's exactly the same time Sandy got his call, and the same as I received mine."

The three boys stood in dumfounded silence, trying to think what could have happened.

"It's impossible," Rex argued. "How could Michael call each one of us at exactly the same time?"

Unable to come up with an answer, they turned their attention to the softball game.

When Rex arrived back at home, his parents were waiting for him at the front door. He could tell by the look on their faces that something was seriously wrong. "What is it?" asked Rex, noticing the telegram that his father clutched in his hand.

Mr. Stirling put his arm around Rex's shoulder, and in a strained voice replied, "Son, your friend Michael was stricken with acute meningitis three days ago. We received a telegram from his father, but your mother and I decided against telling you because we didn't want to upset you. Another telegram arrived a short time ago. I'm sure they did all they could for him, but Michael passed away."

Rex exploded with angry fury. "It's not true! You're lying to me!" Mr. Stirling's arms merely tightened around Rex's shoulders. He made no comment.

Rex was pleading now. "But Dad, how can it be? Sandy, David, and me were talking to Michael tonight on the telephone. He called each of us from England at 6:30 p.m. and said he was fine."

Mr. Stirling slowly unfolded the crumpled telegram and showed it to Rex. It read: "Regret to inform you Michael passed away at 6:30 this evening." The name typed out at the bottom indicated the telegram had been sent by Arlo Grobin.

Slowly but surely, modern technology is making its way into reports about supernatural phenomena. The story about the boyhood friends in Newfoundland is an incident of "fetching," the reaching out by a person at death to friends and family members. This may be one of the first fetchings to utilize the telephone.

12

YESTERDAYS AND TOMORROWS

SEEING THE FUTURE

Forerunners, foresight, and double vision are serious-sounding terms that describe supernatural warnings or clear indications of approaching events. These occurrences may be good or bad, or sometimes neutral. Traditionally they are connected with impending death and deep personal tragedy.

That a death will occur in a house may be signified by a bird beating against the windows or becoming trapped somewhere within the building. The whirring sound of invisible wings can sometimes be heard late at night, long after most birds have returned to the safety and security of their nests. Are these the sounds of owls? Perhaps. But the flight of the owl is usually silent, the better to surprise its prey as well.

Disaster is supposed to follow shortly after a mirror or a picture falls from the wall. In another version of this belief, whoever causes a mirror to break shall suffer seven years of bad luck.

The music of an organ, choir, or violin may be heard several times preceding an event. If there is no apparent source or cause for the music, it is a bad omen. Three short, distinct knocks at the front door of a house or at the formal door of a room are the classic summons to something that is invariably unhappy.

Many reports of early Canadian forerunners were collected by Dr. Helen Creighton for her book *Bluenose Ghosts*. Most of her tales originated with people of Celtic descent, suggesting that these legendary previews have their source somewhere in the folklore of Scotland and Ireland, countries whose fog-shrouded rocky crags and glistening emerald valleys abound with tales of spirits and the supernatural.

The area around Halifax, Nova Scotia, was, and still is, rich with stories about foresight and forerunners. And all across Canada, one can find people who believe firmly in superstitions connected with these phenomena. As people from different countries have emigrated and intermingled across our vast landscape, so too have their views on life and death.

Some beliefs are handed along from generation to generation, seldom challenged. This chain of faith is incredibly strong. If a family member happens to die shortly after a picture falls from a wall, the old belief is reinforced for all involved. When a death does not occur very quickly after the event, the incident of the broken mirror is conveniently overlooked and forgotten. Whenever a famous individual dies, people come forward after the fact to relate that they knew it would occur. There are claims that U.S. President Kennedy was warned not to make his fateful trip to Dallas only days before he travelled to that city to meet his death at the hands of an assassin's bullet. John Lennon's slaying was followed by similar after-the-fact statements. For every high-profile tragedy, there is always someone who comes forward to say, "I knew this would happen."

Given the highly selective memories of most people, it is difficult to separate an actual chain of events from mere coincidence. And perhaps a differentiation should be made between what is accidental — possibly even natural — and what is truly unusual. Pictures fall from walls all the time due to numerous natural causes, but three sharp knocks on the door when no one is about are understandably most unnerving as they are hard to explain.

Forerunners come in many forms. Sometimes they merely involve a sudden, inexplicable mood change. One woman in Country Harbour, Nova Scotia, related a personal experience that illustrates this phenomenon.

Clarissa MacTavish was bringing in her dried wash from the line at dusk one late summer's day when she was struck suddenly by a powerful feeling of loneliness and utter desolation. She let her laundry basket fall; her body collapsed and she lay huddled on the ground beside the back porch of her home. There was no physical reason for this profound reaction but she could not restrain herself, and began to weep uncontrollably. Something was very wrong. She couldn't explain this bizarre behaviour on her part; she was happy with her life and job, and was in the best of health.

Early the next morning, Clarissa learned that two of her best friends had died tragically in a highway accident caused by the gloomy light of early evening. The time of the mishap matched exactly with that of her attack of extreme sadness and anxiety. Such "coincidences" happen frequently enough to warrant attention.

A forerunner may take the form of a specific noise or a change in mood. In this respect, it varies from foresight, a phenomenon that, as its name implies, involves a visual experience. Foresight seems to occur most commonly, for some unknown reason, among people of Scottish or Germanic descent. But being from a different heritage does not preclude one from experiencing a foresight; nor does being from Scottish or Germanic lineage guarantee that one will see into the future.

A man who is already dead may appear before his startled widow, or keep an important prearranged meeting with a close friend. These appearances are usually quite brief, with only a very short time allotted for last-minute communications. We do not know why some people move around after death while others do not.

Some supernatural warnings are general; others can be quite specific. In many cases, only one person observes the event connected with a case of foresight. (This is not the case with forerunners, which can occur in several different physical locations at the same instant in time.) This presents a major problem. Very few people wish to discuss such an experience because they have no evidence for the story but their own word. They are reluctant to be pinned down about something that they themselves find difficult to accept. Also, some of the visits are of a highly private and personal nature.

The first automobile was seen by those with foresight long before its actual arrival in their isolated communities. They had no idea what sort of creation was noisily passing them on the back-country laneways, and were terrified of the strange apparition. Phantom trains, cars, and carriages were seen and accurately described well in advance of their physical appearance on the scene.

The implications of foresight for the notion of self-determination gives one pause. Do we base our actions upon rational decisions, or are we all moving in a previously determined pattern? Certainly it would be most disconcerting to have someone inform you that your funeral procession will shortly be passing along a certain road en route to the local cemetery.

What is even more unnerving is that all human attempts to prevent the fulfillment of foresight and forerunners have failed. Somehow, no matter how hard one struggles, or how ingeniously one tries to improvise, circumstances always combine to prove the accuracy of the prediction. A cortège trying to find an alternate routing will soon discover that the road has been flooded out or that a serious traffic collision has closed the way. It will be forced back onto the path indicated by that earlier, predestined vision.

Many people claim to possess foresight or what they refer to as "extrasensory perception" or ESP. It would be more accurate to refer to "higher sensory perception." The supernatural is not beyond the ability of our senses; it is simply a potential capability that we have yet to develop fully.

In most cases, there is a way to check out claims of foresight. Have the individual write out a memo the next time anything odd happens. They should include a detailed description of what has occurred and what they think it means for the immediate future. Then have that person tell someone, preferably yourself, and turn the dated memo over to be checked later.

If the predicted sequence of events actually comes to pass, with no interference from either of you, the foresight may indeed be genuine. These are very difficult conditions to meet, since such experiences may occur only once or twice in a person's lifetime. It is quite common for someone claiming the ability to back off from being subjected to any testing. They consider it to be a matter of faith, and expect you to believe their predictions without question.

Only recently have we been able to work with extra sensory perception as a definable and measurable entity. Most of the earlier work was done under the auspices of the military, in the United States and in the former Soviet Union. These results were classified, and some remain so even today, many years after the experimentation was carried out.

The Maimonides Medical Center in the United States was the first research facility to release test results on extrasensory perception to the general public. These disproved a few earlier misconceptions. For one thing, the Maimonides testing revealed that men were better telepathic receivers than women. Emotional messages were more likely to be received than unemotional ones, and distance had absolutely no effect upon a person's perception abilities. It was also demonstrated that some people could successfully predict the future in a laboratory setting. In other words, dreams or visions really are the key to the future, and we can learn from them.

The Maimonides tests also indicated that mood plays an important part in the ability to receive messages. The best subjects were generally those who were either happy and confident, or very unhappy, insecure, and dejected. These test results make it easier to understand the unusual mood swings associated with cases involving foresight.

The scientists concluded that there was a "definite correlation between mood and the individual's ability to perform extrasensory stunts in laboratories." Self-confidence was found to be very important, reinforcing the old adage that many things can be done if we only have faith in our own abilities. Not all extrasensory skills are practical, however. A person's ability to predict what shapes or cards will appear next in a sequence does not necessarily allow that person to forecast whether you will pass an examination or successfully secure the job for which you have just been interviewed.

THE CLOCK TURNS BACK

Hindsight is much the same as gazing backwards in time. People who have experienced this phenomenon have described it as watching a movie set in a previous period that has been researched with great care and accuracy. It generally involves the passive observation of a real event that occurred at some time in the past on the same spot.

The astonished viewer may be utterly ignorant as to the historical significance of the sighting. No textbook, no play, no motion picture, regardless of how authentic the dialogue or set design or costumes, can ever re-create the accuracy of such an experience.

The people participating in the actual historical event take no mind of the modern intruder, and act as though this presence were invisible to them. They are not affected in any noticeable way by the interloper from the future in their midst and their actions remain completely neutral.

This phenomenon has been likened to travelling backwards through both time and space. The result can be a distinct feeling of disorientation and mental confusion.

One of the most celebrated incidents of what we call hindsight occurred when two women visiting Versailles on vacation abruptly found themselves displaced back in time to the setting of the royal palace, immediately prior to the chaos of the French Revolution. The buildings were in their original positions and structural condition. Gone were the signs of the passage of two centuries with their attendant wear and tear, neglect and urban pollution. Vanished were the colourful clusters of tourists and the vulgar signs for food concessions and souvenir stands; it was also impossible to find a public convenience.

Recovering from the initial shock, the two friends, both well-educated, wandered about at will, fascinated by the tableau before them.

The women were not noticed by any of the individuals they encountered, despite their casual modern clothing, which would have seemed outlandish in the period into which they had stumbled. It was as though they had become invisible. Had they been seen, their presence in the protected royal gardens would have provoked a definite response from the French courtiers and members of the Royal Guard.

From this experience it is evident that some supernatural phenomena can work in completely opposite directions. They can bring the past forward into the present, in the form of a ghost that may be seen by some, and felt or heard by others. Or, they can transport representatives of the present backwards through time, into what we call history, through hindsight. The main difference is that those who experience hindsight have little or no impact upon their temporary surroundings. A ghost, on the other hand, can, and often does, thoroughly upset the present-day existence of any number of people.

The past, it seems, is rigid, and cannot be altered by any actions on our part. Conversely, our existence in the present is fluid, and therefore subject to the whims of such things as spirits from the past.

Many works of fiction are based on the premise that an individual can go back into time and space in order to alter historical events. While this is a fascinating concept, it is riddled with problems and is not supported by existing research into the supernatural. We cannot go back and refight wars, prevent catastrophes, or even change the fate of a single character who has lived and died and who is now a part of history.

In Canada, most reports involving hindsight are from the seaboard areas of Nova Scotia and Newfoundland. Perhaps this is because so many adventures took place in the waters off these two provinces during the days of the earliest sailing ships.

Vessels of all sorts appear unexpectedly in the Maritime tales. Some sport ancient rigging and are manned by buccaneers in their colourful traditional dress, their fierce eyes daring one to a fight. Once-dangerous privateers still row ashore in the dead of a calm night to bury their bloody treasure in a cave, and then with great stealth return in silence to their waiting mother-ship. And when it is darkest, just before the dawn, coasters and freighters that were wrecked upon the treacherous hidden reefs that stretch out to sea repeat their tragedies in graphic detail for contemporary observers armed with binoculars who watch from the safety of the shore.

Hindsight viewings recall the tales of legendary shipboard fires that destroyed men and cargo without distinction and then, finally, engulfed the carrier. Long-forgotten ships move soundlessly across the open harbours, trailing shooting sparks and ghostly sheets of flame as they prepare to settle forever beneath the waiting sea.

Ghosts from the past and glimpses into history become intermingled. Sometimes it is difficult to determine whether the past has come to us or if we have temporarily moved backwards out of our own place in time.

THE YOUNG TEAZER

The Young Teazer was a privateer operating along the Nova Scotia coast. One day in 1813 the ship, out on one of its dangerous and illegal junkets, was surrounded by armed warships in Mahone Bay. The vessel was trapped; its crew could neither fight nor flee. Rather than subject themselves to ignominious capture by the reviled British, some of the privateer's company decided to destroy their own craft and, with it, all evidence of their criminal activity. *The Young Teazer* slid slowly to the bottom of the bay in a fiery blaze of crackling timber, her flags defiant to the end as they swirled from the main mast.

This tragic event took place almost two centuries ago. Under normal circumstances, that would have marked the end of the affair, which might have rated a minor mention in a dry, impersonal volume of history. But the same ship is still reported to this very day, afloat and ablaze, by reputable witnesses both on shore and in boats in Mahone Bay itself.

The sightings of *The Young Teazer* are complicated. Some people see the ship, while others, situated on the very same spot, are unable to do so. Perhaps this is because some people are more receptive than others to the ghostly ship's return to repeat its destruction. Or perhaps *The Young Teazer* sightings are brief, but exciting, hindsight experiences, in which some people actually view the original sinking of the ship.

Other cases of hindsight can be equally hard to pin down. When someone encounters an oddly costumed individual from some other period in an isolated setting, it is impossible to determine who has travelled in which direction through time.

Representatives of past generations have been seen in hindsight incidents. Some individuals are seen at the wheel of great, vintage touring cars; others trudge along dusty country roads leading packhorses, or bent under the load of burdens they bear on their own backs. When vehicles are sighted they often repeat road accidents that were duly recorded in the annals of local police forces years ago.

It may be that any incident that makes a great impression upon the minds of one or more of the people involved becomes indelibly etched into its surroundings. Given the proper circumstances (and we still do not know what these are), the event is capable of recurring over and over again, an instant and detailed replay of real life. The same or similar circumstances can also allow one or more of us to visit the past for a limited but wondrous moment. We have yet to learn how to initiate, control, and terminate such phenomena.

TO BELIEVE, OR NOT?

Among the highly intelligent and well-educated, among those who have dropped out of high school, among the pillars of the clerical establishment and those who hold no firm faith or religious belief, you will encounter people who accept the existence of psychic phenomena. There are no vocational, religious, gender, social, or educational barriers to an interest in the supernatural. These people are not gullible simpletons who blindly accept, without argument and reasonable proofs, all that they are told. They are simply prepared to listen and consider, to debate and then reconsider. Their minds are receptive to new ideas.

Ghosts and other supernatural experiences are becoming more respectable lately as subjects of debate. Possibly because they are often seen on television, some people appear willing to accept their existence too easily, just to be in style. In Canada today, though the number of authenticated sightings is small, many people show a strong and growing tendency to accept the supernatural in its many and varied forms with little serious scrutiny or challenge.

There is a great difference between those who chew over a new tale of the spirit world thoughtfully, with a little skepticism, and those who gobble up the entire story whole like a trained seal swallowing its reward for a trick well-performed. Young people are particularly vulnerable to unquestioning belief. While keenly aware of the contradictions within their own system of values and those of their parents as well, they are frequently unable to understand the discrepancies that still exist in the study of the supernatural.

Teens are highly susceptible to new, unproven theories and care must be exercised to prevent them from turning to self-seeking individuals who profess to have all the answers.

There is no one solution to the many puzzles surrounding the various manifestations of the supernatural. Just as the young challenge politicians, educators, current sexual standards, the clergy, and their own position in modern society, so also should they question evidence of the supernatural.

One indication of the increased contemporary interest in the spirit world is the popularity of psychic bookstores, some of which overlap into such areas as holistic medicine. Books on the supernatural find a large acceptance in Canada, as they do in many other Western countries. A few short years ago, there was a mere handful of people writing on the supernatural. Now they can be found in virtually all parts of the country, having a marvellous time tracking down stories old and new.

What does this increased interest mean? It is not necessarily a reflection of a healthy, receptive attitude: it may conceal a terrible need to escape from the reality of everyday life. It is especially dangerous for susceptible individuals to approach the supernatural world on the level of uncritical emotion. There are those who can cope easily with new and unusual concepts; others require the patient wisdom of a dedicated guide to steer them through.

Just what kind of trouble can come from indiscriminate delving into all the varied aspects of the supernatural? Unethical leadership is the greatest threat. As Owen Rachleff of New York University put it, "Most occult-niks are either frauds of the intellectual and/or financial variety, or disturbed individuals who frequently mistake psychosis for psychic phenomena." Unscrupulous individuals can take advantage of those who lack the ability or the will to stand up and challenge the theories and demand empirical evidence before committing themselves to a potentially disastrous course.

But just as dangerous as being too gullible is to harbour suspicion about everything, to view the world through negative eyes and to close one's heart and mind to hope. Many evangelical and fundamentalist Christians regard every nuance of the occult as a threat of demonic proportion. They refuse to concede that the world of the supernatural might have something of value to offer, a possible vehicle to allow us to learn something more of the world in which we find ourselves. These naysayers cannot be expected to deal rationally with the increasing modern interest in occult matters. Those who rank Casper the Friendly Ghost alongside Demonology tend to miss the middle ground between the two extremes, the area that bears the greatest degree of human interest and fascination.

People who deny a belief in ghosts have admitted having experiences involving inexplicable manifestations. Some of these incidents are amusing, others quite frightening. But, to date, our Western theological teachings do not account for, or allow, the existence of another world or dimension in which souls and spirits wander about aimlessly for varying periods of time, occasionally intersecting and intervening in the lives of some of us. These apparitions appear to receive no guidance from a higher power as some of us have been led to expect. They are simply there, wherever "there" is.

These ephemeral visitors show no consistency of purpose to indicate that their shadowy realm is a planned state. The realm of ghosts seems to be a mixed limbo into which both the forces of good and evil have been flung haphazardly, a random amalgam of the unknown. Perhaps spirits that interact with us are at a developmental stage of transition. Whatever their world is like, since it is becoming increasingly difficult to deny the existence of ghosts, the logical approach would be to make room for them, very carefully, in our worldview and to learn how to cope with their persistent and often shrouded demands.

Unless they are confronted with a major incident affecting them personally, people tend to associate ghost stories with strange, uncomfortable tales uttered in whispered tones by grandparents or by adolescents around smoky campfires. Even when faced by such an event, many respond by denying the evidence of their own senses and proclaiming that nothing unusual occurred. These individuals are as sadly mistaken as those who swallow whole all manner of bizarre material without first questioning the chef.

Canada's "supernatural heritage" draws on the folklore and legends of the many races and cultures that have contributed to forming the country. It is part of the character and moral fibre of Canada itself. To presume that supernatural phenomena did not exist in the past, and to pretend that they do not occur with regularity today, is to deny historical fact — and to cast aspersions upon the integrity of a great many Canadians who have encountered such manifestations.

Some of the people whose stories populate the preceding chapters may have been guilty of falsification for reasons known only to themselves. Others may have been honestly mistaken about the inexplicable experiences they have endured. But I seriously doubt if you can convince yourself that they were *all* in error. There are too many consistencies in the stories from across this country.

Ghosts have been with us since the days when the first humans dwelt within this vast and vibrant land. They created havoc from the very beginning of humanity; they will no doubt continue to wreak confusion well into its future.

CONTRIBUTORS

Anne Marie Antoshewski

W. Ritchie Benedict

Jack Brisson

Kenneth M. Brown

Louise Buchholz

Vera Butler

Colin W. Clarke

Adrian Coles

Mrs. Milton Dallar

Gene Doucet

Dean Palkenburg

Alan Hustak

Mrs. Marcus Jones

Maryon Kantaroff

Adam Lebor, *Globe & Mail*,
    May 30, 1994

Arlene Lessard, "Alive & Well,"
    Nov. 1981

Neil A. Matheson

Harvey & Lois Macklin

Keely Osland

Joyce Radchenko

Francis & Kathy Rousselles

Dr. Frank Scott

W. Rex Stirling

Ray Skrepnek

Ralph Surette, *Maclean's*,
    Aug. 10, 1987

Jim Telfer

Nikala Travis

Marlene Urzada

Eric Ward

Brenda Warren

Lee White

Branda Wilson

Morley Wilson, *Toronto Star*,
    Mar. 12, 1995